Bourton Bridge

BOURTON BRIDGE, BOOK 1

MIA FOX

EVATOPIA PRESS

For my Family — I love you.

Chapter One

A SIGN ABOVE THE WEATHERED DOORWAY READ, 'Welcome to Bourton Bridge,' although those familiar with the proprietor's gruff demeanor suspected it had been hung without his knowledge and in jest. The tiny co-op shop was meant to stock all the essentials, but it offered only a meager selection of goods, as its owner preferred to keep visitors at bay. The weather was improving and soon, the English village in the heart of the Cotswolds would attract tourists eager for a photo atop one of the stone bridges that crossed its river and lent the rural community its name. As he did most mornings, Luke paused outside the shop, seemingly giving himself resolve before entering.

"Morning, Wilfred." Upon hearing Luke's voice, the orange tabby that had been asleep on the entry steps bounded up and wound himself around Luke's legs, before jumping onto the ledge under the shop window. From inside, the proprietor banged on the pane and sent Luke an angry glare. Luke merely smiled back, and the cat paid no mind to the noise.

"Don't go far. I'll be right back," Luke scratched the cat under its chin, shifting his chef's whites away so as not to collect any wayward fur. He entered the shop and immediately got a bollocking from the proprietor.

"Stop encouraging the pest." George complained, as was his natural instinct. "He was 'ere when I arrived and I tried to shoo him away, but get this…" Luke raised his eyebrows in anticipation of George's news. "He looked right at me and hissed, as if to say he was waiting for you." George carried on at an elevated pitch. "How many times 'ave I told you, Luke? Feed a stray and he'll stay for more."

"Come on, George… ol' Wilfred wouldn't do you any harm. Maybe you can find a soft spot for a creature without a roof over its head. The way I see it, he and I are your best customers. I'll take a coffee for myself and a tin of tuna for Wilfred."

The shop assistant, Brianne, gave Luke a curious look. "How do you drink the stuff?" she whispered as her grumbling boss went to fetch the murky brew from a pot tucked behind the counter.

"If I don't, who will?" His eyes crinkled with his smile, the slightest start of crow's feet daring to expose themselves on his otherwise flawless face.

"You're a chef for Pete's sake. You should have better taste," she admonished. "Maybe I could show you a thing or two. You know, spice things up a bit?" Luke had heard innuendos from Brianne before, but always managed to sidestep them.

Saving Luke from an immediate reply, his phone dinged with the arrival of a text.

Better drink your sludge today. Gallagher party at 5. Mom of the bride has already texted twice… in the last hour.

Luke imagined his boss, Elizabeth, sipping her own coffee right now, but it would reflect her sophistication and be a distinguished, French roast. Pointing to his phone, he replied, "Duty calls."

Brianne rested her chest suggestively on the counter and smiled at Luke, unable to help herself. Unexpected turns in Luke's life made him shy away from dating, but given his striking looks, women still tried to get his attention. Although not interested, it wasn't in Luke's kind nature to be rude. "In answer to your question, I've been walking past George's shop longer than I've had good taste, so my loyalty rests with him, not my stomach. He means well."

Looking doubtful, she replied, "If you say so… The offer still stands."

Taking in the conversation, George chased away Brianne, saving Luke from further interaction. He handed the coffee over in a styrofoam cup. "That'll be 50p for the coffee and another for Mongrel's food," came his surly tone, which Luke blissfully overlooked.

"It's Wilfred. He seems to know the name… after all these months," Luke added with a smirk.

"Peachy," George replied.

"Hey, George, remember that talk about paper cups? Good for the environment; good for business?"

"Not interested in more business, but just so you don't feel the need to check in regularly, this is the last of 'em," he pointed to Luke's squeaky cup. "You didn't expect me to throw out perfectly good inventory?"

Luke knew when to pick his battles. He reached for a lid, then slid an arm behind the counter where he knew George had a can opener stashed. "I ought to remove that thing," George complained.

"You're talking about the can opener, not the cat," Luke confirmed.

"Both!"

With Wilfred fed and on his way to explore, Luke returned the can opener to George and offered a casual toast of his coffee before bringing it to his lips. He swallowed hard and closed his green eyes briefly. His lips puckered and his strong jaw set into a hard line. The first sip was always the hardest. This morning's cup tasted as if George had left the pot on a low simmer since yesterday, making the coffee thick with bitterness.

Brianne crossed her arms and cocked her eyebrow in an "I told you so" fashion. Luke smiled, but refused to complain.

"Everything alright, Luke?" George challenged.

In spite of his curmudgeonly ways, the locals had frequented George's shop for thirty years, choosing convenience over conversation. George had a soft side, although he concealed it well. Even though he complained about Wilfred, Luke had seen him "accidentally" leave a portion of his sandwich outside. He had been married for twenty-five years and his wife could talk until a year of Sundays. That alone told Luke that there was more to George than most people saw.

"Coffee's just fine." Luke opened the door and felt a morning chill that the sun had yet to chase away. He turned up his collar, covering his neck just below his coal-colored hair. "This'll keep me going for a busy day," he said, tipping his cup. "The Gallagher wedding rehearsal is taking place later." Luke turned to leave, but stopped when George uncharacteristically continued the conversation.

"You're doing the Gallagher dinner?"

"Well, myself and Elizabeth, of course. Why do you ask?"

"Bonnie, the grumpy one… allergic to mushrooms."

It came as a surprise to Luke that George recognized grumpiness, let alone knew anything about the family. "George, you know how Elizabeth loves to cook with morels."

"Fancy cooking talk," George grumbled. "Like I said, no mushrooms. It's that simple."

Luke smiled. "I'll let her know."

George nodded once and turned his attention to his phone — his daily allotment for conversation more than fulfilled.

"I'll be on my way."

Brianne, looking longingly after Luke, made one last attempt for his attention. "See you tomorrow!"

"Come on, Mopey. Chin up and back to work." In an uncharacteristic fashion, George handed Brianne a muffin, stale at best, but she accepted and gave him a sideways stare, suspecting that his heart was bigger than he let on.

———

Le Pont Restaurant took its name from the centuries old bridges that covered the waterways of Bourton Bridge. Elizabeth, the owner and head chef, had herself bridged the gap between her French upbringing and England, skillfully melding the cuisines to acclaimed results. Locals originally questioned her menu, but Elizabeth wouldn't succumb to their expectations. Traditional items such as fish and chips — or even worse, "fish fingers" — were upgraded to Sole Meunière, and the whispers of doubt were banished once people tried it.

Her principles mirrored her proper appearance. People tended to sit up a little straighter in her presence. She mainly kept to herself, but in the restaurant her guests always felt welcome. Without cajoling, she inspired them to do the unthinkable in the English countryside — they ventured beyond the familiar and embraced a new food experience.

"Que faites-vous ici? C'est inacceptable!" Elizabeth rarely fell into her native French tongue, except when extremely happy or equally angry.

How long have you been sleeping in my storage room!? The Food Standards Agency isn't known for turning a blind eye, and neither am I."

That one-sided conversation occurred five years ago, but it felt like another lifetime. Elizabeth discovered Luke's hideaway, but rather than tossing him to the street like a stray, she employed him. She gave him a life he never knew existed. He assumed it was because she had once been young and looking for work. Much later, he learned she grew up in an orphanage, which explained both her stoicism and the kindness that was deep in her heart, but kept close to her chest. Today, as he entered the restaurant to hear Elizabeth in the midst of a rant, all in French, Luke was reminded of their first meeting.

"Absolument pas! Êtes-vous fou?"

The food supplier receiving the unwanted attention turned when he saw Luke. With a helpless shrug, he implored an explanation. "What is she saying?"

Elizabeth was pacing and shaking her head, a motion that Luke had seen often when she tried to calm herself.

"Well, my French isn't very good, except for food and cooking terms. However, I do know that 'fou' is crazy and she seems pretty adamant that whatever you're suggesting, well… it's never going to happen."

"Jamais!" Elizabeth shouted in agreement. "Never."

The supplier turned back to Elizabeth. "But these frozen meals are a pub staple."

"Le Pont is not a pub!"

Only fresh ingredients were used in Elizabeth's style of Provençal cuisine. Frozen cottage pies or bangers and mash weren't found on her menu. Some quintessentially British entrées did make the cut, but only if she and Luke could reimagine them with a French flair.

The traditional "Sunday Lunch" of roast beef was elevated to include a red wine reduction sauce and caramelized onions. The accompanying boiled carrots and peas served at other pubs were adapted into *Carrots Vichy*, alongside *Petits Pois à La Française* that featured sweet pearl onions. Rather than simply roasting potatoes, she served Pommes Anna, a minimalist dish of thinly sliced potatoes arranged in overlapping layers and drizzled with butter. Even Yorkshire pudding got a makeover to Elizabeth's *Chausson*, delicate puffs of pastry baked in the shape of a slipper, their translated meaning. So popular were these airy delights that guests began asking for them daily and thanks to the support Luke offered, Elizabeth was able to meet the demand, allowing guests to order them to accompany any meal.

Luke had proven to be a quick study and relished in the fineries of French cooking, perhaps because he rarely had a home-cooked meal growing up. Freezer food had been the norm for him, and he suspected that this was the root of Elizabeth's argument with the supplier.

"Scampi? As in a butter sautéed shrimp seasoned with garlic?" Luke confirmed.

"No. His idea of scampi is frozen shrimp that we reheat," Elizabeth said the words with an expression of distaste as if she had just ingested the very food she was rejecting.

Luke's response was to turn to the door and hold it open for the supplier, indicating he should leave before losing all of his business dealings with Elizabeth. "Mate, you should probably be on your way. She's never going to come around to frozen scampi. Try the Greyhound Pub," he suggested.

The supplier grabbed his tablet and muttered under his breath. "Nothing? You want nothing?"

Elizabeth was annoyed, but not enough so to ruin the relationship. "I'll take two sacks of flour, a pound of rolled oats, and Luke… anything else?"

"We're low on cinnamon."

Elizabeth nodded. "Right. Cinnamon too."

"No starters? No mains?"

Elizabeth narrowed her eyes at the man and took a deep breath as if it was all she could do to not break out into French obscenities once more. "Our vegetables come from local farms. Our proteins are all ethically sourced. Those are the ingredients that we use to create starters and mains. From scratch!"

Once the supplier left and Elizabeth's sense of calm returned, Luke inquired about the Gallagher dinner. "George wanted me to remind you that Bonnie is allergic to mushrooms."

"Mon Dieu! I forgot. George told you this?"

Luke nodded. "I was as surprised as you."

"He may have saved the day," Elizabeth noted.

"Don't tell ol' George."

"Never." She smiled a mischievous grin and her blue eyes sparkled.

Her eyes reminded Luke of someone else. Someone dear to both of them. The warnings of melancholy were daring to creep into his mind, and he didn't want to bring Elizabeth down. Often, he buried his feelings to protect hers. He turned on his own smile, a practiced expression. "I better get organized. Sauces to make… Lives to change," he uttered the silly phrase that he and Elizabeth coined.

"Go on," Elizabeth indicated the kitchen. "No mushrooms." She locked the front door after the supplier left so they could begin preparations without interruption. Looking out the bay window facing the street, she noted, "Looks like rain. Hopefully, that's good luck for the bride and groom," and she went back to writing the specials board.

Luke glanced out the window, his expression clouding over like the sky. Elizabeth noticed and reached a hand to his arm. "Come on, now." Her tone was gentle, but insistent. "I feel it too…" She let her thoughts fade. "Best to stay busy."

Giving the sky one last look, Luke nodded and walked into the kitchen.

Chapter Two

An ocean away, in a suburb north of Los Angeles, Jade rested on her back, her arms extended overhead. Her gaze was directed at the stars that shone through the ceiling hole in her backyard's yurt. A delicate charm of a colorful bird on a silver chain hung from her neck, taking flight along the grace of her collar bone. The charm caught the flickering reflection of a candle's flame, which also illuminated Jade's brown eyes, transforming them into a warm, caramel hue. She closed them and began to relax when a small voice interrupted her meditation.

"I had a nightmare. Can I lie with you?" Jade's daughter, Emilie, popped herself down atop a pile of blankets.

"It's awfully late for you, little bird," but Jade patted the blanket next to her. "Lie down and relax. I'll take you back to your room for a story in a moment." From the first night that Emilie came home from the hospital as a baby, Jade loved spending time with her. She had become pregnant right out of college. It was too soon for her boyfriend, but he "married her anyway" and never let her forget that it wasn't part of his plan.

Jade ran her fingers through her daughter's hair. "Close your eyes. Breathe in, slowly exhale out."

Emilie did as her mother suggested, her chest rising and falling with her inhalations.

Turning toward her, Jade whispered softly, "Do you feel better?"

Emilie's voice took on an exasperated tone. "I don't know if I'm doing it right."

"Auntie Willow says it's about how you feel," Jade explained.

"Dad says there has to be a right way."

Jade's smile faded. "Maybe we just have to 'be' and the right path will find us."

Frustrated, Emilie shook her head, more to herself than her mother. "Dad told me to have a *plan and purpose*. Otherwise, he says it's just *pie in the sky*," she said, imitating a gruff tone.

Jade's lips pressed into a tight line, recognizing the words of her husband. She inhaled deeply again, trying to center herself and practice the teachings her yoga friend imparted. "Purpose is important, but there's nothing wrong with pie." With ease, Jade changed the subject. "Unless it's your birthday, which happens to be in two days. What kind of cake are we having?"

Emilie laughed. "I don't think he meant that kind of pie. But for my birthday, can I have a Genoise cake with raspberry filling and Chantilly cream?"

"Whoa, that sounds delicious… and complicated. You've been sneaking in baking videos?"

Emilie nodded happily, the earlier conversation all but forgotten. "Sometimes when you go out, Daddy gets busy and I get bored. That's why I had a nightmare. I called out, but nobody was there. So, I came out here."

The news wasn't a surprise. Jade nodded, more to herself

than Emilie. "I didn't know that Daddy left the house. But I'm never far away. As for your birthday, I'll do my best, but I think you might have to be happy with a regular chocolate birthday cake." She reached for Emilie's hand and gave it a little squeeze.

———

A prep chef carefully carried a three-tier cake into the larder and promptly returned to the kitchen to finish his other duties. One of Elizabeth's most important lessons in the kitchen was efficiency. As such, she followed the Brigade de Cuisine — a hierarchy of sorts so that every person knew what was expected of them. Elizabeth had come to see Luke as her right hand, the head chef. Thomas was next in line as sous chef and a rotating staff of prep chefs were there to support them.

Frying pans sizzled and pots boiled. Knives against chopping boards created a musical percussion. Luke breathed in the smells of the restaurant — sauces fragrant with garlic, ovens steaming with bread. It smelled like what home should be. Something that Luke never experienced. Now stirring a broth within one of Le Pont's tall stew pots, Luke thought about the conversation that marked one of his last nights at his father's house.

"Where'd you put the damn keys?" Luke's father yelled. "You good for nothin'. I know you got 'em hidden." Luke remembered the altercation. Out of anger, his father tossed back half the whiskey in his glass and threw the remainder at Luke.

His father had been drunk and passed out most of the day after losing a job to a competing construction company. Once his dad had passed out on the couch, Luke removed the car keys from his father's pocket. He knew his dad would wake up by nightfall and start the whole process again. At the time,

Luke figured it better that his father's aggressions were directed at him rather than unleashed behind the wheel.

Luke grew up in a council estate on the outskirts of Oxford. He sought a quieter life in Bourton Bridge in the Cotswolds, mainly to avoid his father. He hoped that his meager cooking skills could translate to a job. For as long as he could remember, if he wanted to eat, he was the one who had to cook. The idea of working in a restaurant didn't come from conceit, but to escape the fate his father cast on him. Like many Englishman, his family's surname was a reflection of the trade predetermined for them, but Luke had no intention of joining his father on a building site. The name Barrow, a gussied up version of wheelbarrow, was as close as he would get to construction work. It's not that Luke had anything against getting his hands dirty. On the contrary, hard work suited him. Elizabeth had put him through his paces when he first asked for a job and he never shied away from it. It was his father that he chose to repel and with good reason.

Luke stole a glance through the swinging kitchen doors each time Elizabeth or another employee entered. He would catch a momentary glimpse of the restaurant's front window, and out of habit, he kept an eye out for his father. Bourton Bridge was just far enough away from Oxford to make it inconvenient for his father to stop by, but close enough that it wasn't altogether unlikely. After a particularly bad bender, his father would stagger into the restaurant wanting to start a fight. Today, Luke's heart did a little jump when he glimpsed a male figure outside. He held the swinging door open and then felt relief to see the person was too tall to be his father, and in fact, was an old friend.

Standing on the front steps, Harry towered to the height of the door. When he saw Luke peer out the kitchen porthole, he raised his hand in a wave, his bicep naturally flexing. Luke wiped down his hands on the front of his apron and went to unlock the door. He greeted Harry with a fist bump that exploded into a convoluted series of hand slaps dating back to their childhood. "You're up early. What brings you to the countryside?" Luke asked his old friend.

"I was hoping to bum a coffee off you. The only place open is George's and my stomach just can't… well, stomach it," Harry smiled broadly, a beautiful set of teeth shining in bright contrast against his face.

"Yeah, come on in. Elizabeth won't mind. Have a seat."

Harry shook his head. "I don't want to intrude when you're getting the place ready. I brought my thermos," he indicated.

Luke looked surprised and gave a little chuckle. "You came with your own thermos?"

"It's for work. Construction jobs have been slim lately, but a new one is starting," Harry paused. "Just down the lane, actually. The old farmhouse…"

Luke knew of the property. The neglected building and the land it stood on had been vacant for years. It was probably charming when first erected, but today it was in terrible disarray. Structures were like people and needed looking after, particularly as the years wore on.

"Now that you mention it, I noticed the *For Sale* sign was gone. I just assumed it fell off — like everything else on that farmhouse. Well, good for you, Harry. It'll be great to see more of you. It's been too long."

Harry paused, and turned his eyes downward for a moment. When he returned to meet Luke's gaze he sighed heavily. "Luke, there's another reason I came by. I'll be working for your dad. He's the GC on the job."

Luke's breath left him as if he had been sucker punched. He shook his head and rolled his eyes. "GC? Is that what he told you? Listen Harry, my dad is not a general contractor. Never passed the exams. He forged the paperwork."

A pause in the conversation caused Harry to sigh outwardly. "I guess I'm not surprised… seeing what he's done over the years."

"I wouldn't wish time with him on anyone, let alone an old friend. There must be something else for you."

"I'm studying for my contractor's license, but I need an income while I wait to sit for the exams. There's no new construction taking place in Oxford; and handyman work is too temporary. This job is the best I've found." Luke remained silent and Harry turned to leave.

"Hey, nothing will change between us," Luke reassured him. "Just watch out for yourself."

Grateful for Luke's words, Harry turned back and embraced him, pulling Luke to his massive chest. "Maybe the steady work will change him," Harry offered, but Luke couldn't respond. He knew his father too well.

Chapter Three

LUKE HAD A LONG HISTORY OF KEEPING AN EYE OUT for his dad whenever passing a construction site. It had become his own superstition, much in the way people avoid walking under ladders. If ever he did see his father, he made a mental note of the day and time so as to avoid him in the future. It seemed that practice was now a necessity, and as best as he tried to not let it interfere with his work, the preoccupation was distracting.

With determination, he brushed off his apprehension and locked the front door following Harry's departure. Just an hour remained until opening, and there was still much to accomplish. Elizabeth was writing the specials board in her elegant scroll, but looked up sensing something was off with Luke. "Coffee's ready... when you finish your mud," she said referring to George's brew.

"I'll have a proper cuppa with my elevenses," Luke said, now entering the kitchen and referring to his mid-morning snack. To Elizabeth's chagrin, Luke had come to enjoy experimenting with baking, but it seemed terribly unfair to her that he could indulge without his toned physique ever changing.

Some movement caught her eye outside the front door. Seeing who it was reminded her of why she was careful with her weight. Luke followed her gaze with trepidation, but was relieved to see Ben, one of Le Pont's regulars. "It's still chilly out; mind if I open early?"

"You're a good man, Luke. Ben is lucky to have a friend in you."

Luke gave a small shake of his head and sent her a knowing smile. "I think we both know that he's more interested in developing a friendship with you."

"Nonsense," she said a bit too quickly.

"I guarantee he doesn't show up this early for me… and every day at that!" Luke left her side to open the door for the gentleman, who Luke judged to be in his late 50s with a Santa Claus appearance minus the belly. "Morning, Ben," Luke greeted amicably. "Coffee and croissant?"

"Thank you, Luke. That sounds lovely."

Ben put in the same order everyday. Luke suspected the simplicity of it was purposeful so as not to be any trouble. He would sit with his book and observe the comings and goings of the customers. Always observant, but never a gossip. In Luke's opinion, he was the ideal match for Elizabeth. After returning from Ben's table, Luke encouraged Elizabeth to join him.

"Go on."

"You took care of him. I don't want to hover."

"He wants you to hover. That's why he arrives before we get busy."

"You don't know what you're talking about, but strictly as part of my duties, I'll say hello."

"Yes, of course. And maybe, as part of your duties, you should invite him to dinner to try one of the specials."

Elizabeth opened her eyes wide as if the idea was completely preposterous. Yet, she carefully pressed non-existent wrinkles from her dress and smoothed down her hair before disappearing from the kitchen.

Luke continued directing the preparation for the day ahead. Soon, organized chaos ensued and through it all, he kept his cool. He sautéed and simmered using multiple pans, created delectable sauces, and set examples for Thomas of how he wanted each dish plated. The results mimicked a meal from a Michelin restaurant.

But while Elizabeth and Ben chatted in the front of house and Luke focused on a new recipe, a loud snap and hiss sounded near the stove. One of the station chefs cried out. Like a mother hawk, Elizabeth immediately heard his wail. She bounded up from Ben, who was just a step behind her, both moving faster than one would expect they could.

"Chef! Problem here!" another kitchen worker called out.

Luke turned and saw the start of an oil fire. Flames flicked upward, dangerously out of control. His memory went back to the night of his last altercation with his father. *"Poncing about with your cookery? Having some girlie fun?"* His father stood menacingly close, his drunken breath ripe with stench. To put an end to Luke's meal preparations, his father tossed his drink at him, but succeeded only in dousing the flame with his alcohol. Luke had been caught off guard as the fire reached beyond the pot and burned his hand.

"Chef!" the younger man shouted. Desperation laced his voice and pulled Luke from his memory. Instinct kicked in, and he sprang into action. He turned off the gas, but the flames still rose and dared to extend their tentacles toward his arm. Above the burning frying pan was a canister of baking soda, which Luke reached for. Flames nuzzled underneath him as he began to pour the powder onto the flame. At the same time, Ben burst into the kitchen with Elizabeth on his heels, but the elder man held out his arm blocking her from coming closer. Acting quickly, he reached for the fire extinguisher resting in its harness on the wall. The combination of the extinguisher's foam with the baking powder caused the fire to die out. The sizzling sounds were replaced with a quiet hiss. All was quiet until Elizabeth's stern voice rang out.

"What were you thinking?" she shouted at Luke. "The fire extinguisher is here for a reason."

"The soda was closer."

"Your hands are your gift. Where would I be without them? Let me see." She took his hands in her own and turned them over to examine them. His fingers were long and graceful, his nails manicured and clean. Only the scarring of his previous accident, caused by his father, marred his hands. He weaved his fingers between hers and gave a slight squeeze before releasing.

"I'm fine. We work in a kitchen."

"Modesty in the eye of danger is known as stupidity," she reminded.

Luke turned to Ben. "Thank you, Ben. You knew exactly what to look for. Are you okay?"

"Right as rain," the older man answered, seemingly quite proud that he could be of help, particularly in front of Elizabeth. His modesty returned just as fast as the fire had broken out. "I'll just be at my table, finishing my tea."

"Thank you, Ben," Elizabeth nodded.

The worker who allowed the flame to leap out of control spoke quietly. "I'm sorry, Chefs. It was my fault."

"These things happen. Let's just get back to work." Elizabeth, now satisfied that the kitchen was in order, and more importantly, that Luke was unharmed, exhaled deeply. Once the staff was busy, she spoke in a quiet voice to Luke. "That was an unnecessary risk, being that close to the flame."

"Have you tried my bordelaise sauce? It's definitely worth saving," Luke smiled.

"Don't joke. I couldn't bear if something happened to

you…," her voice caught in her throat, but she finished her thought, "… to you, too."

"I know," Luke said gently. He knew there was more to Elizabeth's emotions than just the fire.

Elizabeth held out her hand. "Give me your apron."

"What? I'm fired now?"

"I should coco." It wasn't like her to use cockney rhyming slang, but the better part of 25 years in the country had taught her a few key ones. "Go on, take a break before the lunch crowd. I'll see you in an hour."

Knowing that there were only so many arguments he could win with Elizabeth in a given day, Luke untied his apron and handed it over. As she stepped closer to take it, he surprised her with a kiss on her cheek.

"Scoot! Can't have that sort of display here."

Elizabeth had a tough exterior, but Luke knew another side to her. "Ahh, there you are! I was worried you were going soft on me, like those caramels you make at Christmas. A hard chocolate shell that hides the gooey inside."

"I don't have a gooey inside," Elizabeth protested.

"Of course not," he smiled back.

Jade had never been a particularly accomplished cook, but she made up for it in creativity and vision. Jumbo soft pink marshmallows became her inspiration for Emilie's princess birthday theme. Jade dipped each one in chocolate and was now wrapping them in pink cellophane. Her best friend, Willow, a lanky woman with black hair and almond eyes that seemed to read into one's soul, had never missed one of Emilie's birthdays and now tied each delectable package with a silver ribbon.

"How long did it take you to do all of this?" she asked, surveying the spread that extended across the kitchen's island.

"Two days," Jade answered. "The decorating and cooking was not nearly as difficult as keeping Emilie away from it. Speaking of which…," Jade angled her head to the next room where Emilie was playing. "Can you check on her?"

Jade carried on with the final preparations — dishing spaghetti into a large bowl, plating the garlic bread, and skewering fruit balls — while Willow seemed to glide in and out of the room. In Willow's effortless way, she played games with Emilie, reminded Jade to breathe and stay grounded, and in between, she managed to tap out social media posts for her clients.

"You've been an enormous help," Jade said to her friend. "What would I do without you?"

"Fortunately, I can work from anywhere so you never have to find out. We're twinsies." Willow wrinkled her adorable button nose at her friend and held up her pinkie finger to intertwine with Jade's.

"Nearly forgot…" Jade glanced at the kitchen table. "The most important thing for a princess party…" Atop each pink paper plate sat a silver napkin and on top of that, she placed a silver tiara.

"Practical and beautiful," Willow noted.

"Definitely," Jade replied, happy for her friend's humor. "Should we call in the birthday girl?" Jade's voice purposefully rose as she knew Emilie was lurking nearby. Jade opened the swinging door to the kitchen to find her daughter just on the other side.

Immediately, her mouth turned upwards into a wide grin. "Wow, this is… It's amazing, Mom."

"Not every day my sweet girl celebrates a birthday… although I'm highly in favor of celebrating un-birthdays."

"Wait until you see the cake," Willow added with a mischievous smile. "It's huge! And pink! No doubt, amazingly delicious."

Noting that Willow had her hands behind her back, Emilie craned her neck. "Oh, let me see it."

"Emilie, I can't hold a towering pink cake behind my back, but I do have this." Willow revealed a present decked out in a pink bow to match the theme. Although her voice held its characteristic whispery tone, she encouraged Emilie, "Go on, rip it open!"

"It's too pretty." Emilie carefully slid a finger under the seam.

Willow smiled and shook her head with amusement. Glancing at Jade, "Wonder where she gets this?"

Jade held up her hands and shrugged her shoulders. Emilie finally extracted the gift from its wrapper to find a beautifully carved, wooden box with a hinged top — an artist's set of paints, pens, and colored paper. "Thank you! I love it, Auntie Willow!"

"*Auntie* Willow?"

The three of them turned at the sound of the stern voice that came from behind.

"A term reserved for good friends and better people," Willow replied without missing a beat. "Nice to see you, Grainger."

Jade shot her friend a look. *Don't make things worse,* her eyes implied.

"Started without me, I see," Grainger noted with a tight voice.

"You said you would be late," Jade reminded. "Her friends aren't arriving for half an hour, so you haven't missed anything."

Grainger moved in close enough behind Jade to speak directly in her ear. "Having a party here after I've endured a long day is really quite selfish of you." He then uttered his opinion about Willow's gift. "And that…," he said with distaste, "is simply useless."

Jade was used to Grainger's vocal opinions, but she didn't want Emilie to be hurt. With relief he had kept his voice to an exasperated whisper. "Please, not now," Jade said quietly. "It's her birthday."

"You shouldn't encourage silly flights of fancy," he insisted, taking no note of Jade's request. "Here, darling," he said proudly, handing Emilie his own gift. "It's something you *need*."

Emilie opened it and although it wasn't a gift that would typically appeal to an eight-year-old, she remained gracious. "A calculator!"

"A graphing calculator," Grainger corrected. "It's much more complex than the run of the mill kind. You can calculate complex equations… plot graphs. You'll be able to calculate risk factors. Then when you're rich, you can hire someone to make a cake…," turning toward Jade, he added, "and not waste all day doing it yourself."

Jade sent her daughter a tight-lipped smile. They sat in silence until the ring of Grainger's cell phone caused him to move into the next room. Willow and Emilie resumed their conversation, but Jade was focused on Grainger's. His booming voice could be heard by all of them: "Excellent news! I'll be there next week."

He returned to the kitchen and Emilie immediately tugged on his arm. "Daddy, do you want to try a dipped marshmallow?"

"In a minute, honey. This is important. I need to talk to Mommy."

Seeing Emilie's smile fade, Jade tried to send him a look indicating that certainly nothing was more important than his daughter. "Can it wait until after the party?" she asked brightly, trying to bring the focus back to Emilie.

"I said it was important."

Jade nodded, resolved that it was easier to go along with him than argue. "Willow, can you…" she indicated Emilie.

Willow was used to the dynamic between them, and without missing a beat, she stepped in to help. "Emilie, let's go practice the dance we made up." Willow mouthed 'it's okay' to Jade and took the little girl outside. Then, as an afterthought, she said aloud, "Good thing we bought the yurt."

She knew the comment would wind up Grainger, but she just wasn't as accommodating as Jade. Ideas came to her freely and she shared her opinions openly. This was good for her job in marketing, but not where Grainger was concerned. In truth, it was hard to hold her tongue around him. He was rude and arrogant, everything her friend wasn't. Taking Emilie by the hand, she was happy for an excuse to not be in the same room with him.

Even in college, Grainger proved to be a difficult personality. Before he came along, she and Jade were inseparable. Their shared experience of both losing their parents during secondary school years created a bond akin to sisterhood. After graduation, Willow suggested they travel to Hong Kong before starting their careers. She wanted to show Jade where she grew up and help her get her first passport stamp. Hearing this idea, Grainger put a fast end to it, citing crime rates and reminding Jade that she had barely left Los Angeles during her lifetime. Since Grainger met Jade, he had systematically wedged himself between her and Willow. In spite of Willow assuring Jade that they would be perfectly safe in her native country, Grainger ended the possibility once and for all. "What about the baby?"

Willow never forgot Jade's hurt expression that matched her own. "I was going to tell you. I wanted to ask you to be the baby's godmother. I just… the right moment hadn't come up," Jade said with tears in her eyes. Willow nodded and said, the words that would become something of a mantra when Grainger was around… "It's okay." Yet she knew that he would do his best to tarnish the sisterhood she and Jade had cultivated.

After Jade's pregnancy was revealed, she shared another hard truth with Willow. Grainger never earned his degree. Although Jade wouldn't reveal the reason, Willow suspected academic suspension. She had seen firsthand the way he would cut corners — buying essays and paying people to take his exams. One time she questioned him and he proceeded to tell her she was the fool for working harder, not smarter.

Perhaps it was the pregnancy, but Jade was taken in by Grainger's gumption and drive. She started making excuses for him and told Willow that he didn't believe in the traditional path to a career. Hearing a sliver of his phone conversation, Willow hoped he wasn't about to launch into yet another get-rich-quick scheme. "Just holler when you want us," Willow said, opening the door to the backyard for Emilie.

With Willow out of earshot, Grainger barreled on with his news. "The loan was approved. I got that property in the Cotswolds. Gonna do a quick flip of it."

"That's great." Jade nodded, although she hadn't been told any details prior. "Let me know if you need anything." She hoped her fast acknowledgement could bring his attention back to the party. "But maybe later? The girls will be here soon."

Grainger sighed again, this time heavier than previously as he tried to make a point. "If you would just let me finish. What I *need*," he said emphasizing his words, "is to go there to oversee it. Don't want to be paying a mortgage on a property that isn't turning a profit. I've got four months."

Jade looked worried. "Four months for what?"

Matching Jade's worried expression was Grainger's annoyed one. "To refurbish the old farmhouse. All the celebs are wanting a country manor house now. This will be perfect. And, I've got a handle on a contractor. Apparently, his crew is cheap and fast."

"Four months sounds really quick. What kind of interest rate is on this loan? What happens if it takes longer?"

Grainger cut her off, "First off, what do you know about anything? You're a mother; you've never worked a day in your life."

The comment was one he always resorted to, but she never considered raising a child to be without merit. "I just meant that working there means not working here."

"Sometimes you have to follow the opportunity. Now stop worrying for nothing. Mark my words, by Christmas we'll have a hefty profit in our pockets." He opened the back door and shouted out, more to be contrary to Jade than conciliatory toward Emilie. "Emilie, don't we have some candy to sample?"

Chapter Four

L E P O N T S T O O D O N O N E S I D E O F B O U R T O N B R I D G E, while Elizabeth's house rested on the other. To traverse between them, one had to pass through the village center. Though Elizabeth typically drove, Luke preferred to take a more meandering route home, opting to cross the meadow and find a moment of quiet. At the meadow's edge, where it met the river, Luke paused atop one of the village's bridges to collect his thoughts as he watched the peaceful glide of swans beneath him. He hadn't told Elizabeth about Harry's news because he knew it would upset her as much as it did him. He also knew that talk would have to come soon.

He carried on toward the lower village, past the shops and the majority of homes, until a gravel driveway, secluded by a box hedge on both sides, appeared. If you weren't looking for the parting, you would certainly pass right by. As the lane continued, tall cypress trees provided even more privacy until one reached the circular turning at the very end. A house with a red door stood on the far side, cheery and inviting. Reaching into his pocket, he secured his wallet and removed £50, placing it into an envelope and sending it through the letter opening in the door. No note accompanied it. No details were left on the envelope. But satisfied nonetheless, he continued down a narrow pebble path behind the house.

Up ahead was the home's guest cottage. A lone weed protruded from the corner of one of the paving stones in the path. Luke immediately bent down to remove it, and deposited it into the compost bin behind the main house, doubling back for a minute. Although Luke wasn't the owner of the house, nor the cottage, he took pride in its upkeep and the sense of belonging he felt every day he spent there.

Fashioned similarly to the main house, the guest cottage was made of Cotswold stone featuring a slate roof and limestone walls. Positioned on the wall adjacent to the door was a ceramic placard that read "Halcyon Cottage" with a single, colorful bird with plumes of orange and blue. Greek legend stated that the Halcyon was a symbol of calm and tranquility. From the first day he found himself living at Halcyon Cottage, Luke felt at peace.

He squeezed the Warwick iron entry handle, and entered, bending slightly to avoid hitting the door frame with his six-foot height. A few books were stacked on the entry table, a painting of a beautiful girl hung above it. Luke kissed his hand and gently, pressed two fingertips to the image, as if he had done so often and even in person. He stood for one moment longer, staring at her image before he picked up a duffle bag that sat in the entry and no sooner, turned to leave the way he came.

———

In spite of the busy day, Jade couldn't sleep. The party went off without a hitch. Emilie and her friends had a great time. When the parents came to pick up their girls, everyone commented on the array of happy smiles. And although Jade wore her own, the expression was one that was practiced and polished to keep the peace with Grainger and provide stability for Emilie. At times like this, when she lay awake with worry, she wondered how she continued to find the strength to wake each day and plaster on the happiness.

After the festivities faded and Willow bid her farewell, Grainger's supposedly joyous news had the opposite effect on Jade. It was bad enough that he had launched them into a pricey investment, but now, the extent of his plans unfolded. Far from embarking on his journey alone, he insisted that the entire family relocate to England. Passports, once safely tucked away, now lay on the kitchen table. Jade had scanned them quickly, hoping an oversight had occurred, but none had expired. Everything was in order. She didn't know how long he had secretly been making plans for the family to move, but with less than two weeks' notice before they left, the enormity of the decision hit Jade.

"Maybe you should initially go alone, set us up, and see what's what?" Jade suggested after the guests had left.

"What's what?" he mocked. "If you aren't clear on what's what, let me enlighten you."

Grainger proceeded to tell her that he would be too busy to set up house and that was her job anyway… "because she didn't work."

"What about Emilie's school?" Jade fretted, putting it all together in her mind. Emilie would be leaving her teacher, her friends, and Jade didn't even know if the local school would accept her mid-year.

"Jade, stop bringing me problems. Find solutions. You're coming. Emilie is coming. That's that. If you can't wrap your head around it, then I guess you will stay here, but Emilie will be moving to England. You know I would never leave her."

Grainger left the house shortly after his tirade. Jade never knew where he was headed, probably a bar, maybe to someone else, but she preferred the time alone so she never asked. Reflecting on his words, Jade knew he wouldn't change his mind and she would never allow Emilie to go without her. She tried to be optimistic and consider that living in a new country might be a wonderful learning opportunity. But it was a lot to process. She couldn't imagine not having Willow nearby. Jade never spoke ill of Grainger, but Willow saw through the facade.

It started at a university party, a bit too much wine, and the assurance from mutual friends that she and Grainger were meant to meet. She let him drive her home, although looking back at the night, he had probably drank more than she had. It was a pattern that she had come to see in him. But at the time, he had taken control of the situation and her younger self had found that to be sexy. One night was all it took. She found herself pregnant.

Ironically, the friends who introduced them, broke up. They weren't the best judge of character or what made a relationship work. Jade had argued that relationships were at the heart of everything, even work, but Grainger scowled at her and said she wasn't cut out for work. During her four years of school, Jade studied art history and worked with a top interior designer, sought after by many of Los Angeles' celebrities and business moguls. She was a quick study and the clients loved her. With the pregnancy, Grainger told her to make a choice: family or work. When Emilie reached school age, she reasoned that she could return to the work she loved, and then Grainger questioned if she actually loved their daughter. He always gave her the same ultimatum: take care of the family or he would take away the family. She always chose Emilie, and for her daughter's sake, Jade was resolved that she would make England work.

The duffle bag, now empty, sat on the floor of a rowing scull. Luke's long legs were positioned over it, bent closely against him. His muscles tensed as he slid the seat back, stretching his legs to their full length, before pulling forward again. His sculling stroke was smooth and regulated. Back and forth, using his legs and arms with precise timing. His technique propelled the narrow boat along the River Widenbrush, moving slowly at first and then gaining speed with each stroke.

Throughout the year, Luke trained with a team of rowing scullers for various regattas, the Henley Royal Regatta being the main one of the season. Yet, he also went out alone nearly every afternoon. Using a sweep boat without the support of a coxswain to aid in steering was grueling, but effective for clearing his mind. The sound the oar made as it sliced into the water, the feel of the breeze on his face, the warmth from the sun on his face and shoulders — all soothed him.

Some days it was easy to put his past behind him; other days, however, his thoughts betrayed him. Around Elizabeth he did his best to maintain a sunny exterior. It wasn't just because she was his employer. She didn't deserve any more hardship in her life, and he certainly wasn't going to be the one to dampen her days.

He continued rowing for another two miles, passing a few other boaters before stopping in the midst of the river where the water was calm and he could rest. He took a deep breath and filled his lungs to capacity before he exhaled slowly. He began to relax, his thoughts floating away as he slid onto his back, bringing his arms behind his head. He gazed toward the cumulus clouds above him, his mystery-filled eyes reflecting a sadness as he stared deep in thought.

———

Having stowed his boat and returned home to shower and gather his chef's whites, Luke then made his way back to the restaurant. The cobblestone lanes were now bustling with activity. The afternoon had drawn workers back to their jobs after the lunch break, and tourists took in the offerings of the Cotswolds.

As Luke walked in the direction of Le Pont, he stole a glance at the lane that intersected the river walk where the derelict building stood. The main streets of the village were laid out in a cross shape and had he wanted to, he could continue straight and avoid seeing the building altogether. But it was within sniffing distance to the restaurant and curiosity, or call it concern, got the best of him. He noticed a few construction workers heading in the direction of the old farm-house, and saw Harry amongst the ones who were already there.

As if sensing his presence, Harry turned from his vantage point atop a ladder and waved his hand in greeting. Luke was determined not to let the news of his dad affect his longtime friendship, and raised his own hand in acknowledgment. He and Harry had studied for exams together and passed notes about the answers together. Harry was the first person to ride with him when he got his driving license. And while in school, they always admitted when they liked a girl, and never went after the same one.

But with all the good times, also came a few bad. On more than one occasion, Luke found himself sleeping at Harry's place. His parents were always welcoming, but he could tell they were uneasy that trouble might follow Luke, particularly when he showed up with a black eye and one time even worse, a broken arm. Luke was surprised that they were okay with Harry working for his father, but he assumed that at this point in Harry's life, he made his own choices. Luke hoped for Harry's sake that the choice wouldn't lead him astray.

Not seeing his father around, Luke started to breathe easier. As he continued on his way toward the restaurant, Luke spied his father standing with his back to him.

"Dinner one night this week?" Harry called out.

Luke indicated that he had to get to work, and hoped Harry would realize that his father was right there, but Harry didn't understand his hand motions. "Ah what the heck. Just hang on a minute; I'm coming down." Harry removed his tool belt and started to climb down. He jumped to the ground, skipping the bottom two rungs, obviously having done this many a time.

Luke called out, "Hey, I know you're busy; we can catch up later." His desire to move on went without notice.

"What?" Harry shouted.

Luke's voice was drowned out by a loud mechanical groan from above. A crane with a pallet hanging from it, swayed awkwardly. One of the holding ropes was frayed and starting to tear. The sound came from the grinding of gears as the crane operator tried in vain to control the inevitable. The heavy pallet tilted off-balance, held by only three corners as the rope tore completely.

Chapter Five

DEBRIS RAINED DOWN TO THE GROUND AND LUKE shielded his eyes from the dust. As if the entire scene was too much to grasp, two workers stood glued to their spots. Their reactions were limited to the horror on their faces; their feet stood immobile as if unable to register what was happening. There was little anyone could do to stop the fall of heavy bricks and stone.

As each piece fell, gravel sprayed from the breakage. The sound of the men's warning shouts were drowned out by the crumbling stone. Finally, quiet took over as the pallet containing the bricks stopped swinging now that most of its weight had fallen.

Luke could hear the angry shouts of Clive, his father, inquiring as to who was responsible. His mind was muddied about priorities, or perhaps it was just his nature to be more concerned about money over people. His questions and placing of blame weren't echoed out of concern for his workers, but rather, his annoyance over the loss of materials. The men shuffled their way back to their spots, ready to resume their work. A couple of them immediately began to collect the broken stone and clean up the site.

From his vantage point, Luke could see that the fallout from the accident was not over. It was clear that only three ropes would not support the remaining weight on the pallet. The workers, including Harry, had their heads bent toward the ground as they shoveled stone and picked up broken bricks. Initially, only a bit more dust started to fall, certainly not enough to cause the men to look up or move. It seemed like it was just the settling of grime that had already been stirred up with the earlier crash. Too angry with what had occurred, Clive ignored or simply couldn't be bothered to look upwards at the swinging pallet that now teetered even more precariously. However, Luke saw the inevitable.

He darted across the street and toward the scene, grabbing the arm of the closest man and pulling him away from where he crouched. Others noticed and backed off as well. But Harry remained. Having believed everything was back to normal, he had secured his earbuds in place and now hummed a song, unaware of what was about to befall him. As the second rope tore, more debris fell, and Luke pushed him out of harm's way.

Harry was built solidly and more muscular than Luke. They used to wrestle when they were kids and it was always Luke who tapped out, rhythmically slapping his hand to the ground in defeat. But in this moment, adrenaline took over and the force of Luke's push landed Harry a few feet away. Luke stumbled backwards to the ground as a brick crashed onto his shoulder. Yet, he rose to his feet in what was perhaps a cruelty of fate. Rather than his strength saving him, it placed him in a more dangerous spot. The pallet swung to a vertical position and every remaining brick toppled to the ground. The deluge of debris struck Luke repeatedly until he succumbed, and remained unmoving.

Luke lay with his eyes closed, motionless. In his own darkness, he dreamt. Darkness wasn't a scary place, but more like a welcome slice of shade on a hot day. Cool and inviting. As his body accepted the darkness, his thoughts morphed. He was no longer in a cavernous abyss, but instead, on his rowing skull, passing underneath one of the river bridges.

He felt peaceful, happy actually. There was a comfort to the darkness. It felt almost like an embrace from a woman he knew and loved. And then he realized she was with him. Her back was turned toward him, her face hidden, and yet, Luke knew her well. His arms wrapped around her waist, pulling her against his chest. He held her close, nuzzled her neck and smelled the scent of honeysuckle. Whether it wafted to him from her own perfume or the nearby vines, he couldn't be certain. It didn't matter. He relished in the gentle rise and fall of his chest against her.

As the boat continued its glide under the bridge, a flock of birds startled. They had been perched under the eaves of the bridge, but the intrusion caused them to leave. Their sudden flight made the woman lean forward in surprise. As she did, Luke felt a terrible need to hold her close once more.

The whispering rustle of the wings dissolved into Luke's consciousness. He woke to find a nurse wrapping a bandage around his torso. The pull of the bandage from its cylinder and the starch of her uniform echoed the sound of wings from his dream. It took Luke a moment to push the fogginess from his brain and recognize that he was in a hospital bed.

"Hey there," the nurse greeted him gently when she saw his eyes open. "You had a long sleep."

"Did I?" Luke replied, pressing the fingertips of one hand to his right temple.

The nurse jutted her chin in response to his action. "I imagine that hurts. I'll get you something to ease the headache. You have a concussion… among other injuries."

Luke took a moment to glance at his prone body. In addition to the bandage wrapped around his chest and ribs, smaller ones were interlaced across his forearms.

"Keeping that concussion company are two broken ribs, lacerations on your arms and face, but take a look at these…" She maneuvered his hands gently to where he could see them. Not a scratch on either one. "You're lucky."

Luke nodded. "I am. I need my hands for work. Well, I suppose everybody does, but I'm grateful. How's the other guy?"

"I heard how this happened… you pushed someone out of harm's way. I imagine he's fine. You're the only one from the site who was sent to us. A man from the construction site called the ambulance and your work apparently. So, you don't need to worry about anything other than resting." Her gentle hint came with a more stern action of indicating Luke should lie back as he tried unsuccessfully to press himself to a seated position.

"If you really want to watch television or sit up, use this button." She handed him the remote attached to the bed. "No ab work. You've got plenty anyway."

Luke smiled. "Thank you. Do you know how long I've been here?"

She paused, glancing at the clock on the wall. "Well, it's nearly dinner time."

"Oh, just a cat nap."

The nurse shook her head. "Dinner time… the following day. You took quite a hit. I'll check on you in a bit."

She moved to leave and then stopped in the doorway. "Oh,

I nearly forgot. A man… your father, he said, came by. But, he said it was just to check if…" she let the unspoken words fade away. The meaning was clear. "He didn't stay when he learned you would be okay."

"I'm not surprised." Luke's mouth turned downward as he said the words.

"Is there anyone I should call?" the nurse asked gently.

"As long as my work knows," his voice trailed off. "There's nobody else."

Jade felt terribly alone.

Earlier in the day, she and Willow sat in her backyard yurt. It was Willow who had insisted she buy it as a personal retreat. When the idea was presented, Jade initially repeated Grainger's words that it was an unnecessary extravagance. Thankfully, Willow's insistence won out and the yurt was readily used. They would do yoga together. Afterwards, they felt a bit lighter and would laugh together. Sometimes they would indulge and eat Cheetos dipped in ranch dressing together. And today, they cried together. But in spite of Willow's pleas for her to stay in California, she was determined to honor her marriage, even if that meant feeling isolated.

Grainger's angry words interrupted her thoughts. "Damn wheel on my suitcase broke. Probably from all those times I had to haul the stuff that didn't fit into your case."

Jade remained tight-lipped as Grainger grumbled. She remembered past vacations slightly differently, such as when she carried the suitcases while Grainger stayed busy 'dealing with the desk clerk' or 'sorting out the car'.

Grainger shoved an array of heavy coats along the closet rack, angrily squeezing them together. He bent low to maneuver past the coats and deep into the closet crawl space to find a more suitable suitcase from where they were stored under the stairs. With an obvious show of annoyance, he threw the first case into the open hallway nearly hitting Jade.

Ignoring his angry actions, she took a deep breath and tried to defuse him. "Do you need help?"

"You think?" he responded sarcastically. "I'll grab the ones from the back and you pull them out."

"How many are you getting?" When no response came back from Grainger, she poked her head into the space behind his back in order to be heard. "Grainger, why do we need so many suitcases?"

"Just in case the build out takes longer than expected. Might as well bring things for two seasons, if it comes to that." He didn't say more and she didn't dare argue.

Grainger tossed two more suitcases behind him and Jade pulled them into the hallway. She stared at them with dread, unsure of what to do, but determined to figure out something. Grainger backed himself out of the closet and into the hallway. They faced each other, the suitcases piled between them.

"Jade, try to wipe off that sour expression. Most people would consider this a wonderful adventure."

"*Most people* wouldn't have been surprised about such a big decision." It wasn't like Jade to speak freely to Grainger. Usually, she worked to maintain the peace, but the change of circumstances made it hard to hold her tongue. Yet, the moment she spoke her mind, she was reminded why she typically kept quiet.

Grainger's eye narrowed and he stared at her with an expression of hatred. "Jade, if you ever question me again, I will question your competence as well. I'll keep Emilie from you, and you'll be on your own. By the way, I've rented out the house. You truly will have no place to come back to you, if you try to return early."

For the life of her, she couldn't fathom why he even wanted her around. He rarely, if ever, spoke with love or anything resembling a partnership. As she turned to leave, she got an answer as to her purpose.

"Jade, be useful and make me a cup of tea."

———

Luke replaced the kettle onto its heating element after pouring the steaming water into a mug. He dunked the Earl Grey teabag a few times, then carried the mug to a built-in window seat with a view of the garden. Leaning against the cushions lining the wall, he grimaced slightly from the movement. Yet, in spite of the accident, his frame still appeared strong. He sat shirtless, the bandages protecting his broken ribs, hugging the muscles of his torso.

He inhaled slightly to test his ribs, then took a sip from the mug and reflected whether he had been in the right place at the right time or altogether the wrong place. As if fate wanted to give him insight, a knock sounded at the door. Luke maneuvered to rise, but the discomfort made him rethink the effort. "Come in," he called out, deciding it was too much trouble to stand on ceremony. But when he saw his father, he forced himself to his feet, not wanting Clive to come all the way into his home.

There were times when he could have used more space than the cottage provided, but Elizabeth owned both properties and always made him feel welcome in the main house, particularly when he wanted to use the larger kitchen to test a recipe. Now wasn't a time when he needed more room. He was relieved that he could maneuver to the front door in relatively no time at all, serving to keep Clive from entering beyond the vestibule.

"You're not going to invite me in?" he bellowed.

Typical for his father, the man didn't wait for a response, but barreled on with his intended message. "No matter. I have no intention of staying."

Luke knew his father well enough to know this wasn't a social call. "What can I do for you?"

"I came by the hospital."

Luke's head moved in a slow nod, waiting for his father's delivery. There was always a point, never random conversation.

"I saw Harry there. He was waiting outside your room. Checking to see how you were doing. In case you're wondering, he was thankfully okay."

Luke began to lean against the wall, feeling that his instincts were wrong. Perhaps, a thank you for what he did to save Harry or a show of concern for himself was forthcoming. He let his guard down, and feeling tired from the effort of rising, he took a seat on a small bench by the door. "I'm glad I was there to help." He turned his gaze downward and adjusted the bandage that had slipped.

Unexpectedly, his father's reaction was swift and forceful. Grabbing him under his arm, Clive hauled him to his feet. Memories of similar encounters from his youth flooded Luke's mind. Despite now being taller and more muscular than his father, Luke had momentarily forgotten the need to remain vigilant. His father took advantage of the situation and leaned into Luke, holding him roughly.

"What are you talking about?" Clive's tone was angry and appalled. "I'm certain that this whole thing probably happened *because* you were there. No doubt you distracted my *men*."

He placed emphasis on the final word, his distaste for Luke evident.

"You can leave," Luke replied evenly.

"I'll leave when I've said what I came to say."

"Foolish me, thinking you were here out of concern. So what is it?"

Clive leaned in closer to Luke, his voice growing more menacing. "If you're not going to help with my business, stay away from it."

It was then that Luke detected the familiar stench of alcohol. It emanated from Clive, releasing from his pores. Luke had gotten used to it growing up, even finding gratitude in its warning. That repulsive smell was the unmistakable precursor to his father's descent into violence.

This time was no different. Clive shoved Luke, slamming him backwards. Luke grimaced as his ribs were pressed against the wood frame of the entry. The small plaque that hung outside the front door tilted with the force of Luke being thrust against the wall.

Luke had always seen his home as a place of refuge, and like the name on the placard implied, a place of peace for him. "Get out!"

"I'm done here," Clive spat and walked the path that wrapped past the main house.

Luke watched to ensure his father continued toward the street. He saw with disgust that his father's angry haste caused him to nearly barge into Elizabeth as she made her way home. But she was strong and stood her ground, refusing to maneuver to the side, but instead forcing Clive to side step her.

"Get outta the way, old woman."

She ignored his choice words, and approached Luke's cottage rather than continue into her own home. Shaking her head, she spoke. "You may have left his business, but he does a good job of nosing into yours." She paused, "Not like you to raise your voice. Did you deck him too?"

"Very funny."

"Now that the unpleasantness is gone, onto this…" She

waved the envelope that Luke had placed through the letterbox earlier. "How many times have I told you that your paycheck — all of it — is for you?"

Luke smiled for the first time in the last hour. "As many times as I've told you that I want to pay rent."

Elizabeth patted the side of his upper arm. It was a gesture he had come to know over the years, not entirely different to how she greeted Wilfred. Elizabeth might have been French by birth, but living in England for so many years had certainly rubbed off on her and affection didn't come easy. She was as 'stiff upper lip' as one came, but where it counted she had tremendous warmth. "At least come around tonight for dinner. I'm trying a new recipe and you could use some looking after. Win-win."

"I'm capable of taking care of myself. Bandages and all."

"Indulge me." Elizabeth's expression changed and her tone turned serious. "Luke, all joking aside. You've been through an ordeal. You can take some time off."

"I never want to take advantage of your kindness," Luke said with similar seriousness.

"You're not. Never have and never will."

Chapter Six

"YOU MUST BE JOKING." WILLOW STABBED A LETTUCE leaf without the desired results. Her fork merely made a screeching, scraping noise against the china plate. She tried again. The sound mirrored her fury, and finally she simply plucked it up, graceful as always in spite of using her fingers.

"Look at me. I can't even eat properly; I'm so upset."

"I don't know what to do." Jade pushed her own plate away. Her appetite had been nonexistent since the day prior when Grainger delivered his news and ultimatum.

Willow sat back in her chair when the waiter approached, silently signaling that she was finished. She waited for the waiter to clear the table and leave their side before continuing with her thoughts.

"Jade, I'm not just upset. I'm worried." She hesitated before speaking again and placed a gentle palm on her friend's hand. "If it's hard here, it's going to be harder there. It'll be just you. Dealing with Grainger."

"Well, it's not like I have family here."

When a tear escaped down Jade's cheek, Willow stopped her. "You've got me. I'm your family."

Jade nodded, but cast her eyes downward, not wanting to meet her friend's gaze for fear of releasing more tears or Willow's reproach of what she was about to say. "You're stronger than I am, Willow. I wouldn't dare wind him up the way you do. You've always stood up for yourself."

"Don't make me out to be brave. I don't have to live in the same house with him. Forgive me, but I could never live in the same house."

"I made a vow," Jade said simply. "I have to see it through. Good times and bad."

Willow took a moment to reflect on Jade's words. She was right. It was easier for her to stand up to Grainger's ugliness when she could leave. Admittedly, Willow often asked whether Grainger was home before agreeing to visit. He was that unpleasant to be around. Yet still, one nagging thought remained. "Jade, I know it's not easy and I respect your character. You are strong to hold onto those vows. But, I have to ask you... where have the good times been?"

Jade shrugged her shoulders looking defeated. "It doesn't matter. He booked our flight through some sort of last minute website. Got a deal on the tickets."

"Of course he did," Willow said bitterly.

Jade nodded. "Hopefully, it's only four months," she said as much to herself as to her friend.

The kitchen staff bustled to prepare for dinner. Pots simmered with delectable smelling stews on the large, industrial range. Two prep chefs chopped vegetables and made preparations in unison. Their movements were the culinary equivalent of a dance. The front of house, the term restaurateurs use for the dining area, was closed and as such, quiet during this afternoon time of preparation before the evening crowd would arrive.

The swinging double doors to the kitchen were left open to let the gentle breeze from the front doors cool the actions of the staff. But in with the breeze blew Luke's father, who stumbled against the doorframe and cursed loudly as he continued inside. "Bollocks! Luke! Where you at, Luke? I knows you here. Git yourself outta that damn kitchen."

The visit was unwanted, but not altogether unexpected. Luke's lifetime of having to ward off his father taught him that he liked to have the last word. When he told his father to get out, Luke knew it wouldn't sit well with him. His face reddened with embarrassment as the staff heard Clive's shouts and even worse, saw him overturn a chair as he stumbled against it.

Luke hurried into the dining area. "You're drunk again," he hissed under his breath, trying to set the example that a restaurant was not the place for loud voices.

"I've got a right to an afternoon toddy. Maybe you should 'ave one too. Lighten you up a bit."

"Go home. I don't know what you want, but this isn't the time for it."

"Is that any way to address your father?"

"You lost that title years ago. Now leave. This is where I work."

Elizabeth arrived through the front doors and immediately saw the trouble brewing. "Luke? Is everything alright?" She casually showed that her cell phone was in hand, just waiting for a signal from Luke that she should call for help.

Luke still felt badly that his father had shown up at Elizabeth's home. He was determined to rectify the situation at the restaurant. "He was just leaving."

"I 'aven't said what I came here for. Not yet at least," his father replied.

"Clive, we are presently closed," Elizabeth announced in his direction.

To that, Luke's father uprighted the chair he toppled and sat down like a petulant child.

"No you don't," Luke grabbed him by the collar, hauling him to his feet in much the same fashion that his father had done to him. Luke was strong and healing quickly. "I've got this," he assured Elizabeth and physically walked his father to the door and onto the street.

"Okay, okay." Clive struggled to remove himself from Luke's grip, but it was futile. Luke had a good three inches on him not to mention the muscular frame he gained from rowing. His father's whiskey and beer gut physique could not compete. "I'll leave your *work*," he spat out the last word. "But my new job is a big one and I need extra men on it. Not that you're much of a man, but beggars can't be choosers."

"You are dreaming if you think I'm ever going to work for you." Luke turned to the restaurant, leaving his dad on the sidewalk. He closed and locked the front doors, then met Elizabeth's gaze and sighed outwardly. "I'm sorry. I promise it won't happen again."

Embarrassed, he pushed open the kitchen swinging doors, but Elizabeth's concern stopped him. "Luke, you've always been a good man. Any promise you made, you kept. But this time… with regards to your father… This is a promise you can't keep."

Chapter Seven

THE PREVIOUS NIGHT'S DINNER HOUR HAD BEEN busy, leaving little time for casual talk among the staff. As much as Luke enjoyed his conversations with Elizabeth, he was thankful that the night had been strictly about business. Making his way back to work, he sipped hesitantly on his morning coffee, and hoped the incident with his father was forgotten and behind them.

He was convinced George kept the coffee pot brewing nonstop and his stomach grumbled in protest. This cup tasted as if the coffee had been reboiled a few times and was perhaps two or three days old, but Luke drank it nonetheless to combat his sleepless night. Ben arrived the same time as Luke, and without hesitation, he took his usual table and pulled out a crossword. Luke brought him coffee in a silver pitcher, laid out a croissant basket, and let him wait for Elizabeth. No doubt, he wanted a chance to catch up and find out how the Gallagher party went.

Occasionally, Luke would look up, but Ben took no notice. As if to ensure the topic of the party wouldn't stir up any negative discord, Ben interrupted Luke only once to inquire whether Bonnie Gallagher had given them any trouble. And in fact, Luke proudly reported that Bonnie, who had never been much of an eater, as proven by her bird leg figure, tucked into the offerings with gusto. Her face, normally frozen with a down-turned mouth, wore a smile throughout the evening.

Seeing that his cup was drained, Luke asked, "Got everything you need, Ben?"

"Pay no attention to me. You've got your work. Best get on with it or you'll get an earful from Elizabeth and she'll ban me from these morning visits."

"Somehow I think that's unlikely," Luke assured him. In comparison to last night's rush, the quiet of the morning was welcome and having Ben as a fixture was comforting. Luke continued to work on the day's menu at a table facing the street, until Harry tapped on the front window.

Luke unlocked the front door and Harry smiled broadly. "It's so good to see you at work, up and about. I'm so sorry, Luke, for the accident and my part in it."

"Harry, you didn't do anything. No apologies needed. Can I get you a cup of coffee?"

"That would be great." Harry sat down at the table next to Ben and Luke chuckled to himself that in spite of being closed he already had two tables to serve, although he didn't mind a bit. When he returned with a coffee for Harry and a refill for Ben, both men spoke at the same time.

"You didn't have to bring a refill," Ben protested.

"I could've gotten my own cup," Harry said.

"You two enjoy. I'm just going to get back to it." Luke returned to his seat and poured over his recipe notes. He was just adding a few ideas when he looked up and caught sight of a woman peering into the window.

"You're busy at this hour," Harry joked. "Do you know her?"

With her tiny nose scrunched up against the glass, she

reminded Luke of someone he once was very close to. Her hands formed a tent over her eyes, blocking the glare as she tried to catch a clear view into the restaurant.

A light breeze blew a lock of her hair over her cheek. She turned her chin over her shoulder, trying to negotiate with the wind to keep her hair from becoming unruly. When she took her hand and gently moved her hair behind her ear, Luke reflected on how beautiful her face appeared in the morning sun.

"Never seen her," Luke answered. As he looked up at the clock, he muttered to himself, "Hell with it," and stood up to get the door. It was clear that she couldn't see Luke due to the glare and the dark glass, but when he approached, she looked up in surprise.

"Oh, hello. I wasn't sure anyone was in," she said pleasantly.

"We're not yet open, but I can offer you a cup of coffee." Luke imagined Elizabeth's surprise if she were to arrive to find Ben, Harry, and yet another guest. Although the lunch specials menu was not yet complete, he couldn't imagine not inviting this woman inside and suspected that Elizabeth would be welcoming.

Turning her glance toward Ben and then Harry, she appeared slightly confused.

"We make exceptions," Luke explained, and with a sweep of his arm he indicated that she should come in too.

"Thank you. I appreciate the kindness."

Immediately, Luke reflected on her accent. She wasn't from England. American, he was certain, but he was never adept at placing each regional accent. "You're visiting. I insist on being hospitable."

She nodded and smiled, "From California. Just north of Los Angeles."

"Really?"

Her smile grew. "Why do you seem surprised?"

"It's just that our visitors from the west coast typically sleep in. Jet lag…," he explained.

She shrugged her shoulders and Luke took in their soft curve, the milky white of her skin, and the cute roll she did with her eyes. "My best friend got me into yoga. We're often upside down."

Luke found himself charmed by her sense of humor. He hadn't given any woman a second glance in a very long time and it took him by surprise. "I've always wanted to try it. If you find a good place to practice here, let me know."

She hesitated and seemed as if she wanted to continue the conversation, but at the same time, her smile faded. Luke noticed the change in her demeanor immediately. "I'm sorry. That was terribly forward. We don't even know each other. Please… allow me to me get you a coffee and forget I said anything else."

Suddenly, her gaze went across the street. He followed the direction and saw her brown eyes fill with what appeared to be dread and maybe even sadness. A man walked toward her. Hurriedly she answered, "I would have liked to stay longer," before she turned to leave.

"Hey, grab me a coffee, will ya?" The man shouted from halfway across the street for any passerby to hear. When he reached her side, he reached for her hand possessively, eyeing Luke as he did so. "We're in a hurry," he reminded her, but stared directly at Luke as if to send him the message.

Luke took the hint and smiled tight-lipped. "Two coffees to go; straight away."

"They're not actually open, Grainger."

"It's no trouble," Luke replied.

"There, you see?" Grainger replied.

Luke wished he could be chivalrous and say something to bring the smile back to her eyes. He wasn't raised with affection or warm words, and because of that lack of human connection, he knew the importance of offering kindness to others.

Jade turned her head ever so slightly. Catching Luke's glance she mouthed, "Sorry," but Luke merely shook his head to imply it was okay. Yet somehow, he already knew that for her, the opposite was true.

———

Ben savored his coffee to stay in Elizabeth's presence while Harry hurried off to avoid any rebuke from Clive. The restaurant remained busy throughout the day and although Luke's thoughts occasionally strayed to the beautiful tourist who had so quickly charmed him, he focused on work. Elizabeth made a rosemary lamb roast with all the trimmings while he prepared mini trios of chocolate, raspberry, and vanilla mousse for dessert.

Their customers praised the dishes, particularly Vera and Mary who lingered over their meals. The two elderly sisters had lived together since childhood and were as much a part of the community as their store, *Bourton Bric-a-Brac*. Local residents often donated keepsakes no longer wanted while tourists clamored for the curios and smaller antiques that were perfect for transport home. It created a cycle where one person's trash, or bric-a-brac as it was known, was another's treasure. The sisters, who were charmingly reminiscent of the antiques they sold, never shied away from offering their opinions, and were well known for getting the best deals at the boot and jumble sales.

As they finished their sherry and dessert, Luke stopped by their table to ensure they were satisfied. "It was lovely, Luke." Mary delicately turned her spoon face down onto her plate.

She left the last bite untouched, a gesture of refined politeness that evoked a different era.

"How do you and Elizabeth find the time to prepare all of this?" Vera exclaimed.

"It's our pleasure."

Once the sisters got an idea, they rarely discarded it. "It is delightful," Mary agreed, "but Vera and I were talking, and we think you and Elizabeth work yourselves too hard."

"Yes…" Vera took over the conversation, "…open all the time, catering parties for everyone in the village, and never a frozen meal."

"Oh Mary! They would never," Vera admonished.

Luke smiled both at the sisters' banter and the memory of the supplier recently asked to leave after pushing frozen goods onto Elizabeth.

"We know you and Elizabeth wouldn't cut corners, but perhaps you could take some time off when the holiday season rolls around."

Elizabeth heard the conversation and joined the table. She and Luke each wore a look as if to say that the sisters had just suggested the most ridiculous idea ever. "People love holiday food and I can't disappoint them," Elizabeth explained. "Sausage rolls… mince pies…," her voice trailed off with the memory of Christmas pasts.

"Bûche De Noël," Luke added, referring to the traditional chocolate yule log cake.

In spite of their descriptions of holiday food, Luke and Elizabeth shared a surreptitious glance, each knowing all too well the real reason they wouldn't take time off and preferred the restaurant to take over their lives.

"Well, we best be heading off," Vera spoke and Mary also rose from the table. They each gave Elizabeth the customary kiss on each cheek as they had learned from her French ways before heading out the door.

Elizabeth locked it after them and promptly headed back toward the kitchen. Luke called after her. "We're already prepped for tomorrow."

She nodded. "I'm just going to check on the inventory."

"I did it earlier."

"Well, then I'll…" her voice trailed as if she knew she had no more work to accomplish, but wasn't ready to be alone with her thoughts. The down time was hard for both of them.

"What are your plans for the evening, Luke?"

Luke laughed outwardly. "Oh you know me. I'm going to throw a rager at the cottage, invite a dozen or so young Oxford coeds, and see where that leads me."

"Would it be so terrible if one day, you did? Maybe you would meet someone special."

Luke didn't answer and instead, threw the thought back at her. "With all due respect, what about spending time with Ben outside of here?"

Elizabeth sighed loudly knowing there was no point in continuing the conversation. A tap at the window broke the tension. They looked up to see Harry.

"Hi Mate," Luke opened the door to greet him. "Everything okay? We were just closing up."

"I know. I saw the lights on. I was working late."

"Construction work at this hour?"

Harry nodded. "Your dad has a big meeting tomorrow and said he needed a rush to start putting up drywall. I was wondering if I could buy you a nightcap to thank you properly for saving my life."

Elizabeth and Luke shared a glance, and it was Luke who spoke up. "Harry, that accident probably occurred because my father uses shoddy equipment, works you all to the bone, and ignores city codes."

Harry didn't answer, and turned to leave. "I'm sorry to bother you. Catch you soon."

"Harry, wait," Luke stopped him. "I'm sorry. I just took out my issues on you. I meant what I said before. It was just an accident. Not your fault. That drink sounds great. Elizabeth, join us?"

"Thank you for the invite, but I'm tired," she politely declined, as Luke knew she would. Work, home, repeat. It was their routine, and one that suited Luke just fine. But Harry looked as if he could use a friend. "Have a drink for me," Elizabeth smiled. "And Luke, enjoy yourself." She said the last words pointedly to which Luke nodded, but only out of politeness.

Chapter Eight

FIVE YEARS AGO...

A younger Luke made his way towards the river head, carrying his rowing equipment over his shoulder. As he passed by the restaurant, he glanced through the window at a girl about his own age. She looked up at the same time and sent him a sweet, inviting smile that he imagined would taste like honey. On a whim, he indicated his oars and pointed toward the river, inviting her out through his own made up sign language.

She tossed up her hands cheekily as if she would take him up on his offer, if only she could. As a counter offer, she pointed to a help wanted sign and indicated the tables that needed to be set.

Luke set down his oars by the side of the building and immediately went inside where he lifted the sign from the windowsill. He faced the lettering toward the girl. "What about me?"

"What about you?"

"I'm in the market for a job. I like to eat. Seems like a good fit."

"You like to eat," she repeated. "Is that the only thing that attracted you to this job?"

He noticed the dish towel in her hand and reached for the other end. As his fingers inched closer to hers, he kept his gaze locked on her eyes. When his hand finally met hers, he gently intertwined their fingers. "I'm Luke."

"Emma," she responded.

"It's nice to meet you, Emma."

Another worker arrived and the spell created between them was diminished. Emma released the towel, but Luke held on and began to take over dusting the chairs where Emma left off.

"It's not that simple," Emma said over her shoulder, still keeping one eye on the handsome stranger.

"Winning you over?" Luke asked with a glint in his eye.

"Getting the job… and yes, that too."

Luke smiled and raised his eyebrows in a confident, but not cocky gesture as if to imply, 'we'll see'.

Emma couldn't help but warm to him. "Come with me," she said, taking off her apron and leading him toward the kitchen. "You'll have to inquire with the owner," she nodded her head in the direction of Elizabeth, stern looking and swearing under her breath in French after examining a steaming pot on the stove.

"She's had a bad morning. Maybe you can cheer her up."

For the first time, Luke appeared unsure. "Is that possible? She seems quite… ornery."

Emma nodded. "That she is, but she's also my mom so I might be biased." She smiled after delivering that last zinger, and spying a large clock on the wall, proceeded to turn on her heel.

"Aren't you going to ease the way," Luke whispered, standing closer to her.

Emma smiled, taking in the feel of his warm breath.

"Somehow, I think your charm will do just fine all on your own. Besides, I'm off duty. Good luck."

"Will I see you again?"

She pushed through the double doors leading away from the kitchen into the dining room. "That depends on if she likes you."

Elizabeth looked up to glare at Luke as if to ask why he was in her kitchen.

"Bye, Mom! I found a stray outside. Can we keep him?"

Luke returned to the restaurant every day for two weeks. Initially, Elizabeth wasn't sure if it was the free lunch or her daughter that brought him back. He looked on the thin side, and the way he looked at her daughter was unmistakable. She was correct on both accounts. On the fifteenth day when she turned up and found him already waiting at the doorstep, she acquiesced.

"You're persistent," she said unlocking the door.

"You say that like it's a bad thing," he said and followed her inside.

"I haven't decided yet, but since you seem to be a morning person and I prefer not to be, I'm giving you this." She handed him the key. "Don't ever be late."

"No Ma'am. I won't be. You won't regret this."

"Let's make that a promise, shall we?"

And promise he did.

Luke had gotten used to opening up the place and starting the prep work. He laid the tables, read Elizabeth's notes about the daily specials, prepared the blackboards with descriptions of dishes, and then moved to the kitchen to start cutting vegetables. Elizabeth was a tough, but fair employer, assuring him that he would gain more responsibility and training in cooking as he proved himself. He intended to do just that.

Although he spent most days working with Emma, the busy schedule meant their conversations were limited to the needs of the kitchen and customers. At the end of the day, Luke was so tired he could barely speak. Still, he couldn't help but steal glances at Emma whenever he could, and to his elation he had caught her looking at him more than once as well.

"Mom says you catch on quickly," she said one afternoon during the hours when the restaurant was closed. Emma used this time to prepare the desserts that needed time to bake or set in the refrigerator. She preferred the meticulous nature of baking to the experimentation of cooking that her mom did.

"I'm trying. It's all new," he admitted and watched as she used a small knife to cut a delicate leaf shape out of pastry. A touch of flour was dusted across her cheek. Luke wanted to brush it off, but caught himself and opened a cupboard to remove an apron instead.

Emma smiled as he tied it around his waist. "Very professional. You must be spending a lot of time with my mum."

"She doesn't mess around, that's for sure."

"And do you?"

He knew flirting when he heard it, but in spite of the undeniable attraction he felt for Emma, Luke needed this job and getting involved with Emma was probably not the smartest move to winning over Elizabeth. He ignored Emma's comment, but couldn't help but hold her gaze. She was simply beautiful and he couldn't look away.

Approaching her, he indicated her cheek. "You've got a little…" he pointed, but when she looked confused, he gently brushed the flour from her cheek. There was an electricity between them and for a moment they didn't say a word. Luke looked at her porcelain cheek, touched it lightly with his finger once more, and then backed off. He smiled and composed himself, as did Emma.

"I'm glad you got the job."

Luke nodded. "Prep cook. But I hope to actually cook one day, not just prep. Do you need any help?"

Emma's cheeky nature returned. "Oh, this is a job for a pastry chef."

"Understood."

"I'm kidding with you. Here," she handed him a heart-shaped cutter that remained on the counter. "You can have my heart."

He reached for the heart and their hands touched, staying in place a moment longer than necessary. "Let's hope I'm better with pastry than I am with comebacks."

She smiled. "No comeback needed. You can simply ask me out."

He opened his mouth as if he was about to take her up on it, but promptly shut it again. Emma rolled her eyes. "Am I going to have to ask you?"

Luke motioned toward the closed double doors of the kitchen. Elizabeth's voice carried as she spoke to a supplier. "Your mom is my boss. We work together."

Emma smiled, ignoring any possibility of a problem. "Yeah, it's pretty great, isn't it?"

"Emma, you can tell I'm into you, but I think it's unwise to dip one's pen in the company's ink."

She scrunched her little nose at him, teasingly asking, "Are you saying you want to dip your pen in my ink?"

"I'm truly not very good with words. I meant…"

"Don't worry. I know what you meant. You're obviously a gentleman." She paused and whispered conspiratorially, "Maybe too much of one."

He met her gaze, trying to figure her out, but she mistook

his interested glance for concern and responded, "Hey, my comment… it's this new thing called flirting."

Luke nodded, letting her know that he wasn't as proper as she might believe. He helped her roll out more dough and allowed his hand to brush over hers. His fingers interwove with hers as she rolled the dough into a ball. He let his hand leave hers only to trace a finger along her forearm. She closed her eyes to absorb the feeling and seeing her eyes closed, Luke took his chances. He turned toward her and rested his forehead on hers. Emma opened her eyes to gaze up at him.

"You are so beautiful. Job or no job. I'll never be able to resist you." He whispered the words so softly it was almost an admission to himself rather than a compliment meant for Emma to hear. He leaned in slowly and his lips met hers in the softest of kisses.

When they broke apart, he did so begrudgingly and reached for her hand to maintain some contact. "Emma, you take my breath away."

She turned her eyes downward and smiled. "I guess that means we're going out tonight."

"I guess it does," he agreed, knowing he could never argue. "Where can I pick you up?"

"You already did, but I'll text you my address." She reached her hand into Luke's back pocket. He eyed her with amusement as she removed his phone and entered her contact details.

Chapter Nine

LUKE CARRIED HIS SHELL OVER HIS SHOULDER. Still slightly wet from the river, some water dripped from the narrow boat onto his wide shoulders, a welcome gift as his brow beaded with sweat. He hauled the boat and oars across town, and finally stopped at a house with a flower pot on the doorstep. It might have been a nice addition to the dilapidated house, if it hadn't simply been a pot of dirt. There was nothing welcoming about the place. As if well aware that the neighborhood was as dodgy as the house, Luke stowed his gear in a large storage box around the side of the house and set the combination to a heavy padlock sealing it shut. It was only after giving it a tug to assure its closure that he entered the house to shower and change for his date.

The neglected homes of the council estates — the government provided housing — mirrored many of the families who resided there. Luke glanced at the misshapen cushions on the couch, and confirmed his father wasn't sleeping amongst them. The tatty curtains behind it were drawn and in spite of a tear in the fabric, outdoor light was banished. Luke couldn't help but think that the dimness was a blessing as it camouflaged the decor.

He was fully aware of the difference between a house and a home. This place was simply where he slept. The house was among many on a council estate in Blackbird Stow, situated on the south-eastern periphery of Oxford. Part of the city, and yet, it couldn't be more different. Oxford was known for its distinguished academia and colleges, and the nearby Cotswolds beckoned the stylish set to visit. But Blackbird Stow was a working class ward and civil parish that was the antithesis of refinement.

Luke's house was an exact replica of the one next door and the one next door to that. Most of the day, raised voices and fights could be heard from any one of his neighbors. For this brief and blessed moment, the street and house were silent. With the couch empty, he assumed his father wasn't home. But just as he began to relax in that thought, he heard a familiar pop of a beer cap and the ting of metal landing wherever it fell.

His father's booming voice entered the room before he did. "You're home early. Did you get paid today?"

Luke didn't immediately answer, waiting for his father to fully enter the sitting room. Long ago he developed a system of assessing Clive in terms of how many drinks he had consumed before entering into conversation. One beer and his dad offered unsolicited advice. Two and he started to interrupt. Three and Clive started to mix in hard liquor and grew belligerent. When Clive entered the room, beer bottle in hand, Luke knew not to expect any civility or his father inquiring about his day.

After taking a swig, Clive continued talking. "We're short a player. Boys will be here any minute." Luke saw that the card table that doubled as a dining room table was set with poker chips and packets of crisps. "Looks okay," his father noted, sliding the curtains open. "Welcoming even."

Movement caught Luke's eye and he saw a trio of his father's drinking buddies making their way to the front door. Each one carried a six-pack signaling to Luke that it would be a loud evening. He was thankful he wouldn't be there to endure it.

"Yes, I got paid," Luke replied swiftly and without protest.

"Pull up a chair in that case; add in your ante."

"Thanks, but I've got plans. I'll deposit my share of the rent into the account when I go out." Luke started toward his bedroom, but his father blocked the hallway to challenge him.

"I don't ask you everyday," he hissed. Luke pulled back, smelling the distinct odor of whiskey mixing with the beer and his father's stale breath. Although it was an imperceptible motion, just a slight leaning away, his father noticed and grabbed Luke's forearm. "Those plans have anything to do with that snooty woman and her restaurant?"

Clive turned toward his friends who had just made their way inside. He put on a fake French accent to greet them. "Luke doesn't work in a café. That's below him. His boss owns a rest-or-ront. "Hey Luke, say that fancy pansy word she calls a bakery."

When Luke didn't answer, one of Clive's friends helped egg him on. "Come on, Lukie. You used to be more obedient when you were a boy. Teach your old man something new."

Still Luke didn't answer, and it wound up Clive. He shoved him against the chest. "Where are your manners? You want to get outta here, then answer." He pushed him again. This time using both hands. When Luke gave him a slight shove back, Clive pulled his entire arm back and took a swing.

But the outburst of aggression didn't surprise Luke. He had come to expect it and caught Clive's fist in his own. Luke had learned to use Clive's anger as a rationale to change his life. The temptation to leave being stronger than the desire to ignore his father's demands. Finally, as his father puffed up his chest, daring Luke to retaliate, he took the high road, which he knew would anger his father more. With a perfect French accent, he answered, "Patisserie."

His dad shook his head in disgust and turned away from Luke. Luke let out a sigh, believing the incident to be behind him. That's when his father took a sudden swing and planted his fist onto Luke's cheekbone and then another cross jab that landed on his eye. It was only then that he was ready to join his friends. One of them handed Clive another beer. He opened it and greedily chugged half of it down. After releasing a vulgar burp, he turned to Luke. "A lot of good knowing French will do you," he spat.

Luke turned away, but not before his father uttered one last thing. "One day, that woman… Elizabeth," he said in a mock highbrow accent, "is going to see where you came from and who you really are. You'll have a nice shiner tomorrow. You can wear it like a badge. She'll change her mind about you."

It may have been an idle threat, but it was enough to rattle Luke's confidence.

Chapter Ten

OVER THE YEARS, WHENEVER HIS FATHER BECAME violent, Luke made a promise to himself. He would never be like him. He would work hard. And, he would get out. He certainly couldn't risk leading his father anywhere near Emma. If the man got even a whisper of an idea that Luke fancied her, he would be sure to cause issues. The same was true for his job. If his father got wind that it wasn't just for money, but enjoyment, he would try to ruin it.

It was one thing for him to deal with his father's behavior, but he wouldn't wish the experience on anyone else. He could already tell that Emma was a sweet girl, raised in a good home. As much as he wanted to see her tonight, he just couldn't. He could hear the men in the front room grow more boisterous with every drink. Any interaction with them would certainly result in unpleasantness, so after showering and dressing, Luke crawled out his window and into the rain, but not for the address that Emma gave him. He returned to the restaurant and let himself in with his key. It was cold and dark, but he didn't turn on a light or the heater. It was after hours and he didn't want to alert the neighboring homes that someone was present, nor did he want to increase the electricity bill for Elizabeth.

In just a short week, the job had become incredibly important and not just because he needed the income to keep his father at bay. More than that, the restaurant gave him a glimpse into how other people were raised and lived their lives. Ben Mason was a kind man, and Luke admired his gentlemanly behavior toward Elizabeth. Vera and Mary had obvious affection for each other. Their weekly visit to the restaurant proved that they were friends as well as sisters. For a moment, he wished he had a sibling to share stories and tribulations. But, considering the home he was raised in, it was best he was alone. His father's views on family were selfish. Children were an inconvenience, he often retorted.

In spite of his father's mocking, Clive was right about one thing. Luke recognized the calibre of Elizabeth and the people who dined at her restaurant. They had manners and appreciated the finer cuisine. They brought their spoon to their mouth as opposed to hanging their head toward the plate. They relished the cuisine and never shoveled their meal down. They spent time at the table to enjoy conversation as much as the meal. The white linen napkins were always tucked neatly onto their laps, never inside their shirts. Backs were straight, never hunched. Luke took inspiration from these people, but perhaps what drove him most was the way he felt while working there.

He prepared food to please all the senses. Not just taste, but how the food looked and smelled. The vegetables were cut into uniform sizes. Entrees were placed like a crowning glory on the plate's center stage. The side dishes were the performers that enhanced the star attraction. Sauces were carefully ladled with a portion that only enhanced the food, never masked it.

The result was praise from the customers and Elizabeth.

Luke couldn't remember a time when he ever received accolades from his father, not even as a young child when he would bring an art project home from school or as an older teen when he earned high marks. He thought of this as he lay down in the storage room adjacent to the kitchen.

He was determined to make a new life and learn the restaurant trade. He wanted to go out with Emma, but in the end, there was too much risk. His father couldn't be trusted and he needed to ensure the restaurant was safe. With his loyalty to Elizabeth firmly set in his mind, he maneuvered himself against a sack of flour and listened to the rain pour down against the glass skylight above. He looked up to see the stars, then hunkered down in spite of being cold.

Luke was awoken in the early hours of morning with the sensation of falling. He quickly realized, it wasn't a dream, but Elizabeth pulling a sack of flour from under his feet. It was just before dawn, and he squinted against the light that shone in from the kitchen. In spite of the dimness of the room, there was no hiding the bruises that started to form around his eye and down to his cheek. Indicating them, she said, "I didn't think it was wise to remove the flour bag that served as your pillow."

"Sorry, Ma'am. I'll be on my way," he said hurrying to his feet.

"Mind telling me what happened and why you're sleeping in my storage room? I don't think you're here at this hour to start the breads."

Luke felt the shame rise to his face. He had intended to wake early and do just as she mentioned, start the morning preparations. Instead he repeated, "I am terribly sorry."

Her response was a roll of her eyes and a shake of her

head. "Oh bother." Elizabeth looked at her watch. "Three hours before opening. I guess we'll be making quick breads today. Only a slight change of plans."

The morning light was starting to come through the skylight above. She located Luke's shoes, kicked them over to him, and said, "Hurry up. You're coming with me this morning."

"Ma'am?" Luke held his shoes awkwardly. "I'm not fired?"

"No, you're not fired. You're the best prep chef I've ever had. But hurry up," she indicated his shoes. You can tell me your story on the drive."

Luke put on his shoes, grabbed his jacket, and was straightening the sacks of flour that he had creased when he asked, "Where are we going?"

"Home."

The simple, one word answer caused him to drop the sack he held. Luke stammered. "I…I can't… I can't go back." His voice caught in his throat.

Elizabeth's normally austere demeanor vanished. Her mouth turned upwards in a rare, but gentle smile. She placed a hand, veiny but still strong, to his upper arm and gave him a pat. It resembled what one would do to a cherished dog, but for Elizabeth, it was her way of showing affection. And in that moment, she demonstrated the extent of her compassion.

"That's apparent, my dear boy. Don't you worry. I meant my home."

Chapter Eleven

PRESENT...

Luke swept the walkway in front of the restaurant and as was now his habit, he glanced up the street towards the construction site. Only this time, it wasn't only his father that he kept an eye out for. He saw the beautiful visitor cross the street, her hair billowing gently in the wind, and once again he wished he could brush it out of her eyes. He didn't expect to see her so soon, and found himself surprisingly elated. This time, she held hands with a young girl who resembled her closely, and he assumed she must be her daughter. The man who had gruffly ordered a coffee appeared at their side and took the girl's other hand.

From his vantage point they looked like a happy family and momentarily, Luke wondered if the strife he witnessed from the previous day was imagined. No sooner had the thought come to him when the image in front of his eyes vanished and the man tugged roughly on the young girl's arm. She protested and refused to move; the man leaned down and appeared to shout. Trying to maintain public appearances, the woman scooped up the child in her arms to diffuse the tears.

As if sensing his eyes on her, she turned and held Luke's gaze. They never exchanged names, and yet, Luke began to piece together elements of her life, recognizing it from his own situation.

Her attention was brought back to the dilapidated building by her husband. She set the child down gently and then stood up with perfect posture, her shoulders pulled back, her delicate neck lengthened gracefully. Luke started to take note of the subtle signs of her personality. The manner in which she kept her daughter close when a car whizzed past was protective. The way she smiled when Luke had spoken earlier showed her interest in others. There was much to admire about her that went beyond her physical attributes. But he couldn't ignore those qualities: her lush hair, eyes framed in dark lashes, and her tiny waist that made him want to wrap his arms around her. He shook his head to wake himself from his reverie. He didn't know her, he reminded himself. More importantly, she was married.

"She's a looker," Ben commented, having arrived for his morning routine. "Someone new to the neighborhood?" Ben knew everyone within a few square blocks. He wasn't a busy body, but he had a kind way about him and when someone in the area needed an ear, he lent his.

Luke followed him into the restaurant. "I'm not sure."

"You're not sure if she's a looker? I find that hard to believe."

Luke smiled. "Yes, you're right about that. They might be tourists, but they're spending a lot of time staring at that building."

Ben studied the couple and nodded in agreement. "Seems like they have a definite interest in that place. Not many people are out and about first thing in the morning without good reason."

Luke sent Ben a knowing grin, "Like you?" He had long

sensed that Ben wanted to find the courage to ask Elizabeth out and merely used his morning coffee and crossword as an excuse to be near her. As if on cue, Elizabeth arrived for her day, and Luke gave Ben a smug smile as if to say, "See?"

"Good morning, Elizabeth," Ben greeted, straightening up a bit.

She smiled, but kept her tone professional. "Good morning, Ben. How are you today?" In spite of her intention to do the opposite, she seemed to bustle about with nervous energy whenever Ben was present. "I hope you're enjoying your morning. Let me know if there's anything you need… rather…," she paused, "Luke would be happy to get it for you."

Ben's smile slowly cast itself into a line and he nodded as Elizabeth retreated into the kitchen. He looked out the window again. "Luke, it's nice to have dreams. And just so we're clear… She is a looker."

Luke raised his eyes and let them drift to the kitchen where Elizabeth had retreated.

Ben was too polite to bring his personal thoughts to the forefront of their conversation. "I was referring to the woman out there, of course."

Luke nodded, but with a look that showed he knew the truth. "Ben, you've been coming in for as long as I can remember. I know our croissants are as good as the ones in France; after all, Elizabeth makes them, but I think you're here for more than the food. Why don't you…" Luke made a gesture as if to say 'get on with it.' He saw the way Ben looked at Elizabeth, and for the first time in many years, Luke could relate.

Ben knew of Luke's past, but spoke as if referring to himself. "It's not always easy to swim across a cold lake. It takes awhile to get used to the water."

"Ben, I'd say you've treaded water long enough."

"Well, what about you, Luke? Although, you might have your sights on a difficult catch."

Both men surreptitiously watched the going ons across the way. The woman bent down to speak to her daughter while her husband gesticulated toward the empty building, seemingly growing more annoyed that her attention was not on him.

Ben commented first. "Not much of a gentleman." The man pulled roughly on the woman's arm, driving her attention to what he wanted to point out.

Luke watched the unfolding exchange between the couple. "No, definitely not." His frown deepened when his own father arrived at the scene.

"Isn't that your dad?" Ben asked. "What's he doing with them?"

"God, I hate to think," Luke answered. "But, I need to check on the kitchen. Ben, consider what I said." He jutted his chin to the kitchen where they both knew Elizabeth was stationed. Ben patted Luke's back to show he had heard him.

Luke didn't relish watching the scene across the street fold out any longer. His final glance revealed his father speaking to the man he had heard being called Grainger. Luke's father focused on him, ignoring his wife. Of course he would. Like Grainger, his father had never shown respect to women. Immediately, Grainger dropped her hand and turned to face Clive. The woman seemed somehow relieved, and led her daughter a bit farther away from their exchange.

A look of concern crossed Luke's features as he entered the kitchen. Finding Elizabeth, he asked, "You know anything about the place across the street?"

"Just that it sold and the man out there is said to be the new owner."

"Of all the projects, my father has to be on that one."

"Yes. That man found your dad's website and hired him

while they were still in America. Word is he's on a tight dead-line to finish construction."

"Well, that explains the broken pallet. As if my dad needed more reason to cut corners and do a lazy job."

Elizabeth nodded in response and with a slight shrug of her shoulders, attempted to make Luke feel better. "At least, he won't be around too long."

Although being rid of his father couldn't come soon enough, an expeditious construction timeline meant he wouldn't have long to see the beautiful woman either. Interrupting Luke's thoughts, Elizabeth reminded him, "Let's not focus on your father. Nothing good can happen when he's around."

It was a realistic statement, and yet, Luke prayed that it was just a passing comment. He had already been sent to the hospital once because of his dad's cheap equipment and lack of focus. He hoped that was the end of it and no more harm came to anyone.

"Come on, we've got work to do." Elizabeth handed Luke a plate with a fresh croissant from the oven. "This is for Ben."

No sooner did she hand him the plate, when the bell over the front door rang. Luke hoped it wasn't his father returning for another fight. Peering out the kitchen porthole, he exhaled with relief to see Mary and Vera. "It's Wednesday," he remembered.

"Mary and Vera?"

"Without fail," he answered. "Hey Elizabeth, remember that time when Mary wanted to tell you about a recipe and you ended up listening to her details for 15 minutes? How about you give Ben his croissant and I'll greet the sisters?" Luke pushed open the sliding doors, ready to make an exit.

Elizabeth raised her eyebrows. "You think I should wait-ress now? Since when can't you handle two tables?"

Before Luke could make excuses, Mary's voice greeted

them. "Morning Elizabeth…Luke," Mary called out, making her way to her favorite window seat.

"Lovely aroma in here," Vera added. "I smell cinnamon and cloves. Ooh Mary remember those winters when we used to steep cinnamon sticks and sugar in red wine?" She saw Elizabeth watching her from the double kitchen doors, still battling with herself about going to Ben's table. Vera continued, "It's a long standing family recipe for mulled cider. I can share it, if you like, Elizabeth."

Luke nudged Elizabeth. They were sweet ladies, but they could talk anyone's ear off. "Waitressing or schmoozing?" he whispered in Elizabeth's ear. "You always taught me that every job in a restaurant carries equal importance."

"Let's not get sassy now," Elizabeth replied, knowing full well his reason for wanting her to deliver Ben's croissant.

"What harm could come from bringing him a croissant? That is, unless you have time to learn a new recipe from Vera?"

Elizabeth shrugged her shoulders, but didn't answer. Luke noticed her start to smooth her hair. "You fancy him!"

"I'm too old to fancy someone."

Luke rolled his eyes. "Age has nothing to do with love."

Chapter Twelve

FIVE YEARS AGO...

Emma bustled about the restaurant with a nervous energy that erupted from disappointment. She told herself not to care that Luke stood her up. She barely knew him, she reasoned. Why should she let it bother her? Besides, it was just a first date. Better to see his true colors right away.

"You're not going to wallow," she said aloud. She took advantage of being alone in the restaurant to give herself a much needed pep talk. "In fact, you can't even call these feelings sadness. They're just misplaced emotions that have no business entering your mind. Just see them to the door and give them a good kick in the you know what."

And yet, they seemed to connect. His personality was friendly. He took time to ask her questions when she would talk about her interests. She enjoyed hearing his stories as well. And then there was the other thing... he was very attractive. His lips turned up in a playful smile. Green eyes that danced when they met her blue ones. The way he drew a hand through his wavy dark hair made her want to reach out and do the same. The curve of his biceps as he carried his rowing shell.

"Stop it!" She shook her head, willing the thoughts to leave.

"Miss Emma, did you call?" one of her mother's dish-washers inquired.

"No, sorry. I was just talking to myself. But have you heard from my mother this morning? It's not like her to be late."

"She left a note…" The worker reached into his pocket to produce a post-it, and explained that he found it on the walk-in freezer door. "Sorry, I assumed you saw her earlier."

Emma took the note and absently said, "No, she was already gone when I woke up. Reading the note, Emma furrowed her brow. "Errands to run… will be in before the morning rush. Do your best if I'm late." It wasn't like her mother to run last minute errands, and Emma couldn't imagine what took priority over the restaurant.

Elizabeth sat in the driver's seat of a two-seater, MG open sports car. It was British racing green with an engine that roared to life, causing her to smile every time. Seeing her behind the wheel of the classic car gave Luke a glimpse into what she might have been like in her younger years.

She maneuvered the car through the curving, narrow streets with ease. Her white curls were secured under a bright turquoise scarf, and as she sped along, they blew lightly in the breeze. They drove for about five minutes, past the river, and turned down a long path. The gravel sprayed as she came to a stop in front of a house beautifully built from Cotswold stone. Heading toward its red door, she shouted over her shoulder. "We'll get your things later. Maybe there will be a good time to gather them from your house." Her meaning was clear…

when his father was not around. "And if not, we'll just buy a few necessities."

"I can't ask that of you," Luke protested as he followed her.

"If we buy a few items of clothing, you can pay me in small increments, whatever is comfortable for you. And by the way, I won't accept rent or utilities payment."

"That's too generous."

Elizabeth pointedly said, "Not if you learn the business and stay at the restaurant for many years to come."

"I will, Ma'am."

"Just Elizabeth… we don't need the formalities. At least not here."

As she finished her sentence, Luke saw what 'here' meant. Elizabeth entered the house only to lift a key from a metal wall rack, and then leave again. "Shall we?" She led the way across the drive towards the back of the property. A quaint lychgate with a pitched triangular roof and an arched opening beckoned them to come through. On the other side stood the smaller groom's lodge — a cottage so tiny and quaint it looked reminiscent of a fairytale.

A sash window with white shutters and a flower box with full blooms was situated to the left of a thick oak door. The fragrant scent of red rhododendrons reached anyone who visited. Luke was no exception. Although he had not even entered, it already felt like home. He felt an overwhelming sense of emotion. Nobody had ever shown him such kindness and he took a minute to close his eyes and say a silent prayer of gratitude.

"Are you ready?" Elizabeth gently touched his arm and smiled, sensing his hesitation. "Or perhaps, I should let you do the honors?" She handed him the key, which was surprisingly ordinary given the ornate detail of the door handle plate.

The polished metal showed a Victorian egg and dart design, symbolizing life and death.

"I had a new lock put on last year, but kept the vintage plate. New double-glazed windows keep the cold out. Nearly everything else is original. These bricks…" she indicated the exterior of the cottage, "match the main house and were excavated from Oxfordshire in the 1600s."

"It's beautiful," Luke's voice choked as he spoke.

"Come on, let's see the inside." She nodded her chin to the door, encouraging Luke to open it. Once inside, his attention went to a large fireplace that dwarfed the room. Its opening was outlined in the same oak as the front door and a pile of logs was stacked neatly in the recess next to it. Thick wooden beams clung to the low roof that wasn't much higher than seven feet. The beams provided an inviting accent to the creamy white paint on the ceiling. In contrast, the walls were painted a warm, deep rust hue giving the cottage a decidedly masculine feel in keeping with the title of being a groom's cottage.

"This is pretty much the extent of the place," Elizabeth explained. "The kitchen isn't more than a two-burner stove and sink. Beyond there…" she pointed, "is the one and only bedroom and bathroom. The bedroom has a slightly pitched roof, but you should still be careful. You'll get used to the low ceilings."

"Keeps the place warm, I imagine," noted Luke, who was still standing with a bit of a hunch to his shoulders. As if he realized this for the first time, he glanced up, and seeing that he wouldn't actually hit his head, he let his posture improve to his full height.

"It's small, but as you said, it'll keep you warm in the winter and give you a place to rest your head."

"A million times better than a sack of flour," Luke smiled.

"Indeed," Elizabeth nodded. "I'll bring by some sheets and

towels later. There isn't much storage space, just a cupboard under the stairs. But there is a standing wardrobe in the bedroom that may have some things you need — clothes and whatnot."

Luke took in her comment, wondering whose clothes they had belonged to, but decided not to push. He was too taken by his good fortune to question anything.

"One other thing," Elizabeth added. "The tiny kitchen is fine for heating things up, but not suitable for cooking. Feel free to use the kitchen in the main house, especially if you want to practice your skills. Just be mindful of Emma's space."

———

Emma laid the tables, dusted the chairs, and then retrieved a platter that they used to display the restaurant's baked goods. She dipped a corner of a cloth into silver polish and scrubbed at a non-existent smear. Vigorously she rubbed and stopped only long enough to note with annoyance that everything was clean. There was nothing else to do except prepare the lunch specials and she wasn't a chef.

She thought of Luke with annoyance, and then continued to polish, trying to settle her thoughts. An internal voice kept repeating like a mantra that she was fine without a man. Her mother had taught her to be self-sufficient. She grew up without a father and had seen her mother's strength and echoed it. Sure, it would be nice to feel strong arms wrapped around her, but she reasoned that a good romance book would do her just fine. She checked the hands of the pine grandfather clock that stood in the corner, wondering why he wasn't at work either, and then muttered to herself, "Forget about him. You're being pathetic."

A couple tables were already occupied. An older man with hair color more salt than pepper sat with his wife at a corner table. The Randolphs came every Friday morning and Emma knew their coffee orders without having to ask. A vanilla latté for her and a cinnamon latte for him. She sighed wistfully remembering a story the wife had told her when they first started coming to the restaurant. Apparently, the husband had only drank his coffee black for the first 20 years of their marriage until his wife suggested they "spice things up". She had, of course, meant it in a way that extended beyond coffee, but he took the suggestion literally and ordered a cinnamon latte. One day, the wife winked at Emma and told her the latte was the first of many welcome changes.

As Emma went back to the kitchen, she reflected on her date with Luke that never transpired and wondered if she would find someone to spend 20 minutes with, let alone 20 years. Hearing the bell above the front door, she turned to look out the kitchen double doors.

Her mother bustled into the kitchen as if nothing was unusual.

"Where have you been?" Emma asked in a tone reminiscent of her mother's when she was a teen and stayed out too late. But like Emma had done years earlier, Elizabeth took no notice of her disapproval. She merely repeated the message of her note. "I had an errand to take care of."

"It's not like you to show up after opening."

Elizabeth took a quick inventory of the restaurant. "You seem to have handled everything."

"I said that we only had continental breakfast available... the muffins and croissants that were in the case. I'm not a chef. Speaking of which... Where's Luke? Did you fire him?"

"I gave him the day off."

It wasn't like her mother to do that either, and Emma noted that her answer came rather quickly. "Why would you do that?" Emma asked suspiciously.

"Well…" this time Elizabeth's thoughts stayed in her mouth.

"Why, Mum?" Emma repeated.

"… to sort through some of your father's clothes and clean up Halcyon Cottage." Elizabeth spat out the words in rapid succession.

Emma's mouth dropped open in both surprise and shock. "Why would he need to sort out the cottage?"

"He's moving in."

Chapter Thirteen

DESPITE HER HECTIC SCHEDULE, EMMA FOUND herself consumed by nervous anticipation for Luke's return. Annoyed with her own feelings, she couldn't tear her gaze away from the cursed grandfather clock that didn't have the manners to pass faster. She couldn't begin to fathom what had gotten into her mother.

Working with Luke was one thing, but having him live in the guest cottage and share their kitchen was altogether another. Particularly since he provided no explanation, nary a text message, on why he stood her up. Certainly, had her mother known about his behavior, she wouldn't have offered him residence. Mother always said that rude behavior didn't go unnoticed and yet, somehow Luke had dodged her mother's wrath and won her over. Emma eyed the clock once more.

When it was finally time to close for the afternoon break, Emma found herself lagging around. She searched for more tasks to avoid what would happen when she returned home. Finally, she grabbed the sign they always placed in the window, a powder blue wood placard with a delicate white scroll in English and French that bid their customers well. It read, "See you soon… à bientôt," and as Emma balanced it on the windowsill, she muttered under her breath, "Yeah, I'll see you soon," and finally headed out the door.

By the time she arrived home, she had maneuvered her emotions past rejection and closer to anger. It wasn't a great improvement, but certainly an emotion with a backbone. The car tires sprayed the gravel as she came to a sudden halt. She slammed the door, marched down the path avoiding the main house, and headed straight for Halcyon Cottage where she pounded on the door. When there wasn't an immediate answer, she pounded once more.

Nerves and paranoia were getting the best of her. When Luke still didn't answer, she wondered if he saw her through the window and was avoiding her. After all, he decided not to show up for their date; anything was possible. She was about to turn around and go to the main house when he answered.

To her annoyance, her anger quickly vanished, replaced by the same fluttering she felt in her stomach after he had kissed her. Luke stood in the doorframe wearing only a towel, appearing muscled and gorgeous. Emma forced her eyes away from his torso and toward his face. "You didn't just dip your pen in the company ink, you've added your name to the letterhead."

He could see she was upset and he knew why. It wasn't like him to kiss someone he barely knew. It was even more out of his character to do so and then be rude. "Emma, I'm sorry."

"That's it? You make arrangements to live here with my mom, but you don't have the decency to call instead of standing me up? Or, give me any explanation?"

"Technically, if I called you, I wouldn't be standing you up. Something came up."

She was about to bristle over the vague comment, wondering if "something" was actually a "someone" when her mood suddenly softened. As Luke turned his head, she caught sight of the markings of his bruises.

"What happened here?" she grazed his cheek with the back of her hand.

"It's not something I want to share."

Emma pulled back and shook her head, resolved that anger was safer for her heart than rejection.

He could see the pain in her eyes and hated himself for causing it. "Emma, look at me," he indicated the bruises. "Why do you even want to spend time with me outside of work? Your mum has given me a job and now a place to live, but I don't want to see myself as a charity case. I will pay her every week from my paychecks."

Emma felt her cheeks flush. "I want a date, not to offer charity. I'm not that desperate. I thought we… never mind."

She started to turn away, but Luke caught her elbow swiftly. "I didn't mean it that way. Emma, please wait. Let me throw on some clothes. Will you take a walk with me?"

———

They walked in silence, but not the awkward sort. Emma's shoulders relaxed down her back, the tension of the day melting away. Luke's arms swayed gently at his sides. When his hand brushed against hers, it felt natural that his fingers intertwined with hers. When they reached Bourton Bridge, the one the village was named for, they stopped to admire the view above the River Widenbrush. Underneath, a few punting boats floated by, their slow progress a reflection of the peaceful stillness that had settled around them.

Luke sighed, "One day…"

Emma looked up at him with a questioning gaze, leading him to explain.

"Maybe we will find ourselves floating on the river and you

can tell me everything you want me to know about you. And that, will be the best day ever."

She smiled at his simple wish. "Won't you share too?"

"I'm sure my story isn't as nice, nor my future as bright."

Emma noted his wistful tone. "Why is that?"

He furrowed his brow, drawing his eyebrows closer. His expression was a mixture of contemplation and hesitancy, but after a beat he revealed his truth. "It's the reason why I stood you up. It had absolutely nothing to do with you, Emma, and everything to do with my family — my father. The night we were supposed to meet, he had friends over. They were drinking."

Luke continued to tell her the story of that night and explained that it wasn't an isolated incident. He told her that his face or some other body part inevitably got in the way of his father's wayward fists. "I couldn't put up with it any more, and I went to the restaurant. You know the rest."

Emma let her hand gently graze the bruise on his face. "I'm sorry I was so… heated. It's just that…" she paused again, searching for the words. Finally, she admitted, "I care. Maybe more than what is normal considering our short time together."

Luke wrapped his arms around Emma's waist and with her back against his front, he held her close. "I feel the same."

"I could stay like this for a very long time." She pulled his arms around her even closer. "Still… we should set some boundaries. You deserve privacy, Luke. I wouldn't want to hover…"

He turned her around to face him. "You do know that the cottage doesn't have much in the way of a kitchen? I'm going to be the one hovering."

They continued on their walk, feeling a little lighter than when they headed out. Luke added, "I'll have to store some food in your refrigerator. And, I'll be experimenting with preparing that food in your kitchen. Your mother insisted."

Emma smiled, knowing where this was going.

Luke continued, "And, your mother also invited me to eat the food that I store in your refrigerator and prepare in your kitchen. In fact, she invited me for dinner tonight."

Emma laughed. "You build a strong case. Are you sure you don't want to study law?"

"I'll stick with cooking and baking. Maybe I'll become a proper chef or pâtissier one day." They slowed their pace as they were in no hurry to end their conversation or time together. "Emma, what's your future?"

"I've been studying philosophy at Oxford. In between classes, I help with the restaurant because it's nice to have the freedom to do both."

Luke laughed lightly, "What do you do with a philosopher at your door?"

Emma shrugged her shoulders stumped.

"You say thank you and pay him for the pizza."

Emma nodded, "Very funny. You don't believe in education without a distinct career path?"

Luke shook his head to himself. "I don't know why I joke. I sound like my father. Truth is, I can't think of anything more admirable than education. It doesn't have to lead to a trade. Life leads us to where we're meant to be."

"Who's the philosopher now?" Emma kicked her heel back against Luke's bottom in a playful move.

"You're rubbing off on me."

"Well, one of the reasons I wanted to study at Oxford is because they call it the city of dreaming spires. I've always been a dreamer. My other hobby, maybe one day a career… is just as much a castle in the air," she admitted.

"What is it?"

"Art," she said without hesitation. "I've drawn and painted since I was young. When did you learn to cook?"

"Like you, when I was young. There was never any good food at home so if I wanted to eat, I had to cook. Not that I don't have a lot to learn from your mum."

"Speaking of which… Luke, can I ask…" Emma hesitated. "Where's your mum?"

"She died when I was young."

"Like my dad," she added. "You and I have a lot in common. I believe that people come into one's life for a reason."

Luke bent his head down to Emma. She gazed up and their eyes met. Luke placed his hand against her cheek. "Emma, you have all the makings of an excellent philosopher. So tell me, considering that I made a huge mistake the other night, would a kiss be an act of foolishness?"

"You'd be a fool not to kiss me."

With that, Luke brought his lips to hers in a kiss that was tender and sweet, and filled with promise.

Chapter Fourteen

THEIR CONNECTION BECAME INSTINCTIVE. LUKE glanced through the kitchen porthole window and Emma would naturally turn to meet his gaze. Emma would enter the kitchen to collect an order and Luke brushed her hand as she passed. And it seemed as if both wore a permanent smile.

"Aren't they sweet?" Mary said to her sister, Vera, pointing to Emma. "I see her looking at that handsome young man."

"She has very good taste. I've found myself looking once or twice as well."

"Oh Vera, stop!" her sister chastised.

Elizabeth had been unnecessarily straightening a pile of menus nearby in order to listen in on their conversation.

"More clotted cream?" Vera offered her sister.

Elizabeth furrowed her brows knowing that no more information would be imparted. She had a mind to see about this news for herself, and as such, she let her eyes sweep between Emma and Luke. She noted that Luke seemed a bit distracted. Emma made more trips into the kitchen than necessary. And the kicker, when Emma surreptitiously waved to Luke with her pinkie finger, that was enough.

"He's working," Elizabeth admonished her daughter from outside the double doors, but loud enough for Luke to overhear.

"It's my fault," Luke answered immediately, stepping out of the kitchen.

"This is ridiculous, Emma replied. "Nobody has done anything."

Elizabeth stood up a bit straighter as if adding to her height would make her more intimidating. It didn't work, and Emma simply rolled her eyes.

"I'm doing my job; everyone is happy." Emma waved her arm to the full restaurant of customers who indeed were eating and chatting happily.

"That's besides the point," Elizabeth answered with a fast shake of her head.

"It's my fault," Luke repeated, causing both women to stare at him.

"You're merely half the equation. I'm sure she has something to do with it." Elizabeth sent her gaze back to Emma. "Are you going to let him take full blame?"

Emma considered and then batted her eyes at Luke. "Thank you," she mouthed to him to which he smiled back.

Elizabeth raised her eyes toward the ceiling as if praying to an unseen god. "If you weren't my daughter, I'd have to fire you for distracting our new sous chef."

For the first time, Luke responded without any fear or guilt. His answer was pure excitement. "Sous chef? Seriously? Elizabeth, I mean… Chef… thank you!"

"Elizabeth is fine, even here," she answered. "Now remember, you're still learning my recipes. Later, I'll expect you to train the prep chefs. You can get creative on your own lunch time, and just maybe some of your creations will make it onto the menu. We'll see how you do and take it from there. Just don't cut yourself because something or *someone*…," she said pointedly, "takes your focus off work."

Emma and Luke made their way through the winding streets of the Cotswolds, stopping for a 99, the British creation of inserting a Cadbury Flake bar into a soft serve ice cream cone. They walked as they licked their treats, occasionally using the flaky chocolate finger as a makeshift spoon.

"My mum pretends she doesn't like 99 ice creams, but seriously, how can you not love these?" Emma dipped her flake bar into the ice cream and brought it to her mouth, then replaced the candy into its center and licked her fingers of the chocolate.

"I can't imagine your mum licking her fingers," he said dabbing a napkin to the side of Emma's cheek where she missed a small drip.

"True. What we're doing would horrify her."

Luke looked worried. "Because we're spending time together?"

"No silly, I meant that not only are we licking our fingers, but we're walking while eating. Completely uncivilized behavior as far as the French are concerned… but not for an English lass," she said while taking a lick.

Emma took the last bite of her treat and held up her hands, now completely clean, as a hint for Luke to hold one. He naturally did and after walking another block, Emma stopped unexpectedly and leaned against one of the stone walls that decorated the village. "Luke, it's perfectly safe at this hour. I can get home if you have something else you need to do." In spite of her words, she cheekily leaned closer and wriggled her finger to beckon him closer.

There were so many times at work when Luke saw Emma

and wanted to be near her, but they remained respectful. But now, Luke felt his resolve melt. "I don't want to take up too much of your time. Sometimes I think I should turn away before you decide that I'm like leftovers…best left alone."

"I want you to take up my time." She pressed onto her toes and then, leaning in closer, she whispered, "I gotta secret."

"Oh yeah?"

"Yeah. I like you, Luke Barrows."

"I like you too, Emma."

Although she was close enough to kiss, Luke stepped back. It wasn't that he didn't want to feel her lips against his again, but they were standing on a public street, and he was decidedly British. Ice cream in public was one thing, but kissing was altogether different. Emma may have been half French, but Luke had no influences other than having grown up in conservative England. So, instead of kissing her, he settled for giving her hand a reassuring squeeze.

"There's something I want to do," he said, motioning for her to keep walking. They continued through the village center, passing the market cross, a historical structure that stood at the intersection of the village's three main streets. Taking the street uphill led to Le Pont. Heading to the left would lead toward the construction of the old farmhouse, and below them led to Elizabeth's house. Luke bent down and collected two short sticks and they continued in the direction of Elizabeth's house, first pausing atop Whiteley Bridge, another one of Bourton Bridge's famed five stone bridges and the one closest to her home.

Luke held up the two sticks. "You choose first."

"Are we playing Poohsticks?"

Luke nodded, pleased that Emma immediately knew of the childhood game. Although both sticks looked practically identical in length and width, Emma took her time choosing, determined to select the one that would win.

"Are we playing for anything in particular?" she asked, having made her selection.

"You appear to be a pretty savvy player."

Emma went to one side of the bridge and then the other, checking for the side where the water flowed upstream. "That I am. Since this is your first time playing Poohsticks with me, I'll let this game be just for fun."

Luke held out his hand and Emma shook it — a deal having been made.

"But next time…," she teased, pretending to mean business.

They counted to three and both dropped their sticks on the upstream side of the bridge, then hurried to the opposite side where the water flowed downstream to see whose stick appeared first. When Emma's stick came into view well before Luke's, he whistled under his breath, "Impressive."

"I've got mad skills."

He smiled, captivated. Emma was like no girl he had ever met. Without a doubt, he was utterly smitten and couldn't believe the luck that fate brought him. She made her way over the bridge and he followed, knowing that she could lead him anywhere. When they arrived at Elizabeth's house, Luke paused at the main house before turning toward the path that led to his cottage.

The living situation was still new and their attraction was making it more complicated. Unsure of how to navigate the situation, Luke uttered a simple 'goodnight' and turned toward his cottage.

"Goodnight," she replied back.

The hint of disappointment was evident in her voice. The kiss. Lord knew, he thought of doing it again. But Emma had also indicated that she didn't want to risk them growing tired of each other. His thoughts vacillated back and forth. Like a punting boat, he debated how to steer the relationship. To continue the evening or say goodnight, either could have consequences.

"Goodnight?" She repeated, but this time as a question.

He turned back, remembering something he had tucked into his pocket. "I almost forgot." He removed a small paper bag and opened it to reveal a single scone. "I experimented today... chocolate chip scones for breakfast or afternoon tea."

Emma took a bite from the corner of the perfectly shaped triangular pastry. "Oh it's perfect, Luke. A light crunch on the outside, but soft inside... kind of like my mum," she joked.

He brushed away a dusting of sugar that had decorated the top of the scone and now rested on the corner of her mouth. "Food seems to find its way onto you," he smiled.

"Maybe you shouldn't waste all that lovely sweetness," she responded coyly. Then more boldly, Emma stood on her toes and lightly kissed the side of Luke's jaw. With her proximity, he twirled a strand of her hair before allowing his hand to graze her neck. The whole time, he held her gaze and moved his head even closer to hers. Their mouths were just a whisper away from each other. Emma tilted her head upwards.

Luke smiled, but still held his ground.

"You're not going to kiss me?" Emma's voice held a note of surprise.

"I'm just enjoying the moment."

"You might enjoy it more if you..."

Luke's finger traced her lips, causing her not to finish the thought. When she exhaled softly, it stirred a craving within himself, but still he maintained his control.

"What were you saying?" He kissed her cheekbone, then her jaw.

She closed her eyes and he did the same to the other cheek, all the while moving his mouth closer to her lips. "Nothing..." she mumbled.

Until finally, his mouth was over hers in the lightest and

most tender of kisses. He pulled her body in closer to his, protecting her from the early evening chill and wanting to feel her against him. As he did so, their kiss intensified.

They stood at the entry to his cottage. It would be a welcome move for him to turn the key and take her inside. And although he wanted nothing more than to do just that, he maintained his resolve. "You have an early day tomorrow. You should get some sleep."

"Is that what you want?"

He kissed her again, this time with the promise of a future. "You know I don't, but it's the right move for tonight. We have a lifetime ahead of us, and an early day tomorrow."

Chapter Fifteen

PRESENT DAY

Grainger had rented a tiny flat that smelled like a menagerie of cats had been the previous renters. But in its favor, it was just a short walk from Le Pont, making it easy to get a morning coffee. As he walked briskly toward the work site, Jade and Emilie struggled to keep up.

"Daddy, wait!" Emilie called out.

Grainger barely slowed, but turned over his shoulder to call out. "You know I'm late, Jade. Just keep up."

"We'll meet you there. I'll stop and bring you a coffee," she replied, holding onto Emilie's hand and trying not to drag her along.

Her reply was the one thing that did cause Grainger to stop. "Do not... I repeat, do not cause interruptions. If she can't keep up... if you do not arrive the second that I do, well... let's just say, it'll look bad."

Jade picked up Emilie, who was trying to rest by plopping down in the middle of the sidewalk, exhausted from the fast pace of the walk that was thrust on her. "Why do you want us in tow?"

Grainger shook his head in frustration. "I've told you. I don't want Clive thinking we're not on the same page with the construction and this project. You know how builders are… they get wind that there's some discord and they start playing one person against the other. Next thing you know, he'll be talking to you about fixtures and fittings, you'll say you want the more expensive ones and he'll say something asinine like 'she's got a point'."

"Oh yes, that would be crazy."

"Don't start," Grainger wagged a finger at her. "This is exactly what I mean. Just come along; do your part."

"Grainger, exactly what is my part? This whole project seems really risky."

"I've got it under control. It's a great investment. Just be agreeable. No matter what." He leaned closer, "And keep Emilie quiet."

Jade nodded, thankful at least for Grainger whispering his last sentiment and Emilie not hearing it. She knew that there was little point in arguing with her husband. Over the years, she had discovered that doing so only made matters worse. Being 'agreeable' as he requested was the easiest way to avoid strife.

"There he is," Grainger nodded toward the abandoned property. He grabbed her elbow, and holding onto it firmly, led her across the street. It was his preferred way and Jade always felt it akin to how one leads a horse. She couldn't imagine Grainger tenderly holding her hand or protectively wrapping his arm around her waist. In fact, she had trouble remembering what had drawn her to him years ago. It seemed like another lifetime.

"You with me?"

His words shook her thoughts away. Jade inhaled deeply and sent a practiced smile in Emilie's direction. Excuses came easier over the years and as in the past, she responded to the nagging voice in her head with new justifications. She told herself that jet lag must be the culprit for making her worry. Lack of sleep must be the cause of his irritability.

"Yes," she said simply. It was what he wanted to hear.

When they caught up to Clive, he extended his hand to Grainger and the two launched into small talk, excluding Jade. When Clive finally acknowledged her presence, it was with a tight-lipped smile and a brief nod, more of recognition that she existed, rather than a welcome. His demeanor suggested he wasn't pleased to see her. She didn't really care if this man liked her or not. But call it instinct — something was amiss. She found herself constructing half-truths to ease her discomfort. It couldn't possibly be the scent of alcohol on his breath; perhaps it was merely a cough lozenge. His gaze didn't linger on her chest; surely, he was just looking past her.

Perhaps Grainger felt shades of doubt too, or at least Jade hoped he did, because he launched into questions about the construction. "So, you've assembled your team?"

"Yes, already started some demo." Clive waved his hand to the building proudly, although in its current state it hardly warranted the action.

"Everyone licensed and insured?" Grainger pressed.

Clive took a beat before answering and even then, took another to turn on what Jade saw as a crocodile smile that exposed yellowed teeth and opened the way to lies. "You're going to be very happy with my team. They're fast and hard working."

"Insured?" Grainger repeated.

"Listen Grainger, you hired me to get this job done on time. Let me tell you something about this industry... all that licensed and insured stuff is bullshit." He turned to Jade and saw her glance at Emilie, who stared up at Clive. "Err, sorry... I mean silly stuff." Clive regained his smile and sent it down to Emilie, who now hid behind Jade's back.

"What do you mean?" Grainger asked, still pulling for an answer.

Clive's tone became more aggressive and the cadence to his words sped up. "They're experienced. That's what you want. Licensed and insured? You want to pay more for a piece of paper?"

Grainger took a moment to look at the building. The crew had left without clearing up. Broken bricks littered the sidewalk, never having made it into the rubbish container. A rusted ladder was propped up against the side of the building. Dust and rubble were everywhere. Grainger was a stickler for cleanliness often citing that it was indicative of one's pride in their work. Jade followed his gaze, hoping that he would see this as reason to get out of the deal.

Clive also noticed him taking it all in, but rather than get defensive over the shoddy job that was already becoming apparent, he put a spin on the situation. "See how fast we jumped into action? You paid an advance while in America, and I've made good on my end. We have a deal and I aim to bring this job in on time. Your second payment is due once the demo is complete," he added quickly.

In what Jade hoped was finally a moment of sound judgement, Grainger replied, "But going back to the permits... Isn't it the law? Doesn't someone have to be licensed? You're licensed, right?"

"Look here," he said, pointing to the building. "My crew can do the work twice as fast and for less," Clive replied without answering Grainger directly. "You get these fancy Oxford builders and they'll insist on tea time every hour on the hour. The city will charge for every permit and the approval process will slow everything down."

"But..." Jade inadvertently let the one word escape from her lips only to be sent a warning look from Grainger. She immediately shut her mouth and let her husband continue.

Certainly, he would make the right choice in this sort of situation. It was too important.

Grainger fixed his gaze on Jade, an assertion of dominance evident in his narrowed eyes. Having made his silent point, he turned back to Clive. "Then how exactly do you get around the permit issue?"

"I have a contact," Clive replied briskly, a touch of smugness seeping into his tone, though the vagueness of his statement was palpable. "But I'd advise against prying too deeply."

As Grainger contemplated, it seemed to Jade that he was bowing out. She released a relieved sigh, hopeful that they were nearing the end of this ordeal with Clive. She longed for the familiarity of home, where Emilie could resume her studies and she could find solace in Willow's presence. Inhaling deeply, she dared to believe that closure was within reach. Yet, Grainger's unexpected response jolted her. "I want to get it on the market in four months."

Even Clive seemed taken aback, not only by Grainger's acceptance of his lies, but the increased pressure as well. "I thought you originally said six?"

Grainger reached into his pocket and fished out a £100 note. "Is it a problem?"

Clive snatched at the offering. "Not at all."

Grainger nodded. "Good. I've nothing against saving time and money. From what you're telling me, I can even send some more of this your way and still come out ahead. You catch my meaning?"

"Don't you worry, boss." Clive pocketed the note and Grainger puffed up his chest at the new title he was bestowed. The two men shook hands and Jade's apprehension grew.

In times like these, Willow always made her feel better with a witty comment that would turn her mood around. But it was still too early in California for Jade to consider calling. Without Willow to confide in, Jade considered stopping into

Le Pont to seek solace with a warm cup of tea. She remembered the chef's kindness towards her. But then pushed the thought away. It was his job to offer food — nothing more. She chided herself for thinking otherwise. A wave of apprehension and loneliness washed over her. She typed out a quick text to Willow.

Miss you. Wish you were here.

When she looked up from her phone, Grainger and Clive remained deep in conversation. Her presence went unnoticed, and Grainger made it clear that he didn't want her involvement. Silently, she clasped Emilie's hand and departed without a word.

Jade found an open table at a nearby Greek restaurant called Taverna Nico. She knew that Grainger would follow in the direction she left, but for now, she needed the solace of sitting quietly with Emilie. Her mind brimmed with worry. Clive's method of doing business weighed heavily on her, and the looming prospect of spending Christmas away from home brought sadness.

Willow was like a sister to her and as such, she couldn't imagine not seeing her over the holidays. She stared at her phone, but wasn't particularly surprised when no response came. It was barely 6 a.m. in Los Angeles and Willow was never one for waking early. Trying to distract herself, Jade picked up one of Emilie's crayons and absently started coloring with her as they waited. Grainger arrived and slid into the chair across from Jade.

"Why'd you leave without a word? Damn rude. I need a drink," he said, signaling for a waiter. "A bottle of house red," he bellowed.

Jade interjected. "Maybe you should order just a glass? I'm not having any."

"Of course you're not. Why would you want to celebrate?"

Jade remained quiet and ignored his sarcasm. "Well, you've been very insistent that this is your project."

"It is. But you'll benefit." He spat out the words. "You ready to order?" he asked without looking up.

When she didn't answer, he finally lowered his menu. "What?"

"I'll benefit? You mean, thanks to our mutually made decisions? This sounds sketchy, and I've had no say in the matter."

"What could go wrong?" he asked, and to her amazement he seemed truly in the dark.

"No permits. No licensed contractor. A crew without insurance. You can't be serious, Grainger."

"You are such a buzz kill."

Before she could answer, the waiter dropped off glasses and the bottle of wine. He uncorked it and poured a sampling for Grainger, who swallowed it down greedily. He nodded his approval and indicated for the waiter to fill his glass up. Jade politely shook her head and covered hers with her hand.

"Are we ready to order?"

"Just one more minute," Jade answered.

"I'll be back shortly," the waiter replied as he left.

"Why did you do that? I haven't had lunch today. Make a decision already. I'm hungry." Grainger threw back the rest of his wine.

Jade shook her head, exasperated that they were in this situation. Still not ready to drop the subject, she persevered. "You're meant to improve that building so somebody else will buy it. That means doing it right."

Grainger responded with a false laugh that made Emilie look up, along with someone from a nearby table. "Don't be overly dramatic. It just needs to look better. It's not like they have earthquakes here."

"That's your answer?" Jade's eyes went wide with disbelief.

That set him off. "Listen…" he leaned forward, his jovial act now disappearing as fast as the wine. "You want to be a team? Then, do your job… take care of Emilie and support me emotionally." He poured himself another glass and held the bottle over Jade's glass. "You obviously need to unwind."

"No, thank you," she replied.

"Fine. More for me," he topped off his glass.

"I thought you wanted a clear head for business."

"I do. What's that got to do with anything?"

Emilie looked up from her drawing hearing her dad's voice raise, while Jade did her best to diffuse him. "On second thought, maybe I will have some wine."

"You don't want any. You just don't want me to have it." He poured himself more, and added, "I won't waste it on you. I also don't want to hear you imply that I don't know my limit," he said evenly and then as if to make his point, finished off his glass in a quick throwback. "Let's order," he said looking around for their waiter. "I don't have much time."

"What do you mean?"

"I'm going to London with Clive."

A worried expression crossed Jade's features. For once, Grainger noticed without annoyance. "Relax. It's early and I'm not driving."

She nodded, feeling relieved and believing he meant that they would take a train. It was then that Grainger added, "Clive is."

"Clive is what?"

The waiter returned before Grainger could answer her question. They placed their orders and once he left, Jade immediately pressed her husband for an answer. "Grainger?"

"Clive is picking me up. He's taking me to a new pub for a celebratory drink. I'll have a light lunch with you and then dinner with him. I'll be home by 11… midnight at the latest."

In spite of relishing time alone with Emilie, something that had been less frequent since they arrived in England as Grainger rarely left the flat, Jade worried about how wise it was to go out with Clive.

Grainger took note of her silence. "Relax, Jade. You're the one that expressed concern about us not having any friends here. So I'm making friends."

"But you employ him. It's not good business. And something about him makes me leery."

Grainger's disposition went from trying to reassure her to an explosion. "Good business? Since when do you have good business instincts? In fact, what does any of this have to do with you? I'm tired of you holding me back."

Hearing her father yell always put Emilie on edge and this time, she started to cry, angering Grainger more. "Can you sort her out? That's all you need to do." He threw down a handful of pound notes and stormed out of the restaurant.

"Is everything alright, Madam?" Hearing the commotion, a man who appeared to be the owner of the restaurant came over. "I'm Nico. Can I be of service to you?"

Jade sat in embarrassment, but collected herself for Emilie's sake. "I'm terribly sorry. If our order hasn't been put into your kitchen yet, may I cancel?"

"It's no trouble, Madam. I hope your day improves," he said kindly.

Jade simply nodded and put on a happy face for Emilie as she had done so many times in the past. It was only then that she noticed Luke having a bite while reading a book at a nearby table. Although he didn't gaze up, she couldn't imagine anyone in the restaurant not hearing what had transpired. Her embarrassment prevented her from even saying a polite hello.

Chapter Sixteen

AFTER WORK, LUKE DECIDED TO GRAB A BITE AT THE quaint Greek restaurant a few blocks away. He and Elizabeth knew the owner, Nico, and both parties shared a belief that healthy competition was good for business. They regularly hosted him at their restaurant and took time to support his business as well. Today, Luke was eating solo to be alone with his thoughts.

He reflected about his father's recent behavior. He had always been an angry drunk, but something had shifted in the preceding weeks. Luke continued to see him across from the restaurant. He could hear him yelling at his crew. During a recent catch up with Harry, he asked how he put up with it.

"I look at my paycheck," Harry answered honestly. "My reason to work with him is based on necessity. I deposit the check and buy groceries."

Luke nodded, but wasn't quite ready to let the issue of his father go. "Listen, we have a bit of an issue at Le Pont. I know firsthand how important it is to land a job. I was a stone's throw from being on the street when Elizabeth took me in.

But Harry, we can hear him shouting even when we're inside the restaurant."

"Luke, I'd say that I could speak to him about it, but we both know how far that would get us. Anyway, your cooking is good enough that customers will overlook his noise."

Harry had gone back to work and Luke was left thinking about his answer. Sure, the customers came for the food, but a shouting drunk left something to be desired of the ambiance. With each passing day, it became evident that his father's thirst for his afternoon drink intensified, and with it, his voice grew louder and his demeanor reached the boiling point.

As he ruminated on his dad's behavior, he heard similar shouting from a nearby table. Although his back was turned, within a second he heard the accent and recognized the voice of Jade's husband. Hearing their conversation was unavoidable, and along with it came an explanation to what had triggered his father's recent drinking binges. Her husband and his father were cut from the same cloth. When he first noticed them together, he couldn't be certain that the job posed any particular problems. Now, overhearing Grainger, he knew for certain that his father was up to his tricks. At least this time he admitted that he wasn't a licensed contractor. However, Luke knew that wasn't his father's morality speaking. On the contrary, he had never seen a shred of decency in that man. It was apparent that his admission was meant to put more money in his pocket by saving on a real contractor.

Out of the corner of his eye, he could see Jade collect her belongings. Her discomfort was apparent even from the quick glance that he stole in her direction. He knew she must have felt the sea of eyes that witnessed her husband's behavior, and he didn't want her to think that he was among them. He was sure she had noticed him, but he did his best to fixate his eyes on his book. She rushed out the door without a word and Luke's heart melted.

"Hey Kaitlyn...," he called to the waitress, "can you add this to our restaurants' reciprocal bills?" There were other advantages to becoming friends with competing restaurants in the area. The two owners had decided on a monthly stipend that each party could use for meals. Luke knew that he and Elizabeth were well under their allotment.

"Of course, Luke. Nice to see you," the waitress smiled, while clearing away his plate.

"Feel free to visit. I'll set you up with homemade cinnamon rolls," Luke offered. He then hurried to catch Jade. He knew she didn't want to talk, but it wasn't her fault that her husband had little manners. Embarrassment would only fester and grow. He reasoned that clearing the air was the polite thing to do. Besides, they had yet to officially meet, and in truth, there was something about her — the way she doted on her daughter, the proud way she carried herself, the smile she presented when meeting people — all things that made Luke want to get to know her. Even if it wasn't his place to do so.

He jogged a few steps and caught up to her easily. "Lovely day, isn't it?"

She merely nodded and sent him a tight smile, maintaining her rapid pace, and towing Emilie along. Luke had no idea how the little girl kept up or how Jade managed to move so quickly in heels. His legs were longer and still, he found himself getting winded. He also noted that Jade gave a slight frown at his insistence to stay by her side.

"I'm just in a bit of a hurry," she said.

"No worries. I'm headed this direction too. The fast pace is good for my digestion," he lied, feeling a stitch hit his side. As if on cue, Emilie complained about the same ailment. A small groan escaped her, "Mom, you're giving me a side ache."

"I've got this," Luke smiled and scooped up Emilie without

missing a beat. "At your service," he said to Emilie while ignoring Jade's near immediate protest.

"Emilie…," she pleaded. The unspoken words were clear… start walking so we can regain our dignity.

"Emilie, you might have a better view from the upper deck," Luke teased, talking to her at eye level. She gave him a questioning look, until he bent down and indicated she should crawl up to his shoulders.

Luke positioned the little girl with one leg dangling over each of his shoulders, her hands clenched into his wavy hair as if gripping a horse's mane. She squealed with delight, and once settled, he continued on. This time, it was Jade who followed behind.

"You don't have to do this," she said.

"Like I said, it's a lovely day. I'd rather not enjoy it alone. Is it okay if I walk with you?"

She softened and a genuine smile returned. "Yes, that would be nice."

Although Jade was American, it was apparent that she shared the British trait of wanting to evade public scrutiny. He had finally diffused any tension. They walked in comfortable silence until Luke unwittingly revived the awkwardness, simply by attempting to engage in conversation. "So, you're the new owner of the farmhouse?"

He immediately realized his mistake. Talk of the property reminded her of Grainger and with thoughts of her husband came memories of his recent public behavior. Jade nodded, but didn't offer any more.

Luke rolled his eyes to himself, marveling at his own stupidity. They carried on in silence, side by side, and Luke realized he didn't even know her name or where she was headed. It didn't matter as he was happy to have even a few minutes with her, whether they spoke or not. Emilie seemed content in the silence as well, perched on Luke's shoulders and no doubt admiring the view from a new vantage point. He could feel her shift and he knew she was turning to admire the river with the ducks swimming contentedly.

"Mommy, you should carry me like this."

Luke was happy that her words brought a smile to Jade's face. She looked up at Emilie and answered. "I don't think I'm strong enough to carry you like that. You should thank…," she paused, realizing they hadn't been introduced.

"Luke," he filled in the blank and nodded his head as way of a greeting.

"Jade." She offered her hand automatically, but immediately realized Luke's were occupied holding onto Emilie's knees. "Oh, you've got your hands full," she joked.

"Important cargo." And just like that, any uncomfortableness was behind them. Until it wasn't.

"Mommy, you can't carry me like this, but Daddy is strong enough. Why doesn't he ever do it? And where is he again?"

A heavy sigh escaped Jade. "Daddy is going to a business meeting." She didn't add the part about his plans to go pubbing in London. "We're going home to watch T.V. and then your nap." As if all of the embarrassed feelings had come back, she felt the need to distance herself from Luke. She reached up to Emilie's hand, and instinctively Luke stopped walking. "How 'bout you come down now and give Luke's back a rest?"

"Okay," Emilie said. Luke noticed how agreeable the little girl always seemed and wondered if the trait was inherited from Jade's kindness or fear of Grainger's explosiveness. Luke suspected a bit of both as he bent to help Emilie down.

Immediately upon setting her feet on the ground, Emilie made a beeline for a swing at the edge of a nearby park. "Yes, you can," Jade called out and Emilie beamed. For the first time, Luke and Jade were alone, and he knew it was time to clear the air.

"Are you okay?"

When she didn't answer and started to turn toward where Emilie was swinging, Luke placed a light hand on her arm. He turned her toward him slightly, and gazed straight at her. His expression was kind and concerned.

"We're fine," Jade said simply.

Luke's voice was a gentle whisper. "But are *you* fine?"

Her answer, just a small shrug of her shoulders, concerned Luke. "I'm a good listener."

"I'm sorry that your lunch was interrupted by us."

"From what I saw, you have nothing to apologize for. Does he do that often?"

Again, Jade made a slight motion with her shoulders as if to say maybe, but her eyes revealed that the answer was yes. It didn't matter to Luke. Words weren't necessary and they wouldn't do any good given the circumstances. Luke wanted to say something like he was there for her, but he hardly knew her. He felt a connection; perhaps it was the similarities he saw in the way she had to navigate her husband and he had to deal with his father. He had to wonder if maybe there was something more fated about their meeting.

"Listen, this is certainly not very British… we're raised to make polite conversation and not get too personal. They say we should speak when spoken to so as not to bother someone who is having a hard day. Basically, that adds up to minding our own business. But Jade, what I saw wasn't okay. If you need someone to talk to…"

"I really need to get her home for a nap." Jade indicated Emilie, cutting off Luke and the offer that was presented.

Luke nodded, knowing that he had overstepped. She quickened her pace toward the park, her face looking close to tears. And although Luke's words may have brought them to the surface, he knew he wasn't the root cause. Deciding he would be more appropriate and simply help her get home, he asked, "Are you staying close to the building site?"

"Along the Westing Road. We're renting a flat." Jade offered no more conversation. "This way, Emilie." The little girl bounded off the swing and ran to her mother, who was already approaching the next corner.

"If you don't mind...," Luke started.

Jade stopped, but this time with her arms crossed in a protective stance. "Listen, I don't want to talk about my husband and his rude behavior or the fact that it probably seems as if it runs in the family. I just want to go home."

"I merely wanted to say that you're going the wrong way. Westing Road is that way," he pointed to the opposite corner.

Jade smiled for the first time since Luke had started after her. "I'm sorry. Obviously, I'm a bit upset and I've gotten all turned around. If it's not too much trouble, could you... just tell me where I go from here?"

"Can I do one better and walk you back?"

Jade took a deep inhale, filling her lungs as if to settle her thoughts. "You don't have to. I'm not a charity case."

Her words echoed his own from so many years earlier. He understood Jade all too well. He knew what it was like to feel lost. She misunderstood his silence for a dismissal, and before he could find a way to reassure her, she spoke up, "Just let me be, Luke. Point me in the right direction and I'll leave with my dignity."

He gave her a quick nod and indicated the route she should take. Without another moment's hesitation, she took Emilie's hand and walked off. Luke watched her leave, feeling a myriad of emotions. He didn't understand how Grainger could speak to a woman the way he had, much less his wife. He hoped Jade was alright. More than anything, he wished he could find a way to help her. He watched her walk away, and once he was assured she was safe, he turned and headed the opposite direction.

Chapter Seventeen

JADE PONDERED THE RECENT ENCOUNTER WITH Luke, mulling over every detail. She couldn't shake the thought that he could have simply let her depart when they unexpectedly crossed paths. And when Emilie grew weary, there was no obligation for him to carry her. In parallel situations, Grainger's indifference would have been palpable; he wouldn't have spared Jade a moment, let alone carry Emilie for three blocks. It wasn't good for her marriage to compare the two men, but it was hard not to.

Walking through the lanes of Bourton Bridge, she reminded herself that Grainger was under stress. It was what she always said, what she always did… make excuses. When she applied that tired reasoning, Willow would say it was no excuse for irate behavior. Just last week Jade had brought Willow up to speed, and her friend's concern was evident.

"You don't sound happy," Willow noted. "Then again, you didn't sound happy before you left," she reminded. "Have things gotten worse?"

"In some ways, it's better." Jade tried to sound optimistic.

"There's a lot of history to discover in Oxford, beautiful nature walks to explore, and quaint shops in the Cotswolds.

"You sound like a travel brochure," Willow mused. "Anything else? New friends?"

"The people are warm…" Jade's thoughts drifted to Luke, but Willow misunderstood her pause.

"Anyone in particular?" Willow pressed.

"There's a nice chef in the village."

"A nice chef or a hot chef?"

In uncharacteristic fashion, Jade wasn't able to let her friend pull her out of the doldrums. "Both, and I try not to notice," she said in a reserved tone.

"Hey, are you okay?"

"Yeah, I'm just tired." Jade didn't want to worry her friend and she certainly wasn't ready to share about Luke, hot or not. "I'm still adjusting to the new time zone," she said, making a poor excuse.

Willow had known her long enough to recognize when she was covering up something. "Okay, but remember, it's just a ten-hour flight. If you need me, I can be there in a day. In the meantime, find a yoga class, go to a coffee shop. Find a place where you can meet a new friend. Granted, you won't find someone as witty or wonderful as me, but having someone by your side will help."

"Good ideas. I'll text you soon."

Willow's words from earlier resonated with her. As she walked hand in hand with Emilie, Jade couldn't get the image of Luke out of her head. It had been nice to talk with another adult, even if it was about something uncomfortable. He was kind. He listened to her. He was wonderful with Emilie. But she kept reminding herself of one important fact; she was married.

A friendship with another man wasn't forbidden, but some people might say she was playing with fire. His kindness was having an effect on her. Knowing Willow, she would probably encourage the connection, which made Jade suspect that she should stay far away from the handsome chef. Shaking herself out of this reverie, she paused to look in the window of a quaint store along Waterfront Street — *Bourton Bric-a-Brac*.

"Look!" Emilie's eyes grew with the vision of tiny ceramic statuettes facing out from the window in greeting of would-be customers.

"Do you want to go inside?" As always, Jade put her daughter before herself. She was tired from the day, but this shop seemed like it might lift their spirits. The store was stacked floor to ceiling with shelves displaying keepsakes. One wall was completely devoted to Alice in Wonderland figurines. There was so much to take in that she and Emilie both had the same reaction to simply stop and stare.

"Can I go over there?" Emilie pointed to three uneven and worn wooden steps that beckoned visitors downward toward a basement.

A kindly woman with white curls heard her. "Of course you can, Crumpet."

Jade smiled at the term of endearment that the woman bestowed on Emilie.

"Aren't you the American?" the woman inquired, adjusting her glasses on the bridge of her nose.

"Yes, just visiting. My husband has some business to do here," Jade answered politely.

"Mary, we have a visitor all the way from America!" Jade smiled, amused at all the fuss.

"Vera, she's Californian." Another woman, no doubt the sister to the first, had been dusting a shelf and came over to add this piece of information. "Bought the old farmhouse, down from Le Pont. Going to be quite an endeavor getting that place up to speed. I wouldn't want to be in your shoes."

"As they say, hopefully just a little spit and polish," the

one named Mary added and then seemed to squint at Jade as if she were an unusual zoo animal. "I've seen you at Elizabeth's place."

Jade was surprised that her arrival had caused a stir among the local village. Not to mention, hearing what the locals thought of their purchase did nothing to ease Jade's concerns.

Seeing her face falter, the first sister, Vera, explained. "Oh we hope we didn't offend you. Not a lot happens in Bourton Bridge, and when it does…"

"Let's just say the news spreads," Mary finished her sister's thoughts. "But you'll get to know everyone. We're a close-knit community."

"Has its ups and downs," Vera said as a bit of warning.

Mary continued her thoughts. "Speaking of which, we heard that you were going to sell the place right away. Is that right? Quite an undertaking to just pass it along afterwards."

"Uh, I don't know."

"Well, I'm sure it'll be marvelous, once it's inhabitable," Vera added with a tsk.

And then, as if they had talked themselves tired, Mary pointed to the opposite wall where Jade stood. "You might find something intriguing over there."

Happy to get away, Jade thanked both women and then went exploring. Mary had pointed out a staircase, only as wide as one's shoulders, leading upwards in a higgily piggily spiral that seemed mysterious in keeping with the Lewis Carroll story.

Although she wasn't particularly tall, the low ceiling made one bend over while maneuvering through the tight spaces. It was as if every person in the store had been given a sampling of the mushroom that made Alice grow tall. If only she could have eaten the other mushroom half and shrunk, Jade mused. She also wondered if the sisters had seen her talking with Luke. She remembered the way he had looked at her. At one moment, it seemed as if he was taking in her features admiringly. Then again, with the way Grainger had behaved, it could have just as likely been a look of concern or dare she say, pity.

The idea that she was the subject of gossip made her a bit uneasy. But then again, the sisters seemed kindly and maybe they were just welcoming her in their own way. She tried to take comfort from that thought. It was different here, much like the tale of Wonderland. Its themes of growth and change resonated with her as her own life forced her to look inward.

As Jade reached for a small, porcelain white rabbit, Emilie arrived by her side. "That's pretty," Emilie said.

"It certainly is," Jade replied. Momentarily, she thought what life would be like if a parallel looking glass swallowed her up. But with Emilie by her side, she was reminded of one very good thing in her life.

"Ready to go home?" she asked.

Tired from the day's journey, Emilie nodded in response.

———

With Emilie settled in for a nap, Jade sat down with a cup of tea and scrolled through the news on her phone, but found that most of it did nothing to lift her spirits. With perfect timing, Willow's call arrived.

"Hey stranger!" Willow greeted before Jade even said hello. "I miss you tons."

Hearing Willow's voice and being alone as Emilie slept left Jade feeling lonely. Coupled with Grainger's outburst in contrast to Luke's kindness, she felt a lump in her throat. She choked up and couldn't get a word out for fear of releasing the tears that she had held in since Grainger walked out of the restaurant. She still hadn't heard from him and wondered if he put the incident behind him without so much as to see if she had gotten home alright. She knew Grainger, and he was either still mad or trying to punish her. Either scenario was unacceptable. Logically, Jade knew this, but as with so many times in her marriage, she felt trapped and forced to put up with it.

"Jade? What's wrong?"

When Jade still didn't answer, in fact nary a word had come out of her, Willow spoke in a gentle voice. "Talk to me. Let it out," she coaxed.

That was all it took. A heavy sigh released from Jade and as expected, the tears followed. She tried her best to swallow them, but it was no use. "I miss you, too," Jade sobbed. "I didn't want to worry you last time we spoke, but it's been awful. Grainger has us up to our ears in debt with this project. The contractor is a shady character. I don't trust that anything is going to go well. We fight constantly about it. There's so much to do. I won't be home for Christmas." She let it all out in a rush and then exhaled with the relief of sharing the truth.

"I'm so sorry, Jade. How can I help? Have you met anyone you can hang with? You know, just to give yourself a mental break?"

"You know how it is with Grainger." Jade paused. She had never admitted aloud what Willow had always known. It was impossible to have someone come around when Grainger was home. "He's too volatile. I don't want to risk the awkwardness."

Jade's mind immediately went to Luke who had seen Grainger's behavior more than once. Still, she didn't mention him. What could she say? That she actually fancied Hot Chef?

Jade shifted the conversation to Willow asking about her work instead. The conversation remained slightly stilted and polite because Jade couldn't bring herself to admit that she had made a huge mistake in coming to England. Although when Grainger had threatened to bring Emilie alone, she had no choice. In truth, the mistakes started many years back.

"There is something I can do… I can visit. Immediately, in fact."

"Willow, I can't ask you to do that."

"You haven't. I booked an open-ended ticket the day you left… ready to use whenever you need me. And it sounds like that's right about now."

Jade felt more like herself with Willow's news. "You're the best. I can't wait to show you this adorable village."

"I have another surprise… I'm doing a house swap. So, you have another place in Bourton Bridge for an escape."

"I'm really glad you're coming, but that won't be necessary. I'm fine."

Willow had heard Jade's attempts to be strong for too many years now. "Jade, will you promise me something?"

"Of course."

"Look after yourself and Emilie. I worry about you."

Jade had seen that Luke worried too. She hated being this source of angst for the few people around her who showed her compassion. Trying to put Willow at ease, she said, "Grainger has bad moments, but I have to believe he's not a bad man."

There was a distinct pause in which Jade expected her friend to agree, but Willow said nothing. Agreeing would be the polite thing to do. Even a small 'uh-huh' or nod had they been in person, but Willow couldn't bring herself to do it. Not this time.

"Jade, I've seen you with him for years. I've never thought any argument was even partly your fault. The only thing you have to blame yourself for is marrying him."

When Jade didn't comment, Willow gently added, "And that can be rectified."

Jade remembered her thoughts while holding the Alice in Wonderland figurine and momentarily imagined an alternate life, but just as quickly, she discarded the idea. It was too complicated when children were involved. She couldn't trust

Grainger with Emilie alone. There was too much risk to separate. Finally, Jade answered. "I've already uprooted Emilie enough. This is my life."

"I understand your desire to maintain a family for Emilie. But Jade, when you think about family, is this what you had in mind?"

Chapter Eighteen

WILLOW WATCHED AS ONE PASSENGER AFTER THE next heaved their suitcase from the airport luggage conveyor belt. She stood and watched it rotate, waiting for her Vera Bradley hard case with spinner wheels to come down next. But it didn't.

"Don't be lost. Please find your way," she whispered under her breath.

A woman within earshot gave her a questioning look.

"My suitcase... it has the cutest design; it's called 'Hope Blooms' and I bought it especially for this trip. I thought it would be a good sign because my friend is having some difficulties here. You know, new home, new culture...she's just finding it rather hard to fit in when people don't readily talk to newcomers." Suddenly noticing that the woman held a British passport and was averting her gaze, Willow backtracked. "Not that the English aren't totally welcoming."

The woman gave her a slight nod and moved away.

"Well, that went well," Willow said, still talking to herself, as she continued to keep an eye out for her suitcase. When the conveyor belt remained empty and Willow had finally given up on watching it rotate, she approached the lost luggage counter.

"Hi, my luggage has decided to take a vacation without me," she said to the attendant behind the counter and received a blank stare in response.

"It's lost," Willow clarified.

"Fill out this form, please," the woman handed her a slip of paper as if this happens all the time.

Willow didn't know what upset her more, the fact that she didn't have any clothes or the idea that her suitcase might be having a tropical vacation someplace without her. As she waited in line for a coach into Oxford, she pulled her jacket around her small frame, feeling unaccustomed to the cooler temperature.

She did a little jog in place trying to get her blood flowing after the long journey and to stay warm. When the coach arrived, she found her seat and no sooner realized yet another thing she needed. She immediately asked the coach driver, "Excuse me, is the toilet in the back?"

"Yes madam, but I'm afraid the loo is out of order."

"It's just that I didn't use the loo…" she said trying to assimilate, "before leaving the airport."

"Traffic is light. We'll be stopping right outside Debenhams in about 52 minutes."

"And that is?"

"A fashion shop…a big one. Best take your seat so we can be on our way."

"She did as she was told, crossed her legs tightly and closed her eyes hoping she might fall asleep and forget her physical discomfort."

True to the coach driver's word, they arrived outside the large department store in just under an hour. Without a suitcase to retrieve, Willow was first off the coach and made a beeline into the store.

She looked around at the massive expanse of clothing rounders seeing men's trousers, sport jackets, casual wear, and more. The bright lights of the store and her tiredness from the journey made it difficult to find what she needed. Looking up, she saw the signage that read 'toilets' with an arrow pointing upwards and another reading 'lift' with an arrow pointing to the right.

The need to get to the toilet was unprecedented and she practically ran to the opposite end of the store. A door was clearly marked with the word 'Toilet' and she went in, proceeding directly into a stall. Locking the door, she sat down and exhaled with obvious relief of having made it on time.

It was only then that she heard the entry door creak and the heavy footsteps of work boots. Glancing under the stall door, she saw enormous feet, certainly too big to belong to a woman. It was only then that she had the inkling of an idea that she may have entered the wrong toilets. She looked around her stall and didn't see any of the accoutrements that would normally be available for women. And in fact, there wasn't even any toilet paper.

She waited a moment and then heard the unmistakable sound of a man going to the bathroom. She closed her eyes, said a little prayer, and then mustered up her courage.

"Um, excuse me?"

Her words were met by silence.

"Hello?"

"Hello?" came a decidedly male voice.

"There's no toilet paper in here. Can you hand me some?"

"Well, I'm standing at the urinal and strangely I don't see any."

Willow rolled her eyes. "Very funny. Can you go into the stall next to me? Please?"

"Hold on."

A second later, Willow smiled upon hearing water running and the pump of the soap dispenser. Then, a strong hand reached under her stall with a handful of toilet paper, neatly folded at that.

"What a gentleman. Thank you." A moment later she emerged from her stall.

"For handing you toilet paper or washing my hands first?"

"Both. And the customer service of folding it."

"I'm Willow," she said while washing her own hands.

Harry took in the petite woman whose eyes were shadowed in long black lashes that matched the color of her sleek hair. "Harry," he said, extending his hand after she had a moment to air dry her own.

"This is quite a meet-cute."

Harry sent her a questioning glance. "Meet-cute?"

"Rom-com talk," she said, releasing his hand but not before taking in the fact that they were attached to extremely strong arms. "It's what we'll tell our kids when they ask how we met."

Harry opened his eyes wide in mock fear, but then got over it because Willow's smile was so infectious. "I get it. But most people try a club or pub."

Willow started to vehemently shake her head side to side. "Wait a minute. I didn't come into the men's toilets to pick up a guy. I was lost. I just got off a plane. And desperate."

"Desperate?"

"Not that kind of desperate. Like I said, I came here straight from Heathrow Airport."

He opened the stall where she came out and then immediately came back. "No luggage?"

"Lost. Kinda like me."

He nodded. "We're going shopping."

Willow beamed a smile at Harry as he led the way.

The handles of the shopping bags made their way up Harry's arms like ornaments on a Christmas tree. Two on one side and three on the other.

"I can help," Willow offered.

"Nah, I've got you. Shopping is hard work."

"Finally. A man who understands this fact." Willow's stomach grumbled in agreement of Harry's words.

"You see? How about a cup of tea and a slice of cake? Cafe is on the top level."

Willow answered without hesitation. "I am a bit hungry. But if we eat, then... you know what that means."

Harry smiled as he caught on to Willow's meaning. "Then this really is a meet-cute."

"Our first date," she joked coyly.

Harry had never met a woman like Willow. She was beautiful, but that was second to what most attracted him to her. She was funny, whip smart, and if he was going to be honest with himself, a little odd. And he loved it.

After getting her the items she would need until her luggage arrived, such as a nightie to sleep in that he did his best not to notice, he insisted on walking Willow to her rented flat.

"Maybe we should make one more stop," Harry suggested as they started to move toward the exit. "Indulge me."

He led her to the store's basement level where the food hall was located. It took up the entire basement level and housed a complete grocery store along with an ample deli counter, bakery, and prepared hot food bar. Harry picked out what he considered essentials, filling a shopping bag with milk, tea, a loaf of bread, a wedge of cheese, fresh fruit, chutney for the cheese, and even a chocolate bar if she got late night cravings.

"This is pretty lavish. I won't have to go out for a week," Willow commented as they headed from the store into the cool air.

Having learned that Willow was staying in Bourton Bridge, he pointed out the landmarks including Le Pont. "Don't say that. You'll miss out. Best food in the village, right there. The chef is a good friend of mine."

"Does he make you say that?" she joked.

Harry laughed. "You are something." They walked down the next lane and then Harry pointed out her place. "We're here."

Willow took in the sight of her flat, a tiny house with bougainvillea growing over the door. "Oh it's cute. I've got the code for the lock box here," she said, checking her phone notes. Once the door was open, Harry turned on the lights, deposited her shopping, and hung up her coat.

"Are you always this great?"

"No."

She looked at him with surprise. Maybe he was her ideal man. He was even honest. "Okay, so what's wrong with you?"

"I'm told I snore."

Willow shrugged as if it wasn't that big of a deal. "Wait here." She moved to the chair where she had deposited her purse and dug through it. "Ta-dah!" She proudly displayed a white plastic case containing a pair of earplugs. "Best on the market. I never travel without them. Take them. My way of saying thank you for your help."

He leaned towards her and very gently placed a light kiss on her cheek. "Willow, if I snore, I don't need earplugs. But... you might."

Willow's eyes grew wide, realizing her error. "Oh, you're right."

"Today was very unexpected. But also very nice. It was lovely meeting you, Willow."

"Thank you, Harry. I never thought that losing my luggage would be such a nice experience."

He laughed and opened the door to leave. A steady rain had started to fall. "Got you home just in time. Welcome to England," he said acknowledging the rain.

"It's actually kind of nice. We don't get a lot of rain in Los Angeles... or kind men who help women with their shopping."

"I hope you have a restful evening. If it's not raining too hard and you want to venture out for breakfast, I'll be at Le Pont."

Willow smiled. "I just might see you there."

Chapter Nineteen

LUKE DODGED INTO GEORGE'S CORNER STORE dripping with rain. As he shook off his jacket, spraying an ample amount of water onto the floor, Brianne raised her eyebrows. "You're lucky George is in the back doing inventory."

Luke looked at the puddle he created. "I'm sorry. It's coming down like there's no tomorrow. I forgot my umbrella."

"It's England, Luke. You gotta keep an umbrella in your car." She grabbed a mop that was leaning against the corner wall.

"I walked. Let me help," Luke offered and took the mop from her hands.

"Hmm, walking in this weather... without an umbrella... must be why you're soaked."

Luke smiled in spite of the unwanted sarcasm being dished on him. "Just nipping in for a few essentials."

"You and everyone else. The rain is sure to keep people inside this weekend."

Luke nodded and headed to the closest aisle to pick up

supplies. In spite of what Brianne said, he and Elizabeth knew that people could only stay holed up for so long. Eventually, they would want a change of scenery and a bite out.

He planned to make coq au vin — chicken in wine — a delicate stew that Elizabeth had perfected by adding a scant amount of brandy. The alcohol would burn off as the stew cooked at a low temperature, creating unsurpassed tenderness. Her other secret was to add a pat of butter at the very end of the cooking process to lend a rich decadence to the stew.

However, the bad weather had prevented their fruit and vegetable farmer from making his delivery. So Luke came to George's shop in search of plum tomatoes for a side dish. Luke was reaching into a bin of vegetables that George had on the floor, turning over some limp celery, onions, and potatoes.

Seeing Luke rummage through his produce bin caused George to comment. "Might not be up to your fancy standards, but they'll do the job."

Luke nodded, "That they will. No tomatoes, George?"

"Sold. Some people actually shop here for their fruit and veg."

Luke nodded and gathered up what remained. "Cream of celery soup, it is." He was just getting ready to make his way to the check-out line when he saw Harry.

"What are you doing out in this weather?" Luke asked him.

"I was being gallant and walking a young lady home. And now I thought I'd keep George company until this sudden downpour clears," he said smiling at George, who sent him a scowl in return.

"You could buy something while you're here… Like Luke," the shop owner said pointedly in case Luke also had the idea to use his store strictly as refuge.

Luke's answer came swiftly. "Absolutely, Harry. I'm here for some of George's fine vegetables."

Harry narrowed his eyes at Luke. "For the restaurant?"

"Yes, for the restaurant!" George butted in. "You think he's buying them for ol' Wilfred?"

Hearing his name, the stray cat wandered in from the rain. "Hey, buddy." Luke bent down to scratch the cat behind the ears.

"Don't encourage him, Luke," George protested.

"Don't let him fool you," Harry whispered. "I've seen him put down a box with a blanket each night. Wilfred has landed on his feet here."

Luke smiled, but kept up the act. "Here you are, George," he put down a ten pound note for the vegetables. "Elizabeth is going to be mighty pleased about these. And, use the change for some more tuna for Wilfred."

George nodded and gave Harry a sideways glance. "Just found that blanket lying around in the storeroom. It's not like I brought it from home for him."

"He'll be knitting him a sweater next," Harry leaned over to Luke.

"With booties," Luke replied.

They stifled their laughter, and as they were looking very much like lifelong friends who could read each other's thoughts and finish each other's sentences, Luke heard his dad's booming voice.

"Look atcha," Clive shook his head at Luke. "Darby and Joan comin' out of your mouth, that I'm sure."

His dad's cockney slang for the word *moan* didn't bother him, but his presence put an immediate end to the joking and small talk. "Harry, I'll see you around. We can go for a run along the river when the weather lets up." Luke made a point of referencing the sport that Harry excelled in during their school days. He wondered if Harry regretted pursuing easy money with his dad instead of the slower route toward continuing his education.

Clive side-stepped the two of them to retrieve a bottle of gin from a nearby shelf. He scowled at Luke as he pointedly said to Harry, "I'll see you at the site tomorrow. It'll be a busy day. I'm meeting the 'septic tank' in an hour." He turned back to Luke, "In case you're too high 'n mighty to remember your rhyming slang, I'm referring to the Yank. He and I's got big plans. You'll regret you're not part of them, not like Harry 'ere." Clive put a beefy arm around Harry, before carrying his liquor to the check-out counter.

———

The rain had let up making the walk back to the restaurant more pleasant. Luke did his best to brush off the run-in with his father, greeting a few other villagers who had emerged for some fresh air. He was used to taking long walks to clear his head, but arriving at the restaurant to see Jade having a cup of tea refreshed his mood even more than the cool air. He hurried to put away the groceries and then immediately returned to the dining area to greet her.

"How was your day?" He felt a connection to her, but the last conversation didn't end well. Luke wanted to find a reason to start over. "I baked some cinnamon scones for tomorrow morning, but you can try one now," he said, hoping she would stay longer. "On the house, of course. They would go nicely with the tea."

"That's very kind of you, but I can wait."

He nodded and noticed her eyes darted to the window facing the street. She was looking to see if her husband was around, that he was sure of. Being reminded of her situation and status was enough to stop him hovering. "Well, I'll leave you in peace," he said and turned toward the kitchen.

"Luke…" she reached to touch his arm, keeping him from rushing off. "I did a horrible job of apologizing the other day. I ended up getting defensive and then walking off. It wasn't my most gracious behavior."

He leaned down to her level and looked in her eyes. As if realizing that her hand was still on his arm, she shifted uncomfortably. "I'm sorry." She repeated the apology, but this time he suspected it was for an altogether different reason.

"There's no reason," he said.

"I was forward just now," she gestured her head toward his arm.

A natural laugh burst from him. "You're fine. I guarantee my virtue is intact."

She blushed upon hearing his joke. "As long as you're sure," she smiled and raised her eyebrows for emphasis. He enjoyed the comfortable conversations they had, but also realized that they dissolved just as quickly.

Her smile waned, and a hint of sadness crept into her eyes as she spoke. "I also wanted to apologize for my husband's behavior the first time we were here."

Luke shook his head, wanting to show her that she needn't apologize. "I've been around difficult people my whole life." There was no point, in his mind, to avoid the truth or the subject matter of her husband. He decided right then and there that he wanted to offer her friendship. And like any relationship, one couldn't take the good and leave the bad.

"Listen…," he spoke quietly. "He's part of your life. I'm just offering you an ear if you ever want one. Trust me, I know his personality type." Luke didn't mince words. "I've had a lifetime of something similar while dealing with my dad."

When Jade didn't respond, he continued. "You've met him."

She looked up, her brow furrowed as if trying to recall the details. She knew so few people in England, she couldn't fathom who Luke's dad might be.

"Clive?" Luke offered. "I've seen him talking with your husband."

Jade finally nodded, now understanding. "Perhaps I should go."

It wasn't clear if her statement was meant as a question, but Luke knew what she meant. The connection between their lives became even more intertwined, and not necessarily for the best. But Luke was determined to establish their friendship. "Is your daughter enjoying England?" It was an obvious attempt to change the conversation and simultaneously keep it going.

Jade took another sip of tea, buying herself a moment to compose herself. "She likes it very much. She's currently enjoying an adventure overnight camp." But to keep her situation real and remind Luke of it, she added, "And my husband is celebrating tonight… with your father."

Luke suspected that the reminder about Grainger was meant to deter him, if only it was that easy. "I know you're married, Jade. I respect your situation… although I like you very much."

"I like you, too." Jade had thought the moment of awkwardness had passed, but Luke remained quiet. "Have I done something?" she asked.

"It's not you, Jade. From what I've seen of your husband, and what I know about my father, I've got a bad feeling," he answered honestly. "Are they taking a coach or driving?"

"Grainger said your father was driving, that they wouldn't be too late, although I don't see how that's possible."

Luke nodded to himself and seemed to retreat into his own thoughts. Jade's voice brought him back.

"Hey, in the hope of starting over and the fact that I'm on

my own for a few hours, would you want to take another walk? The rain has stopped. Unless you need to work," she said immediately, feeling foolish for asking him out.

He was surprised, but also elated by her question. "I'd love to."

Chapter Twenty

BEFORE LEAVING THE RESTAURANT, LUKE GRABBED A small bag and filled it with duck food. The owner of a nearby dairy farm, who supplied the restaurant, had ducks on his property and generously shared his feed mixture of seeds, acorns, and vegetation. Elizabeth liked having it on hand for children and even visiting adults. As they neared the river bank, Luke paused and handed Jade the bag of feed.

They took turns tossing the morsels into the river, debating which ducks had more than their fair share. The sun had yet to set and the grassy bank was filled with people, who like them, were enjoying the reprieve from the rain. Some jogged, others walked. The college rowing crews practiced for their annual regattas. Seeing them prompted Jade to ask Luke about the sport. "Have you ever tried it?"

"I have a shell — a boat. It helps me to clear my head, when I need to," he explained. "But it's their season now so I try to stay out of the way of the young guys."

To this comment, Jade laughed. "You're hardly up in years."

"If you saw how out of breath I get compared to them,"

Luke nodded his chin in the direction of one of the teams, "you'd agree with me."

Jade smiled up at him and they fell back into their comfortable silence. As they walked, Luke's arm accidentally brushed against Jade's. He instinctively muttered 'sorry' but also had a strong inclination to wrap it around her.

They crossed one of the river bridges and found a wooden picnic bench where they could rest and take in the remaining part of the day. Luke reached into his backpack and surprised Jade by pulling out a container with charcuterie — cured meats, cheeses, and even some chutney.

"This is a surprise," she said, impressed. "Do you always carry gourmet snacks?"

"I'm a chef so I guess it's my way of being prepared. Some people carry pocket knives, I bring treats."

She laughed, happy to spend time with him. It was quiet and peaceful along the walk and the table was situated under a willow tree, which lent them privacy. George's store was just up ahead and Luke asked if she would excuse him. "I'm just going to get us a drink. The one thing that didn't fit into my backpack."

"Twice in one day?" George noted with surprise.

"Your sunny personality keeps me coming back."

"Watch it, Luke."

Luke chuckled to himself as George rang up his supplies. He turned once over his shoulder to catch another glimpse of Jade seated in the shade of the big tree. His smile grew bigger, but he immediately reminded himself that this was not a date. It could never be more than what it currently was and even that pushed the boundaries.

When he returned from George's shop, he carried a full grocery bag with a variety of ingredients as well as a pitcher. Jade's eyes lit up. "What's all this?"

"I borrowed the pitcher from George. Don't worry. It's clean."

Jade looked mildly concerned. "Is that unusual?"

"Well, I suspect that Brianne, his shop assistant, does it. Anyway, I'm making you a rhubarb cordial. You haven't experienced English culture until you've had one. Since I'm not at the restaurant, I had to cheat a bit and buy canned rhubarb. George opened it for me. But again, don't worry. I cleaned off the can opener."

"Why would you have to do that?"

"The only thing it's used for is opening tuna and kippers for Wilfred — his cat," Luke explained.

Luke proceeded to mix in the rhubarb along with sugar, orange, lemon, and ginger. He poured some fizzy water over the vibrant liquid, added a mint leaf, and then handed the glass to Jade.

"It's delicious," she exclaimed. "The ginger gives it that bit of zing."

"You got it. Kind of like you."

She laughed. "Me?"

"Yeah, you're strong, determined... even when you're lost."

She rolled her eyes. "You mention that moment of stubbornness as if it's a positive trait."

"It is," he nodded with assurance.

Jade grew quiet, lost in the memory and the realization that Grainger was the cause of her angst that day. As if sensing that her mind had wandered, Luke changed the subject by reaching into his backpack. "You had the good snack, now you have to acquire a taste for British crisps."

Jade eyed the assortment that Luke dropped onto the table and immediately wrinkled her nose up. "Eww."

"Eww? You haven't lived until you've tried Thai Sweet Chili Crisps," he said proudly holding up the first packet.

"And what about Roast Chicken and Thyme Crisps?" he held up a bright purple packet.

"Yeah, that sounds like a good combo if it were on an actual chicken, but not on a potato chip."

Luke reached for a red packet. "For the traditionalist… this one is just your everyday crisp."

Jade pointed to a yellow packet and the simple act evoked a response from him. "Interesting choice… sea salt and cider vinegar. Dipping your toe into uncharted territory?"

He held her gaze a bit longer than perhaps he should.

"Sometimes the idea of trying something new is appealing," she replied.

From the intensity of her look, the deep inhalation she took as if to steady herself, the involuntary way she bit her lower lip, Luke was sure they were no longer talking about crisps. He reached across the table and wrapped his arms around her. It was uncharacteristic of him, but he took the chance. They sat in silence, but the proximity of their bodies spoke mountains. There was something innately intimate about a hug in public. It was innocent, and yet reckless. But in that moment, neither seemed to care who saw them.

Luke ran his hand along her back slowly, and then finally, he released his hold and smiled at her. "It's okay."

She nodded, but said nothing. She had to remember that she was living in a foreign country, needing to ensure that she and her daughter were secure. She gazed at the river. She had to do her best to keep swimming upstream with her husband.

Luke broke the silence by crumpling up the crisp bag he had devoured. He squeezed and twisted it, turning it into a tight ball. "Watch this," he indicated a trashcan that stood a good 15 feet away from their table.

"No way," Jade commented.

"There's a trick. That much is true. You finished with that one?"

"It's all yours," she handed him the other crisp bag and he wrapped it around the first, creating a slightly bigger ball. Twisting and squeezing the bags together, he was finally ready. In an overly dramatic show, he lifted the ball toward his forehead, one hand slightly elevated above the other in the way professional basketball players take aim, and he sunk the ball in the trashcan with ease.

"Not bad. You row, bake, and now basketball?"

He smiled and shrugged. "Not sure we can call that basketball."

He looked down to where her hand rested on the table, enticing him to hold it in his own. She caught the direction of his glance and took in a deep breath. Her shoulders fell slightly and he knew that she wanted the closeness as well. But both of them knew better, so he tried changing the subject.

"What are your plans for the property? A hotel, maybe?"

"It's Grainger's deal."

"That was a fast answer."

She shrugged one shoulder. "I feel as if we've established a friendship. It's nice to not always have to say the polite answer."

"We have, and no you don't have to." With that, he took her hand. Screw it. He wanted to and he knew this opportunity probably wouldn't present itself again.

"Luke…"

He met her eyes, expecting her to ask him to stop pushing the boundaries, to stop feeling the way he did about her. Maybe she was about to do just that, but instead when she met his gaze her tone softened.

"Buying this property was Grainger's idea. If I were to live out my dream, I'd buy an art gallery."

For the first time, Luke was the one to drop her hand. She noticed his Adam's apple bob in his throat as he swallowed, although he hadn't taken a drink. He seemed lost in his thoughts suddenly.

"You okay?"

"Yes," he turned back to her and offered a smile, but there was a tinge of sadness in his eyes that she hadn't noted before.

"The paintings in the restaurant… I've admired them. Different styles. It's obviously not one person's work."

She had tried to pull Luke back to his normal light-hearted self, the man who could form a mini basketball with a crisp bag. She realized now how much he had done to improve her mood whenever she saw him. She had always been a bit lighter around him, but now in this moment, something had made him grow serious.

Finally, he collected himself and commented on her observation, but there was a hitch in his voice as if he held back a deep pain. "You're right, the pieces aren't by one person."

"So, who painted them?"

"I did the bad ones."

Jade shook her head. "None of them are bad. You mean the ones that have a less realistic style?"

"Yes, that's a polite way of putting it. I thought you said we were beyond polite chit chat."

"I like them. So, I'm not being polite. I think the colors and brushstrokes are bold and beautiful."

Luke finally smiled the way he normally did. "Oh gosh, there's a soap opera called 'The Bold and the Beautiful'. I think Elizabeth used to watch it."

"It's American. I know it."

"You watch it?!"

Jade opened her eyes wide and shook her head rapidly side to side, "No, my life has enough drama."

She became quiet with the inadvertent admission, and Luke swiftly brought the conversation back to the paintings.

"Thank you for complimenting my art… If it can be called that. The good ones, on the other hand. Those are special."

"Who painted those?"

Luke interlaced his fingers behind his head, glanced toward the sky, and took a deep breath. "The good ones were painted by Elizabeth's daughter."

Chapter Twenty-One

FIVE YEARS AGO...

"Luke? Luke, you've got to see this!"

Emma bounded through the front door of the restaurant. The excitement in her voice carried to where Luke worked in the kitchen.

He propped open the double doors with his hip, revealing that his hands were covered in flour. "Come on in. I'm trying out a new recipe.

Emma joined him and saw that her mother was at the stove. "Hi Mum... didn't know you were here."

"Well, you see darling, this *is* a restaurant and Luke and I have the funny habit of coming here before our diners to prepare the food that they will inevitably order."

"As one would expect," Emma replied politely and in a decidedly more reserved tone.

As if the thought had just occurred to her, Elizabeth inquired, "Do you and Luke typically come here *not* to prepare food?"

Luke shot Emma a look to which she replied, "Absolutely not! So, the reason I stopped by..." She rummaged through her satchel to produce a leaflet. "I found a master's program that combines studio time with art history. It's my dream program… art, philosophy, and all the history behind it."

Elizabeth turned and took the leaflet. She read the first page. "It sounds perfect for you."

"Hey Luke, I found something for you, too." Emma held up a brochure for Luke. "It's a culinary school right here in Oxford."

"My father would flip out. I wouldn't be able to get an application past him."

Emma caught her mom's eye. "Is it alright if Luke receives mail at our house?"

"Of course." Elizabeth gave Luke her affectionate pat. "Emma, do you mind stirring this pot for a minute?"

Emma moved to help her mother and Luke whispered, "You're good at stirring pots."

Elizabeth glanced over, "That she is."

Luke turned to look at Elizabeth. "Golly, you have ears like a… a…"

"Like a bat! Bats have amazing hearing," Emma offered.

"Thank you, Dear. Just the animal I want to be compared to. And Luke, you should know that once my daughter gets an idea, it's hard to dissuade her."

Elizabeth noted the way Luke looked at Emma and smiled, pleased with what she saw. "Dinner is ready."

Luke gave her a questioning glance. "Isn't that for tonight's menu?

"Yes, but I prepared a bit extra for us to try first. Come on you two, sit down."

As Luke and Emma took seats next to each other, Elizabeth placed pies in the oven and then set about dishing out dinner.

Following their meal, Luke disappeared into the kitchen, returning with a plate of six bite-sized pastries.

"This is what I was working on… Chouquette," he announced.

"Oh my," Elizabeth exclaimed and leaned toward the plate to inhale the scent of the airy dessert. "Emma, did you know about this?"

"No. What are they?"

"These were your father's favorite. They are the most delightful and light pâte à choux pastry puffs studded with pearl sugar." She turned to Luke, "Cooking aficionados call them une pâtisseries viennoises."

Emma rolled her eyes. "You see? Whether you attend the school or not, Mum intends to turn you into the chef that I never was and that includes French lessons. You'll be studying from morning 'til night… a real taskmaster."

Luke smiled at their banter. "Somehow I don't think I would mind."

Elizabeth continued, "There, you see? Now, back to these beautiful creations of yours. Throughout France, people eat them for breakfast, or even an afternoon snack known as *le goûter*. Yours are so delightfully puffed and golden. Do you mind if I…" She made a pantomime motion of taking a bite.

"Please, try them," Luke replied. "I want your feedback. I was thinking if you approve, we can include them on the menu."

Emma also reached for one and upon taking a bite, gasped with delight. Elizabeth did the same and immediately asked, "Where did you learn to make them? They are perfect."

Luke answered, albeit a bit sadder. "My mum made something similar. She had never traveled, but loved to try recipes from different countries. Not much of a cook," he said brightening up, "but she loved to bake."

Elizabeth replied, "I would have gotten along well with her."

"Most people did," Luke nodded as he answered, but there was something amiss about his tone. He continued, "My father isn't most people. It sounds horrible, but she's better off where she is now. I miss her. I miss the music she played. I miss the smells that escaped from her oven…" He didn't normally reveal his feelings, and he immediately perked up. "And now, thanks to all of this, I have a bit of that again."

Wanting to lift him up, Emma spoke up. "Luke, put on some music. Whatever you're in the mood for."

Luke took out his phone and scrolled through the songs. "An oldie, but a goodie. My mum would play this one, but when I hear it I'm never sad. I don't think it's possible to be sad when it plays. So, I dedicate it to two of the strongest and wisest women I've ever met."

He held up a chouquette in a toast, and in response, Elizabeth and Emma did the same. The song, *C'est Magnifique*, by Ella Fitzgerald began to play from Luke's phone. It had a melancholy quality that transformed into an upbeat tune, much like Luke's past and his hope for the future.

Chapter Twenty-Two

Luke and Jade arrived at the restaurant following their walk, and he immediately regretted how soon they had returned. "Can you stay?" he asked, and when she hesitated, he implored, "Say yes… I want you to try my dish for tonight. There's still time before we open to customers."

"There's nobody waiting for me at the flat, and with that look on your face, how can I resist? Thank you for the invitation."

Luke beckoned for Jade to follow him into the kitchen.

"Really?" She questioned, excited at the prospect of seeing the kitchen.

"It's not that special." In spite of his comment, and as Jade passed through the kitchen double doors that he held open, he felt in his heart that he was opening the door to a part of his life that he had sealed shut.

"Here, take a seat," he offered her a stool at the butcher block chopping table. As Jade watched, he added final touches to a stew he had prepared earlier before ladling portions into two bowls. Next, he snipped off some fresh herbs that grew in vases prominently situated in the bay windowsill.

"You even grow your own herbs. I'm already impressed, and I haven't even tasted anything," Jade mused.

"This is thyme," he said, sprinkling a bit into the vintage, white crockery bowls. "We also have rosemary, basil, sage, and mint. I use a lot of the mint in our teas and desserts."

He placed the bowls on the counter, but before sitting, he remembered. "Just one more thing. It's the best part," he assured her. He brought over a wood cutting board holding a French boule. He placed it between them, then positioned his own stool close enough that their knees touched. Reaching over, he tore off a section of bread, dipped it into the broth of his bowl and offered the bite to Jade.

Music played softly in the background — the same Ella Fitzgerald song that brought him out of his doldrums when he cooked for Emma and Elizabeth. Jade took the bite from his offering. It was just a piece of bread and it was just a song, but something passed between them.

Jade swallowed. There was a lump in her throat that wasn't from the bread as reality set in. "I need to explain something," she began. "Grainger and I… he wasn't always so gruff. At least, when I first met him. I probably sound like a cliché." She had a distant look in her eyes as if the time she was referring to was long ago. "When I found out I was pregnant, I thought he would be thrilled. He wasn't."

Jade shrugged one shoulder and shook her head. "I love Emilie. But… Grainger and I had different ideas of what our future would be. He wanted to travel the world without any ties. I wanted to create a home for our child. Two very different ideas of how we wanted to live."

Without thinking, Luke placed his hand on Jade's. "It takes two to make a baby."

Jade understood what Luke meant. A tear trickled down her cheek and he brushed it away with his thumb.

"Grainger started drinking… started blaming. I said we should count our blessings that pregnancy came so easily. He didn't want me to keep the baby — Emilie — but I was young and foolish to think he would love her when she arrived. Drinking a glass of wine turned into a glass of whisky and then a bottle of it. His words became more hurtful and in order to tune them out, I tuned out from the marriage. I played the part of the good wife and on most days I accepted what fate dished out to me. I believed that you make your bed and you lie in it."

"But you don't deserve abusive words. And, you most certainly deserve love, acceptance, support."

Jade looked at Luke with an expression of regret. She turned her face down, trying to avoid the thoughts that entered her mind when she saw Luke.

"Jade, listen to me. You're a good mother. You're here with him, so obviously a good wife too."

Jade's expression changed from sadness to something else. She allowed herself to look at Luke and see him as a confidant and friend, but also as a man. "But am I? Am I really, Luke? I think I better turn in for the night. I've shared a lot with you."

"I think you know that I don't mind."

"My best friend from back home arrived in England today. She had been worried about how I would cope here alone. Well… not alone, but on my own…"

"I know what you mean," Luke answered. "You're not alone, Jade."

With the thud of a trash bin overturned, followed by the screech of a cat, Jade woke and turned over to find Grainger's side of the bed still empty. She reached for her cell phone on the side table and through sleepy eyes saw that no messages had arrived and it was past one in the morning.

She lifted a glass of water to her lips, then fluffed her pillow and attempted sleep again, but the restless feeling wouldn't leave. She hoped Emilie was sound asleep in spite of the antics that occurred with sleepovers. As the cat outside launched into a louder ruckus, she imagined little girls talking late into the night. With an audible sigh, Jade threw her legs over the side of the bed and sat up, contemplating how to relax.

Without any word from Grainger, she padded into the kitchen and retrieved the to-go container of the delicious stew Luke had insisted she bring home. She spooned out a couple of mouthfuls, noting that it was just as good served cold. Sitting at their modest kitchen table in the midst of a rented flat, in a country that wasn't her own, she tried to fathom how she landed here and what her future would bring.

Chapter Twenty-Three

WILLOW WOKE UP, SHOWERED, AND FELT
surprisingly refreshed after the journey. She mused that
meeting Harry certainly took her mind off her lost luggage.
She put on one of the new outfits she bought and thought
about digging into some of the snacks that he had insisted on
buying for her. But, the idea of seeing him in person was too
tempting, and like he said, the groceries would keep.

She made her way to Le Pont, following the directions that
he had taken the time to write for her. On the way, she texted
a quick message to Jade.

*Arrived safely yesterday and I'm making my way into the village center.
I hear there's a great place for breakfast… Le Pont? Have you heard of it?*

Jade's phone dinged with the text. Seeing Willow's question, she realized she never told her where 'hot chef' worked
let alone his name. The text left her wondering how much to
reveal. Part of her wanted to reply: *Yeah I hang out there every day
because I'm obsessed with the coffee as well as the chef.*

She knew that Willow would be the last person to judge
her, but still, she just couldn't let herself think of Luke in that

light. She needed to keep it real or she could fall for him. Instead, she replied: *Wonderful food. I'll meet you.*

Even without prompting from Willow, she would have gone to the restaurant to keep her mind occupied. Grainger still hadn't been home and she didn't know what to think.

Willow got to Le Pont as it was opening. She said a friendly hello to the man in chef's whites who was just unlocking the door, and to her surprise saw some people already eating inside.

"Good morning. Feel free to take a seat anywhere you like. I'll bring you a menu."

"Thank you. I think I'll take this seat in the window, but I'm just going to run to the ladies room first."

"Help yourself, but it's a unisex."

Willow nodded and headed toward the back of the restaurant, her mind lingering on the encounter. Had she just met Jade's "nice chef," or was it a given that every restaurant in Bourton Bridge employed chefs who could moonlight as models?

Luke made his way to Ben's table to refill his cup when the front door opened once more. "Busy this morning," Ben noted. "Pretty soon, you'll have to change your hours of operation sign."

"Indeed," Luke agreed and waved to Harry as he came in. Turning back to Ben, he asked, "Would you like a basket of breads while you wait?"

"Wait?"

"Elizabeth should be here soon," he said knowingly.

A light blush rose in Ben's cheeks. "Sounds lovely. Thank you, Luke."

"My pleasure," he said over his shoulder as he approached Harry. "Need that thermos filled?"

"Actually, I'm going to stay and have breakfast," Harry answered, looking toward the front door.

"Really?" Luke said in surprise.

"Yeah, your dad isn't at the site yet. I'm meeting someone… Actually, I met someone. She's great. You'll like her. I'm just going to wash my hands."

"Oh that explains the newcomer. I'll bring some coffees… table in the window."

Harry patted Luke on the back in appreciation and made his way to the back. As he reached the door, Willow exited. "Hey, good morning. We have to stop meeting in public restrooms," she joked.

"Where would the fun in that be?" he said lightly. "The best coffee in Bourton Bridge is waiting for you. I'll be right there."

Luke had just returned from their table having dropped off menus when he saw Jade through the window. He immediately brightened upon seeing her and did a mock jog across the dining room to open the door for her. The moment he saw her expression, he knew something was wrong. "You okay?"

"I'm meeting my friend here, but I'm wondering… Have you heard anything from your father?"

Luke was surprised at her question. "No, but we don't exactly try to catch up with each other."

"Grainger didn't come home," she explained.

"I'm sorry I can't offer any news about them, but is that your friend?" Luke pointed to the table where Harry and Willow were deep in conversation, their heads leaning in towards each other.

"Yes. Wow, she looks happy."

"My friend, Harry, apparently took her out yesterday." Luke paused, taking care to say the right thing. "About your husband. Have you tried the police? Could there have been an accident?"

"That wasn't my immediate thought, to be honest."

Then, understanding her implication, Luke asked, "Does he do this often?"

"I used to worry. I used to miss him. Now, I've come to expect... his behavior." Saying the words aloud, Jade was starting to accept her reality with Grainger once and for all.

"Drinking or women?" Luke didn't want to be hurtful, but he also wanted to understand the situation.

Without hesitation she answered. "Both. And more than one of the latter. After the first, he said he was sorry. Then, he denied it and told me to stop being paranoid. When his drinking became worse, he told me to mind my own business. I thought it might be different here," Jade said, standing a little straighter as if to carry herself with more dignity. "I had hoped the busy schedule would be enough for him... even if Emilie and I aren't."

"Jade, you are more than enough. If Grainger doesn't see you for the beautiful and strong woman that you are, he's missing out."

Hearing Luke say Jade's name, Willow looked over her shoulder. "Jade!" She waved Jade over and threw her arms around her friend. When she pulled away, Willow noticed the looks shared between Jade and Luke, realizing instantly that this wasn't just nice chef, but indeed Hot Chef.

"I'm Willow," she said extending her hand.

"Luke," he said. "Welcome to Bourton Bridge. I hear Harry has shown you around a bit?"

"Funny coincidence... we met yesterday," Willow beamed at Harry.

Jade and Luke both took a moment to look at Harry and Willow, who seemed like they had known each other for much longer than one day. Like couples who come to finish each other's sentences and know what the other is thinking, Willow eyed Harry and he responded. "Jade, I know you're anxious to spend time with Willow, but it's a rare day that I don't have to be at work this early. Would you mind if I stole her for a couple hours?"

Willow smiled at Harry, obviously thrilled at the idea. "Only if you truly don't mind," she said to her friend.

"Go; enjoy yourself. I need to wait for Grainger anyway."

Harry picked up Willow's coat from the back of her chair and held it open for her. She shrugged it on, and then offered him her hand. They may have only known each other for 24 hours, but they looked every bit the couple.

After Willow and Harry left, Jade looked at Luke and her eyes sent him a silent thanks. "Unlike Willow, I don't think I'm very good company at the moment. I don't want to lay my problems on you."

"I thought I've made it clear that I don't mind."

"I know… and you've been a good friend."

Luke nodded. He had heard Jade's subtle reminders before, and each time he kept quiet. This time, he couldn't. "Jade, this probably isn't the most ideal moment to say this, but I care about you…The way I feel about you is more than 'friendly'. I think you're beautiful and sexy…"

Ben looked up from his coffee and Luke shot him a look. Immediately, Ben averted his gaze to focus on his puzzle allowing Luke to continue. "And when I see you, Jade…" he lowered his voice, "I want to get lost in your arms and then some."

Jade opened her eyes wide and stared at Luke. She bit her lower lip and neither one of them responded. "Shit. I'm sorry," he said. "That was inappropriate. If I hear any news from my dad, I'll text you."

"No, you don't understand." She caught his arm before he returned to the kitchen. "Your words, your actions… I haven't experienced a real marriage in years. I wish things were different, but they aren't."

Unable to help himself, Luke took Jade's hand. With a lighter tone, he asked, "Do you want to help me set up for the day? Just to get your mind off things. It's better than waiting on your own. "

Jade brightened. "Thank you, Luke."

"For what?"

"For being you."

Luke gently squeezed her hand and maintained his nonchalant act. He accepted that friendship was the only thing on the table, but he couldn't ignore the way his heart raced in her presence, as if he had just completed a rowing session. He acknowledged its relentless pounding, but knew it stemmed from the simple fact that he was near her.

Chapter Twenty-Four

JADE'S MOOD IMPROVED IMMENSELY WHILE spending time with Luke in the kitchen. "This is how to forget about anything that is bothering you," he said, placing a pile of carrots before her.

"Vegetables?"

"Cute. Let me show you." He proceeded to demonstrate how to julienne the carrots and then handed her the knife, but it was a futile effort compared to his skill. Luke moved around the kitchen with complete confidence. He slowed down time and juggled the preparation of numerous dishes simultaneously with seamless grace. He made everything appear so easy. And sexy. Luke wasn't the only one who had that word on their mind. Jade didn't want to admit it, but there was no denying that truth.

He stirred pots while preparing sauces, expertly used a knife to fillet fish, and with a light hand, he whisked egg whites and sugar before gently folding in a strawberry puree to create a lighter than air mousse.

"You really know what you're doing."

Luke laughed. "You seem surprised."

"Nope, I knew you had it in you." Jade teased and rolled her eyes to make sure he knew it was just that.

Luke couldn't help himself, but to respond in suit. "I've got skills." He looked at her with a wolfish glance. It was enough to make Jade blush as she felt the heat rise in her cheeks. Luke held her gaze a moment longer, satisfied that he had made an impression with his cooking skills and then some. With mock innocence, he asked, "You okay, Jade?"

She fanned herself and took a deep breath. "Kitchens certainly get hot," she noted and returned her attention to the carrots.

Willow and Harry never intended to spend the entire day together, but the time moved rapidly. Initially, Harry simply wanted to show Willow the sites, but soon it was lunchtime and being hungry, they stopped for high tea.

"You might as well immerse yourself in English culture." Harry maneuvered the three-tiered tea stand to show Willow the offerings of finger sandwiches, scones, and cakes.

"Where do I start?"

"That depends. And this is a very serious decision." Harry leveled his gaze to Willow, refusing to crack a smile. "It will say a lot about you."

She gave the plates a once over and then with confidence told him, "I'll take a scone, please."

"Bold move. May I ask why you didn't start with the finger sandwiches?"

She stared directly at Harry, her black eyes assured and her mouth turned up in an alluring smile. "When I see something I want… there's little point in waiting."

"You are so attractive." Harry expertly cut the scone and

spread a portion of clotted cream onto it, topped by strawberry preserves.

"So you admit it?"

"That you're attractive? That goes without saying."

She shook her head slightly. "That you're attracted *to me*."

Harry slid his chair next to Willow's. He leaned in close enough to whisper to her, yet didn't answer, letting the moment unfold. It wasn't until he saw her swallow and the tiniest shred of doubt play across her eyes that he moved even closer with a slow seduction. When his mouth was poised right next to hers, he uttered, "That also goes without saying," and finally kissed her.

"This feels like a vacation," Willow commented as they walked along the river. "Minus the holiday romance."

Harry glanced at her with a 'what did you just say' expression.

Willow shrugged as if her words were completely transparent and obvious. "This isn't just a holiday thing, Harry."

He strode like a man who was comfortable in his own skin, taking long strides with his head held high. Then, as if completely at ease with what she just said, Harry took her hand and lifted it to his mouth where he planted a kiss on it. "You are one confident woman."

"Right back at you."

Harry paused and turned to her. "Willow, this may not be a holiday romance, but I promise you... when you're with me, there will be romance." He leaned down and kissed her cheek, letting his lips stray lower to her neck and then back again. When he heard her sigh, he gave her hand a squeeze and they continued on their way.

"Funny... I feel a little light-headed. Must be the jet lag."

With a knowing smile, Harry responded, "I promise you. It's not the time change."

It was Willow's turn to smile. "Changing the subject slightly… I'm worried about Jade. I flew out not just to visit, but really to check on her."

Harry walked a few more steps before answering. "You're a good friend to come out for her."

"But?" Willow asked.

"I've seen some things involving her husband. I don't know if I should say anything."

"Harry, believe me, I know."

"I can tell Luke is keeping an eye out. If she were in trouble, he would be there for her."

Willow reached for Harry's hand unexpectedly. "I'm glad she's found someone she can confide in. It's too bad they're just friends. This might sound odd, but for her sake, I wish it were more."

Harry looked at Willow as if he wasn't quite understanding. "More?"

Willow lifted her eyes to the heavens coquettishly and shrugged her shoulders. "It's hard to explain. Better if I show you."

They had just arrived at Willow's rented flat and he had every intention of dropping her off and going home. He really liked her and didn't want something good to burn out before it started.

But Willow had other ideas, and who was he to argue?

———

Jade smiled while watching Luke put his final touches on a dish. He spooned a sauce onto the center of the plate, placed a perfectly poached salmon slice on top and then decorated it with a neat pile of the vegetables they had julienned earlier. "It's a work of art," she complimented.

"You're easily amused," Luke noted.

"That I am."

It was comfortable with Jade. Luke enjoyed talking with her, and yet never felt the need to fill in the comfortable silences. She sipped on a cup of tea and watched him work. He had learned to keep his conversation to a minimum when preparing his dishes. It was a lesson most aspiring chefs learn quickly. A cut from a knife, a burn from a pan… concentration trumped conversation.

When he finished what he was doing, he responded to Jade's last comment. "What amuses you most?"

She took a minute to reflect and then answered. "Rom-com movies, baked goods, and sitting by a fire."

"I could get behind those choices."

Luke removed a mixed berry sauce from the refrigerator and placed a teaspoon into it. He offered the taste to Jade, holding the spoon towards her mouth. They had grown more comfortable with each other and this gesture of familiarity seemed perfectly natural, even if that's where their intimacy ended.

"That's amazing. I realize I never asked where you got your training."

Luke chuckled under his breath. "I'm a work in progress. I'm still attending a small culinary school in Oxford. It gives me a more professional outlook on food, but my basic skills I owe to Elizabeth."

He wondered if he should divulge details about his upbringing and paused for a moment before deciding to share. "I wanted to go to culinary school when I first met Elizabeth, but my father didn't support that idea."

Jade remained quiet for a moment. There was something in the air between them. It felt right to share. "I know what it's like to feel…," she struggled for the right words… "as if your ideas are unheard." Her eyes met his. "At least you're pursuing your passion now." Her voice seemed far away as if that same sentiment was out of reach for herself.

Wanting to help, Luke asked, "Tell me your ideas."

"I'll be honest. The idea of leaving my home to flip a property seems like a wasteful endeavor. We can do that in California."

She paused, weighing how much she was willing to share. Grainger had never really listened, despite knowing him for most of her adult life. Her friendship with Luke, though still new, already felt like something deeper. He smiled at her now, his genuine curiosity about her thoughts evident in his gaze. "Turning the property into a boutique hotel seemed interesting to me. Hard work, but also rewarding to give people an escape. Especially if we kept the original feel of a farmhouse. I just thought that city people would love that idea." She took a breath and seemed resolved that it would never happen. "My ideas fall on deaf ears. But, it doesn't matter; I've made my bed. It goes with being married… or at least my marriage."

There was the truth he didn't want to hear. Feeling bold, he countered her statement. "You can change the course of your life. Elizabeth took me under her wing and changed mine." He put down his cooking utensils and looked at Jade pointedly. "Plans change. Life changes us."

She knew they were speaking on two levels, and she decided to share a bit more. "Luke, I may be returning to the United States sooner than I expected. I plan to speak to Grainger about it again. I thought I could support him here, but he doesn't want that. I've been wondering if Emilie wouldn't be happier back in Los Angeles."

"What would make you happy, Jade?" He took her hand in his. "I know it has to be more than rom-coms and baked goods because that's easy. The harder part is sharing them with someone who deserves it." He felt a pang in his heart at the thought of not having her near.

She nodded, understanding his message. The idea of a movie night by the fire with Luke was everything she wanted. It stirred a longing in her that made her wonder if she shouldn't catch the earliest flight home, before her resolve faded and she acted on her desires.

Pots simmered with the evening's delicacies. Fresh bread cooled on the counter. Tables were set with white linens. With the preparation complete, Luke poured Jade a glass of wine. "The prep chefs will be here any minute. Want to get out of here? I've got some time before the dinner guests roll in."

"What about dessert?"

"Are you asking about it or for it?"

Jade smirked. "About it. You've fed me too much lately."

"Flourless chocolate cakes. Already made. They just get a quick pop in the oven to melt their insides."

Jade smiled to herself, thinking how Luke melted her insides as well. But nervous about sending him the wrong idea, she hedged her answer. "I've taken up most of your day. You probably want to get home and unwind."

"What if I walked you home? I never asked where you're staying." He remembered the day she was lost and he pointed her in the direction of the road she sought.

"Thank you. It would be nice to have company. I can show off how I've finally learned the way. Past the market cross in the center of the village, you take the first left, go over the second bridge, then it's just a few flats up."

"Listen to you." He smiled, "You're a pro… even called them flats."

Jade drank the last drop of her wine. Luke did the same,

said his goodbyes to the staff, and they headed out into the brisk air. They had only walked a few meters when Jade pulled her light jacket around herself more snuggly.

"Cold?" Luke inquired, but before waiting for an answer, he wrapped a protective arm around her. Another couple walked in the opposite direction hand-in-hand. They exchanged 'good evenings' as they passed, and Jade realized that she and Luke probably appeared to be a couple as well. If she were being honest, it felt nice having him close.

Without a doubt, he was handsome. She recognized that truth the moment she met him. But now that she knew him, she saw so much more. He was reliable and dedicated to his work. Elizabeth clearly loved him and he doted on her. Seeing someone show so much care toward another person made her aware of what was missing in her life. Jade thought that when Emilie was born, Grainger would change his attitude about family. It didn't take long to recognize that people rarely change. But there was a positive side to that realization. Jade saw in Luke his trait of immeasurable kindness and how it never wavered.

When they arrived at her front door, Jade was surprised that Grainger's car was still not home. She looked up at Luke. "Maybe he is getting dinner with your dad? Would you care for another glass of wine?"

He gave her a sideways glance.

Jade immediately regretted the invite. "I don't know why I said that." She inhaled deeply, filling up with the scent of the night air and Luke's aftershave. "With every sip of wine, my reasons to stay away from you wane," she admitted.

"I don't need wine to know that I'm attracted to you… or that I want to kiss you."

Jade didn't answer and Luke took her silence as an acceptance. He leaned toward her and their foreheads touched. He stayed like that, with his head bowed down to hers, waiting for her to give him a sign to continue. Just a slight tilt upwards of her chin, bringing her delectable mouth closer to his own.

Instead, she shook her head 'no' and placed a hand against his chest. "You were right to hesitate. I can't. I want to, Luke, but I just can't."

Luke took a step backwards, but reached for her hand again, unwilling to completely place distance between them. "I understand. But I don't regret what I've told you tonight."

"Luke, when I look at that derelict farmhouse, it reminds me of my marriage. Something that has seen better days and doesn't seem like it can be salvaged." She planted a light kiss on his cheek. His aftershave smelled of cloves and cinnamon and fresh air. She breathed him in before settling back on her feet and turning toward the door to open it. But just before stepping inside, as if the thought had only just occurred to her, she asked, "Luke, have you ever been in love?"

He nodded and Jade noted that his eyes almost looked sad, but when they met hers, he brightened. "Once," he admitted. "I never thought I would find it again, but now I have hope." With that last admission, he smiled at her — his meaning clear as he turned to walk away.

Chapter Twenty-Five

FIVE YEARS AGO...

Luke sat at the prep station, studying his recipes from a worn leather-bound book that exploded with notes and magazine clippings. The cool metal of the counter was soothing following the frenzied pace he maintained during the dinner shift. The stainless steel no longer seemed like a cold reflection of his life, but a clean slate. The pots and pans that hung above him were no longer a temptation of hope that once seemed too high to reach. Whereas once the kitchen was foreign to him, now it was truly his domain.

He enjoyed these moments of quiet reflection away from the crescendoing clang of dishes and sizzling steam from stock pots. Elizabeth kept a watchful eye on the progress of the kitchen, maneuvering through a delicate balance of giving instruction and allowing the staff to find their creativity. Luke had flourished under her tutelage and today, he wanted to show Emma how much he owed to her mother.

After the dinner crowd had left, Emma let herself in through the front door, and Luke came out to greet her. "I realize this isn't your typical date," he said, leading her back to the kitchen. "And, you've been frequenting this fine establishment longer than I have… but I promise this will be a new experience."

Emma took a place on the stool that Luke vacated, letting her legs dangle and swing, her playful nature never far from the surface. "You don't have to make promises. I'm pretty happy to be wherever you are."

As she settled in, Luke retrieved a small bundle of white and pink flowers tied together with a ribbon. "Apple blossoms," he explained and handed them to Emma. "Symbolic of peace…love… and other things that come with love."

Emma raised an eyebrow. "What sort of things?" As she asked the question, she jumped from her stool and strode closer to Luke. Standing very close, she stared straight into his eyes and turned her chin upwards.

He met her flirtatious gaze and lowered his face toward hers. Emma's eyes closed in anticipation of a kiss, but Luke simply took one of the flowers and delicately brushed the side of her cheek with its soft petals. Slowly, he ran the flower from her cheekbone down to her jawline and lightly traced her lips.

Emma's eyes remained closed until he couldn't resist her mouth any longer. He lightly pressed his lips to hers and with his free hand pulled her in even closer. "This sort of thing," he whispered when they finally broke off their kiss.

He plucked one of the flowers from its stem and placed it in Emma's hair over her ear. "It is said that the ancient Celts considered them a symbol of love and would decorate their chambers with the blossoms to entice amorous nights."

Emma accepted the small bouquet that Luke held out to her. "Luke, I never took you for a kinky type… asking me to the restaurant for an amorous night. What would the customers say? I can just imagine Mary and Vera wagging their tongues at us."

"Let them," Luke loved her sense of humor and flicked a speck of flour toward her, having moved back to his station. "So, I thought you could help me make my famous apple pies."

"Famous? I haven't seen them on the menu."

Luke added butter to the flour using a wire pastry cutter to break the cold blocks into fine pebble-sized pieces. "Well, maybe one day. It's not a traditional apple pie. It has the American filling, but it's combined with a French almond cream… a frangipane. Then, I top it with a crumble to give it an English quality. I thought your mother might not approve of combining the three cultures into one dessert. Hence, the reason why I'm doing it after hours… and hoping you'll sample it."

"I consider myself privileged. Do you need any help?"

"You can tell me if I'm doing it right." Luke started to peel apples, creating long ribbons that curled as they dropped off the fruit.

"You're pretty good, but an expert chef never gets distracted. So what happens if…" Emma jumped off her stool and came to face Luke. She reached her arms around his neck. He responded by circling his own around her waist and pulling her in close. The kiss that ensued was tender, but became more passionate until Luke stopped. With his hands still on her waist, he bowed his forehead down to her head.

"It is taking all of my restraint to not lift you up onto this table right here and now."

"Would that be such a horrible thing?" she coaxed.

"It would't be horrible at all. It would be amazing. But, I don't want our first time to be on top of the prep counter where we both work. And I am going to prove my chef skills to you, so skedaddle."

Emma rolled her eyes, but good-naturedly took her place at the counter while Luke continued slicing apples, sprinkling sugar and cinnamon over them, and then squeezing lemon juice over the top to let the flavors macerate. He reached for a bottle of Calvados apple brandy and drizzled a small amount over the fruit as well. "My secret ingredient," he explained.

He offered the bowl to Emma. "Take a whiff."

She did as he asked. "Mmm, smells like… home. Sweetness and love."

He turned his attention to making the almond cream, a light combination of butter, sugar, eggs and almond flour, which would be added as the first layer of his pie, between the crust and the fruit. He looked up as he whisked the eggs. "Certainly not my home, but it's good to hear that yours was like this."

Emma nodded, both a sadness filling her eyes and a hope. "Luke, things are different for you now. My mom spotted something in you and she was right."

Luke continued to work, arranging the apple slices in concentric circles on top of the cream. "Want to put the final touch on the pie?"

"What's that?"

"Just sprinkle it with the topping," he handed her a bowl already prepared with crumbles of butter, flour, brown sugar and cinnamon.

She smiled and jumped off her stool to stand in front of Luke. She pinched a tiny bit of the sugary blend and let it fall onto the apples. He held her from behind, his hands working alongside hers. His chest pressed into her back and he inhaled the scent of her hair and the small apple blossom flower that was still perched above her ear.

When she finished, he slid the pies into the industrial oven and beckoned her to sit with him. He had brought out a cozy rug and a bottle of wine from his cottage. He laid the rug onto the kitchen floor and then poured two glasses.

She settled onto the rug, lying on her stomach. Folding her arms, she lay her head on them and closed her eyes. "This is a perfect date, Luke. And, I haven't even tried the pie yet."

The timer on the oven sounded and Luke begrudgingly left Emma's side to retrieve the pies. The opening of the oven door immediately released a tempting aroma into the space. As he placed the pies on the counter to cool, both he and Emma leaned in closer to inhale their sweet scent. They were both poised above the pies, standing shoulder to shoulder when the bell over the front door sounded.

"Did you leave the door unlocked?" Emma asked, her eyes widening in surprise. It was nearly eleven o'clock at night, well past the hour that any customer would investigate whether they were open.

"Stay here," Luke instructed as he opened the double doors leading to the dining room. What he saw resulted in him relaxing his stance, but not his mindset. It was his father, drunk as usual. And while he recognized that there wasn't a threat to Emma in the form of a burglar, his father was menacing as always.

"There you are," he slurred. "Get'cha stuff."

Luke placed his oven mitts on a nearby table, aware that his father would surely have a ripe comment about him cooking. "I think you've stumbled through the wrong door. Time for you to go home."

"See you're hanging out with the *bricks and mortar*." His father used cockney rhyming slang referring to 'daughter' when he saw Emma peer out from the kitchen.

"Speak with respect." In contrast to his father, Luke spoke

his words clearly to ensure he was understood. He had rarely spoken back to his father. He knew better. It was impossible to teach him anything and it was never worth the trouble. Until now.

"Don't get up in arms, *china plate*."

Luke had grown up with his father's cockney references and he answered quickly. "I'm not your mate, and certainly not your friend. But as your son, I'm reminding you that you are trespassing and for your own sake, you should go home."

"You know, I ignored that suggestion the first time you said it." His father stumbled forward and then tumbled against Luke, who tried to steady him, yet still his father ended up falling.

Luke stood over him and offered a hand, but believing it was Luke who landed him on the ground, his father came up swinging. Luke dodged easily and once again his father fell over from his own momentum. Luke turned toward Emma. "Call the police. He can spend the night with them."

"Luke!" Emma tried to warn him, but it was too late. Clive had stood up once more and retrieved a large tray that was left at a nearby table. He lifted it high and pulled it down hard toward Luke, striking him on the back of the head.

The blow was uncomfortable, but not hard enough to cause Luke to fall and certainly not hard enough to make him black out. Still, Emma stared in shock and rushed to Luke's side. Luke placed a protective arm around her and reached in his pocket for his phone.

Clive settled a bit from his display and exertion. "You see? She looks at us like we're nothing, just like her mum. She's never going to have anything to do with you."

Luke held the phone up for his father to see, making his intention clear. Then, he led Emma back to the kitchen. "You still have time to get out of here."

But his father was never one to listen to his son. Instead,

he followed Luke and once again got in his face. Standing nose to nose, he began shouting at Luke again. Neither had noticed Elizabeth enter the restaurant let alone its kitchen, until the sudden crack of a large meat cleaver hitting the nearby chopping block sounded. Both the sound and visual were enough to stop Clive.

Still gripping the handle, Elizabeth stared at Clive with as threatening a demeanor as she could muster. "The next strike will result in you losing a finger… or worse," her eyes lowered and her meaning was clear.

Clive muttered something unintelligible and turned to leave, but not before one last parting word. "You can't abandon your family, Lukey."

Once he left for good, Elizabeth shook her head at both Emma and Luke. "When you didn't get home at a reasonable hour I got worried."

"I'm sorry, Elizabeth," Luke started to take the blame for himself and Emma.

"We were just making pies," Emma responded. "Try one?"

"You're both old enough to make decisions about where you are and how you spend your time," Elizabeth replied while taking a fork to a nearby pie. "But you should know better than to have the door unlocked after hours."

Any sign of annoyance vanished immediately when she lifted the fork to her mouth. She smiled as she swallowed and reached above the counter for three plates. "I want a full portion. And this is going on the menu. Immediately," she added.

As they tucked into their pie, a comfortable quiet replaced the stressful environment that left when Clive did. They ate in silence or more so, peace. And through it all, Luke and Emma shared glances.

"Do you two have something you would like to share?" Elizabeth looked from Emma to Luke, but both shook their heads like children who wouldn't come clean on who had eaten the last cookie. "Fine, allow me… Since you both obviously get along well… From now on, Luke, you come home after your shift and we will eat dinner together like a family."

"A family…," he repeated.

"Yes," Elizabeth confirmed. "It's about time you had one."

Chapter Twenty-Six

ELIZABETH CONTINUED TO TRAIN LUKE ON THE preparation of her recipes and he experimented with his own. After the last of the customers left, Emma would settle at the kitchen island watching him and they fell into a routine. They would turn on their favorite playlists — romantic pop for Emma and the blues for Luke. As the music played, the food baked or braised, marinated or stewed, and they danced. Luke wrapped his arms tenderly around Emma and she would rest her head against his chest. Per Elizabeth's insistence, they never stayed too late and always sampled the dishes at home together.

Although Clive had stayed away since the meat cleaver incident, Luke viewed his father's likely return in the same way that mold appeared on bathroom tiles. One could clean up the mess, but if you didn't pay attention, the threat of it remained. Luke had many years of experience with his father's outbursts. They lingered and were likely to surface when Clive drank with friends. It was, unfortunately, a frequent event that exacerbated when he lost his gambles.

Although Luke knew to be vigilant where his father was

concerned, growing up in his troubled house made him more appreciative of his new life. When the knock sounded on his door, he knew it was too light and rhythmic to be his father, and he hoped Emma had found a reason to visit.

"I know it's late, but these just came out of the oven and I thought you might want one before bed," she held out a plate covered in foil. Luke removed the cover and saw two brownies still hot from the oven. The steam of fresh baking created a light condensation on the foil and the rich, chocolatey aroma immediately reached his nose.

"Come in. You're getting soaked." The rain had started to pour down harder and a steady stream fell from the eaves. "You didn't have to bring them in the rain."

For a minute, Emma hesitated. "I didn't mean to disturb you."

"That's not what I meant. Not at all." Luke reached his hand out to her. When Emma accepted it and stepped indoors, the soft light cast shadows over their faces, but it couldn't hide Luke's eyes that roamed inadvertently to Emma's blouse that clung to her frame from the rain. She noticed and smiled to herself, then sent him a lustful look.

Luke shook his head, more a reminder to himself than a message to Emma. "I'm sorry. It's just that you look beautiful."

"Dripping from head to toe?"

"Here, take this," he removed a blanket that had been draped over his own shoulders. As he ballooned it over her, she swiftly took a step forward, ensuring that Luke was also caught up in its warmth.

"Luke…" She only said his name, but her intention was clear.

"Emma, living closely together and working together… It's already complicated. I keep thinking that we can't let this go farther."

She shook her head once. "What do you mean?"

"I care too much about you not to consider what being with me means… my father." Luke gave her a chaste kiss on her cheek — an act that was meant to show he cared, maybe so much that he couldn't go forward.

Yet, when his lips touched her smooth skin, he inhaled her perfume and stayed like that longer than he intended. And when Emma didn't move, almost as if scared to stop what might start, he allowed his mouth to trace a line from her cheek down to her neck. She inhaled, waiting. He let his mouth lightly press against hers, and then no sooner, he recovered and stopped.

"Emma, there are so many reasons why I want to be with you, and an equal number that tells me we shouldn't go any farther." He removed himself from the blanket that enveloped both of them and folded it over Emma's torso.

She looked at him with a myriad of emotions coursing through her — embarrassment, sadness, wanting. "I don't understand why not. We like each other." She paused when he didn't reply, and asked, "You do like me, don't you?"

"Of course I do. But I worry about what my father might do if he found out how much. He destroys everything that is dear to me. Thank you for the brownies. You should go and get some sleep."

As Emma handed him back his blanket and turned toward the door, he saw a tear slip down her cheek. He offered one last word, hoping it would comfort her. "I'm sorry. Please know that."

Yet, his words had the opposite effect. Before she left, she whispered through sobs and the sound of rain, "The irony is… you're the only one hurting me."

Chapter Twenty-Seven

IT WAS A LONG DAY. LE PONT WAS BUSY THE MOMENT they opened for breakfast. During the afternoon break, Luke tested new recipes, and when the dinner hour arrived, so did a steady stream of clientele. It was rewarding to see so many people enjoying his food, but by the end of it, exhaustion weighed on him. He left without hesitation, not even pausing to wait out the rain.

He opened the door to the main house and leaned down to pick up the post that the mail carrier slid through the letter opening. After placing the letters on the sideboard, he walked to the kitchen, sidestepping a bucket that was placed in the middle of the room half filled with water. Aside from a steady drip from the ceiling, the house was quiet.

He stripped off his shirt from work and tossed it into the washer before leaving through the back door toward his cottage. He noted that the door was unlocked and the sound of water came from his bathroom. "Elizabeth?"

The cottage was so small that one could see clear to the back of it from the front. He was just about to call out again when he realized it wasn't Elizabeth checking on his plumbing. Emma emerged from the bathroom wrapped in a towel.

"Oh, you're home."

Luke merely nodded, his words lost at the sight of her.

"The furnace is out in the main house," she explained. "No hot water."

They hadn't spoken since their last interaction, and that one hadn't gone well. When Luke still didn't respond, she mistakenly took his silence as a sign that he wanted to come home from work to a quiet house.

"I'm sorry to intrude." She adjusted her towel and Luke averted his eyes.

He was trying not to be creepy and stare. After all, it had been her artist's studio before he moved in. In what he hoped was a nonchalant tone, he replied, "It's no problem," and bent down to pick up the robe that she discarded on the floor. But when he stood, he noticed her eyes traveling to his shirtless frame. Neither said another word.

Their eyes spoke lengthy conversations — the ones that said not to leave, that they wanted more, and how long they've waited. Luke took a step closer and she walked into his arms. He wrapped them around her and pulled her close. His mouth met hers and their kiss deepened. Her towel shifted and out of gallantry, he held it in place. He didn't want to let her go. He had wanted her for so long. But afraid she might change her mind, he pulled back. He had to be sure of her feelings.

"The other day… I was only trying to protect you. Is this really what you want?" he asked. She placed her hands on either side of his face and pulled him toward her. With a kiss filled with promise and certainty, she murmured against his mouth.

"I'm sure."

She let the towel slip, and this time, Luke didn't try to

keep it in place. His hands traveled down her back and wrapped around her hips. When a gasp of desire escaped her mouth, she eyed him with desire. She nodded her head once and he didn't waste another moment. He scooped her into his arms and carried her to his bedroom.

Emma and Luke arrived at the restaurant the following morning, not just together, but hand-in-hand. Elizabeth took note, but immediately turned and busied herself with tasks far less interesting than the questions that begged to be asked.

She had long known that the only way she and Emma could work together was to give each other space. They never spoke of personal matters at the restaurant, nor did they discuss business problems at the family dinner table. However, this was a time when she wanted to let that unspoken rule wash down the sink, along with the sand that she gently removed from the mussels she washed for tonight's special Moules Marinières.

Emma caught her mother's inquisitive glance, although it lasted only a mere second. Still, she gave Luke's hand a final squeeze and then dropped it. "I'm going to get ready," she whispered, and then as if she had a second thought about the matter, she gave a light tug on his arm and presented a chaste kiss on his cheek before leaving to set up the dining area.

It gave Elizabeth a chance to address Luke privately. "You two seem… happy."

Luke poured himself a cup of coffee, his usual habit before launching into meal prep. "Can I pour you a cup, Elizabeth?" he asked, deftly avoiding the topic.

"No thank you, I've had my fill today."

Luke smiled and began to relax, believing that he had side-stepped questions about himself and Emma. He added cream to his coffee and moved to the pantry to retrieve the flour and sugar he would need to prepare the cakes he planned.

Noting that Luke seemed more at ease, Elizabeth confronted him. "So, you and Emma? What are you thinking?"

Caught off guard, Luke coughed as the sip of coffee went down the wrong pipe.

"On second thought, a coffee would be lovely. Let's take our break, shall we?" Elizabeth said, taking a seat at the island.

"I've just arrived," he said, recovering. He waved his hand toward the kitchen, implying there was work to be done.

But instead, Elizabeth pushed an empty stool toward him.

"Very well," Luke said, defeated and looking truly confused. "What do you mean? She's amazing. You know we hang out."

"I know she's amazing; she's my daughter. And, I know that you two hang out; I just didn't know that you two…"

Luke narrowed his eyes. "I don't think this conversation should go there. Maybe have it with Emma?"

"Luke, you're… you're like a son to me now. And, Emma is my daughter. Therefore, to learn that you and she…"

"Whoa! That is disgusting. I've never viewed Emma like a sister, although yes, you have treated me far better than my own family."

"That's not what I meant. I just meant, I would hate to lose you."

Luke furrowed his brow and shook his head. "How would you lose me? You and this restaurant mean everything to me."

"Exactly. Friendship is one thing, but this… What if you break up?"

"We just started seeing each other. It's too soon to even say that we're together."

Now it was Elizabeth's turn to react with raised brows. "So

I'm imagining that I checked her room last night and her bed was empty?"

"No, I imagine that was the case," Luke answered contritely.

"And, did I imagine that I saw her coming out of your cottage this morning?"

"You may have done so," he admitted.

"And a few hours later, after I may add, that I had been here alone setting up for the day, the two of you waltz in holding hands."

Luke bit his tongue, but nodded his head. "We overslept."

"Late night?"

"It won't happen again," Luke promised.

"See? That's what I mean. What won't happen again? You being late for work? Or you sleeping with my daughter?"

Luke took a deep breath, and tried to shrink within himself, but it didn't work. Elizabeth was still seated in front of him, this time with her arms crossed over her chest.

"The former. I won't be late for work again."

"Wonderful," she replied with sarcasm.

"Elizabeth, we've known each other for months. I was attracted to her the first moment I saw her. Getting to know her was like finding a piece of me that had been missing. And, now she just fits perfectly into my heart."

Elizabeth's gaze softened. "Fine. I approve."

"Thank you, Elizabeth. And for what it's worth, you're never going to lose me. You're stuck with me. And, I'm never going to break her heart."

She nodded. Satisfied that their talk had come to its conclusion, she rose and then turned her head over her shoulder. "Chocolate gateau tonight? Somehow I feel you should make my favorite."

Luke smiled and jumped off the stool, reaching for his apron as he did so.

Chapter Twenty-Eight

LUKE EMERGED FROM THE PANTRY, CARRYING A large ceramic bowl and balancing his baking supplies, when Emma bounded into him. "What did she say?"

Luke steadied his bounty and saw that Emma had gripped the massive bowl from the opposite side. "Let's put this down, shall we? We're about to have flour all over the floor."

She helped him get everything to the baking butcher block and then stood back with her hands on her hips as if to say 'now'. But Luke went about starting his work. He moved to the massive refrigerator to retrieve butter, sour cream, and eggs, went back to the pantry for the vanilla and almond extracts, and then to Emma's annoyance he started measuring out ingredients.

"Emma, would you please hand me the almond paste from the pantry? I forgot to grab it."

"No! How can you just go about your day? What did she say?"

Luke gave her a slight eye roll and went to get the almond paste himself. As he came back, he saw that she wasn't going to let him get any work done until he satisfied her with an answer. But what answer he would or should give was an entirely different question.

Contemplating his response, he started the mixer and began combining the ingredients. When the batter was done and he couldn't buy himself any more time, he took a seat at the island. "She's worried about how we will balance our work life and personal time."

Emma nodded slowly. Her eyes started to glisten and her lower lip began to tremble. "Working together, living together, and spending free time together. It's too much for you?"

He shook his head quickly. "No Emma. It's the best." And when she smiled back, he leaned in close and kissed her. He would have kissed her all day and into the night had the timer on the oven not sounded. When they came up for air, he still held her and replied, "I would happily spend all of my minutes right here with you."

"You're sure?"

"I'm positive."

Elizabeth came in at that moment. Seeing them, she resigned herself that they were in fact a couple. "You two are sweeter than that dessert you're preparing, Luke. And while I find young love to be a joyous thing, the cake will not rise on the butcher block, nor will the sauces bubble while their ingredients are still in the larder.

"Sorry, Mum. My fault. I wanted to know how your talk went."

"It went fine. Do I need to have one with you about work-place etiquette?"

"No, Mum. It won't happen again," Emma smiled and went back to the dining room, practically skipping as she left.

The rest of the day went by as it should. Dishes were prepared with sauces that divinely accompanied them. Customers enjoyed every bite and then indulged in dessert because the enticing aroma of fresh baking wafted into the dining room and was impossible to resist.

Luke and Emma managed to keep a workplace distance from each other, but stole glances whenever they could. Finally, Elizabeth turned to them, "Luke, if you can get back to supervise the prep chefs, Thomas can handle things for an hour or two. Why don't you two enjoy the last bit of sunlight."

"Really?!" Emma confirmed.

"Definitely. Your sweetness is going to give me a toothache. Luke, can you get back in an hour?"

Emma playfully bounded over to Elizabeth to plant a light kiss on her cheek. Luke threw off his apron and didn't wait a second before coming over to pull Elizabeth in for a hug.

"What is all this?" she mockingly complained.

"My love for you," Emma chimed.

"And my appreciation of everything you do and have done for me. I am going to walk your daughter home and be back before the dinner rush."

"Scoot," Elizabeth waved the back of her hand toward the door, but allowed a smile to escape at the sight of them together.

Emma set up her easel in the house's conservatory. One could see both the kitchen and the garden from the glass structure. As she mixed her colors, she could see Luke in the kitchen window. Instinctively, he felt her gaze and turned his attention toward the window. She blew him a kiss and he came out to join her, carrying a crudité platter.

Setting the platter down on a nearby table, Luke peered over Emma's shoulder at her work. The painting showed the Radcliffe Camera, an iconic Oxford University building. Originally built as part of the Radcliffe Science Library, it later became an extension of the now famous Bodleian Library.

Rather than focus on the unique circular library in its entirety, the focal point was narrow — a close-up of a young man and woman, reclining within one of the exterior crevices. The details of the Classical architecture were shown by the man leaning within the building's niches, its rusticated masonry around him. Yet, it was the tenderness of his embrace around the woman's waist and the way she turned slightly over her shoulder as if the man had just asked her something that kept Luke staring.

"It's beautiful, Emma. It's strong and soft all at once." She smiled from his words as she dabbed a streak of paint through the woman's hair. "I just don't feel it's finished."

"It looks perfect. What else is there to do?"

"I'm not entirely sure. It's like a story. There's always the question of what comes next? I look at their expressions and wonder if he's whispering about their dinner plans or something much bigger… their future plans." She looked at Luke to gauge his opinion as she uttered those last words.

He reached for her paint brush to set it aside for a moment. "I see your point." He kissed the top of her head and she rested her cheek against his chest. "I hate to leave, but I promised your mum. I'll be back in a couple hours. Will you still be awake?"

"Most definitely."

"I'll be back before you know it."

When Luke returned, Emma joined him in his cottage. They reclined on the sofa in front of the fireplace with a plush blanket enveloping them. A platter of homemade cookies sat on a nearby ottoman. Luke reached for one and broke off a corner for Emma.

"Luke, that is the most amazing biscuit cookie ever. What is it?"

"Traditional shortbread that isn't so traditional."

She smiled at him. "Will you share your secrets?"

He reached for another cookie. But as he did so, she noticed his arm and reached for his hand.

"Hey hey, I'll share. There's lavender extract and a small amount of rosemary. The combination really intensifies the flavor."

But she looked troubled and didn't release his hand. Instead, she rolled up his shirt sleeve. "I've never noticed… these scars. You're always in chef's whites and when we were together it was dark. Are these from cooking?"

A deep sigh escaped his lungs and he merely shook his head. "No… not from cooking, but they are burns. I suppose that's why he did it where he did. People wouldn't ask questions."

"He?" she asked, horrified.

"My father. Cigarettes stamped out on my forearm whenever I was 'disrespectful' which in his mind was fairly often."

A tear dripped down Emma's cheek and she brought her lips to his arm. In turn, Luke placed his fingers lightly under her chin and raised her face so they were eye to eye. "Don't cry. They have long healed and the pain in my heart left years ago. When I got older and stood taller than he did, he stopped."

She nodded quietly, but it was evident that she was still troubled. "I never knew my dad, but I had all the love I could ask for from my mum, and others. The two sisters who come into the restaurant… Mary and Vera… they've been like aunties to me for as long as I've known."

Luke smiled, picturing the sisters and the obvious admiration and friendship they showed for Elizabeth. "Your mum is wonderful. I feel so fortunate to have her in my life too. But, I have no love lost for my dad. I used to hope he would stop drinking and be the kind of father one sees on television. His actions hurt me far more mentally than they did physically. It helped when I spoke to a therapist and realized that he was sick. Addiction is a terrible disease. I'll never forgive what he did to me, but I'm strong on my own."

Emma leaned in closer and wrapped her arms around Luke's neck. "Don't be an island." She stood up suddenly, letting the blanket fall to the floor. "I need to get my phone."

"Someone you need to call suddenly?" he teased.

"You'll see." Emma tapped on her phone until she found what she wanted. One more tap and a sweet love song cued up. "Wanna dance with me?"

Luke stood and watched her sway to the music. She moved with no cares, no worries. Her smile was contagious and he easily forgot the painful subject of a few minutes earlier. He joined her in front of the fire and placed his hands around her waist. "You cold?"

"I won't be… when you warm me up."

The kiss that followed was soft and tender. He explored her mouth and when they parted, he couldn't help the words from flowing. "I love you, Emma. I love you with all my heart."

She kissed him once more and spoke the words right back against his mouth. "Luke, I love you, too. I'll never stop. Can I stay here tonight?"

"You don't need to ask. You never need to ask."

He moved away from her only long enough to close the iron screen in front of the tiny fireplace before leading her to his room.

Chapter Twenty-Nine

As Luke made his way into the village the following morning, he smiled at the memory of his night with Emma. On impulse, he took a detour to visit TwoLips, the local florist. James, the owner, had a knack for knowing what flower arrangement would connect with his clients. He often worked with Elizabeth when she catered a party. Luke was hoping that James would have the perfect idea for how he could show Emma how much he cared.

James' shop was just past a local gym. It wasn't a fancy place with lots of cardio machines. This one was set up with weights and mats that smelled of rubber and sweat. It catered mainly to body builders — the type who preferred a no frills atmosphere while working out. As he passed, the sounds of grunts and heavy weights dropping onto the floor reverberated out the door. Luke took a glance toward the gym's window as he walked, not expecting the firm shove that struck him from behind.

"Nothin' in there for pansies."

Luke turned as the voice started to snicker at what he

believed to be his own wit. The voice of his father's drinking buddy slurred another threat. "You best keep walkin'."

Luke's father stepped out of the gym. The trouble with the Cotswolds was that the villages were small and people easily traveled from one to the next. With his father now working in Bourton Bridge, it wasn't surprising that he was hanging around. Even a side trip presented the risk of running into him. But for the briefest of moments, Luke wondered if he would put a stop to his friend's disparaging comments. It was a misguided thought. His father's abusive actions had carried on for years and his friends seemed to accept them as commonplace. "Rog, he'll walk on by. That one…" his father aimed a thumb at Luke as he spoke, "that one doesn't have the balls."

Luke knew enough to ignore his dad when he was drunk. But leaving two drunks alone, that was a no-brainer. He started to maneuver past them, but his father carried the added burden of being an angry drunk and today he was looking for a fight. Luke was the passerby who found himself in the wrong place at the wrong time.

"You know I'm done supportin' you," his father spat at Luke.

"When have you ever given even a pence to me in the last five years?" Luke said, his frustration now palatable. "You have it the wrong way around. Every time you get drunk and can't pay your bills, I'm your first stop."

Clive didn't seem to hear Luke's words, or if he did, he was too set in his own mind to change his thoughts. "If you're not going to help on the building site, I'm not going to help you. You can go and be a waiter your whole life." As if aware of his mistake, he added, "Or whatever you do there."

Luke was doing his best to sidestep Clive and Roger when Harry approached on his way to work. Luke and Clive both spied Harry at the same time. Immediately, Harry gave Luke a look as if to say, 'What now?'.

"Harry… he's an example of someone who knows how to work hard. Bet he doesn't disappoint his old man."

"Sorry, Luke," Harry said under his breath. "You need anything?"

"Good to see you, Harry. Just wish it was under different circumstances," Luke muttered so as not to set his father off against his friend.

"His circumstances are just fine," Clive jabbed. "He's not hanging out with some uppity girl who's sure to leave him when she figures out you can't support her. She's not gonna put up with you taking handouts from her mum. Not a girl like that, who sits on her high horse."

Luke had every intention of carrying on as he planned, but walking into a florist shop was a sure-fire way to rile up his father even more. He paused, starting to wonder why he even cared. His father wasn't going to change so why did he have to tiptoe around him? As if Clive knew that something in Luke was faltering, he continued with his relentlessly cruel words. "Or maybe she has jumped off her horse to ride you. Probably all she sees in you."

With that last comment, Luke couldn't muster the self-control. He pulled his arm back and let the punch ricochet into Clive's jaw before he saw it coming. Roger immediately grabbed Luke's arms and held them behind his back to let Clive get his own punch in.

"Let him go," Harry shouted, standing in front of Clive. "You want me to get to work? You get going as well."

"Don't be talking to me that way. I'll remind you that I'm your boss," Clive shouted to Harry from the ground, where he was still getting his bearings after Luke's punch. He spat out some blood and stood, more subdued as if the punch had knocked some sense into him.

"Don't speak of Emma or Elizabeth, ever." Luke shrugged his jacket back into place. "See ya, Harry. Think about what I said before."

Harry nodded, knowing that Luke was right.

"And you think about what I said," Clive yelled after him, watching Luke's back as he continued down the street. "That girl or her mum will resent you one day."

Luke took one last rueful look over his shoulder and walked away.

He walked faster than usual, eager to distance himself from his father's hurtful words. At TwoLips, James suggested a simple white rose tied with a red ribbon—a symbol of new love's innocence and the promise of lasting affection. It felt perfect. But as Luke arrived at the restaurant, he paused for a moment, needing to collect himself.

Instead of going straight to work, he headed toward the river. He knew his father was nothing more than a drunk. He knew that Elizabeth valued him and his work. And, he knew that Emma loved him. But in spite of this, his father's words had an effect on him.

He continued to the boat house and grabbed his punting boat. With the adrenaline from earlier still in effect, he lifted it easily off the rack and carried it towards the water's edge. The weight of the boat seemed to mirror the myriad of concerns on his shoulders.

The narrow boat hit the water with a loud splash, sending some of the murky water onto the bottom of his trousers. He didn't care and jumped into the boat without another thought, positioning his feet and reaching for the oars. He rowed hard, trying to exorcise his demons and make sense of what to do with his life.

After a good fifteen minutes, he reclined onto his back with his arms interlaced behind his head in his thinking pose, the place and position he always came back to when things were rough. Just a night ago, he envisioned asking Emma to marry him. Now, as he closed his eyes and let the sun warm his face, he reflected on whether it was fair to condemn her to a life with his father.

<hr />

When Luke arrived at the restaurant, he was told Emma had left to pick up supplies.

"Did she say when she would be back?" He met his sous chef's gaze. Thomas reminded Luke of himself when he first started. He joined the staff nearly six months ago, and had proven to have raw talent in the kitchen and a head that stayed cool under pressure. He just needed the opportunity to prove himself, much like Luke had needed when he first met Elizabeth.

"No, but she mentioned that she might stop home to check on you. You've been pulling doubles, Chef," his assistant noted. "No disrespect, but you do look tired. You okay?"

Luke was sure that the stress induced by his father contributed to his fatigue. He had thought he was hiding it, but Thomas picked up on his mood. Thankfully, it was Elizabeth's night off. Luke wasn't about to let her down. "I'll be fine," Luke answered in the typical British stiff-upper-lip fashion.

Still, his sous chef had come to be able to read Luke and he sensed something was up. "Chef, why don't you show me how you want everything plated and take the night off? You always say to jump in with both feet. Maybe this should be my night."

Luke thought about it for a moment. He had prepared the dishes earlier and Thomas had made the sauces with him. Preparations were even completed for tomorrow's breakfast. The reservation log showed that it was going to be a quiet night, and Luke realized there was no better night for Thomas to fly solo. After a moment, he agreed. "I think I'll take you up on that. I'll put together our specials menu for tomorrow, and hand you the reins on the kitchen. You've got this."

"Thank you, Chef."

"Do me a favor? If Emma comes back, let her know I've gone home for the night."

Luke was surprised to find Emma already at home when he arrived. He handed her the single white rose, tied with the red ribbon. "For you."

She took his gift and smelled the rose. "Ahh Luke, this is so sweet. And you decided to take the night off?"

He shook his head. "Not exactly, but I needed time to think."

"Something about the way you say 'think' makes me think I'm not going to like it."

He recounted the run-in he had with his father. "Emma, I love you. I love you so much that I worry about inflicting my awful family on you."

She approached him and ran her palm along the side of his face tenderly. "Luke, I'm sorry. Your dad is an asshole."

It was the truth, but he was surprised that Emma spoke so bluntly. He turned his gaze downward and simply nodded. He waited, barely able to breathe, for her to continue. Would she change her mind about being with him? Finally, he met her eyes.

"But that doesn't matter to me," she said quietly. "I love

you." She wrapped her arms around his waist in a hug. "Whatever has put a damper on your day, let me help you forget."

Luke tilted his head down and kissed her. "I can't resist you," he said. "How did you get to be so wonderful?"

"I think my mom had something to do with it."

"That's probably true. And she'll probably have my hide when she finds out I left Thomas in charge of the restaurant tonight."

"He's capable. You deserve a night off and I'd love to spend it with you. But first, I have a quick errand in Stow-on-the-Water. I want to visit James' shop to look at winter arrangements… wreaths, mistletoe, all that fun stuff."

"Do you want me to go with you?"

"I love your thoughtfulness — the flower and your offer. But you've had a day. Why don't you rest and I'll be back before you miss me. I'll take the A29 footpath and be back in a jiffy."

"I can drive you."

She tilted her head from shoulder to shoulder as if considering the options. "How about this? You start dinner. I'll get my exercise in. The timing will be perfect. Half an hour each way. It'll give you time to clear your thoughts from the day and whip something up for us."

"Okay, be safe."

"I love you from here to the moon."

"Is that all?" he joked, his mood already lightening.

She kissed him again and as she left, added, "You're right. To the moon and back… And, for eternity!"

Chapter Thirty

With Grainger's whereabouts still unknown, Jade became increasingly restless. She wished she could say this wasn't like him. The fact that he did this often was the only thing that kept her from calling the police. He usually had an explanation for his whereabouts, citing business meetings, but Jade wasn't a fool. If not for Emilie, she would have outwardly questioned why business always occurred late at night and often on weekends. Unable to relax, she went for a walk. Although the days were now shorter, it was still relatively early and therefore safe in the quiet village.

As she arrived on the main thoroughfare between Le Pont and their new property, she noticed the reflection of blue and white lights at the end of the street. Although she couldn't be certain, it appeared that the police car had parked in front of the old farmhouse. She passed Le Pont first and saw that Luke was speaking to a diner, but his attention was also brought outside.

"Hey," he said, upon seeing her. "Trouble settling down?"

"Grainger still isn't home. It's unusual, even for him." Jade paused, "I just needed to get out and free my mind from worry. But then, I saw that…" she indicated outside.

"Come inside. I'll set you up with a cup of tea. Then we'll find out if it's anything that concerns your property."

Jade agreed, thankful for his gallantry. She took a seat at a table in the restaurant's front bay window, and Luke brought her a pot of Lady Grey tea along with cream and sugar as he had learned she preferred. He followed her gaze to the old property that seemed no closer to a renovation than it did when Luke first met her. Its derelict appearance mimicked his father's, confirming Clive hadn't made much progress with the construction crew that he was supposedly managing.

Indicating the police presence, Jade said, "Maybe it has something to do with permits. It seems every time I talk to Grainger he tells me about another problem."

"My father is supposed to mitigate problems," Luke responded with obvious annoyance. He hated the idea that his father's ineptitude would affect Jade.

"You can't just blame your father. I hear Grainger pushing him to cut corners at every turn."

Luke knew he should hold his tongue, but his disgust escaped. "Those two were cut from the same cloth."

Still looking across the street, worry crept into her voice. "This can't be good news."

It was at that moment that they noticed a police officer approaching the restaurant. When he stepped through the door, Luke took in a deep breath, recognizing the officer immediately.

"Something wrong?" Jade asked, sensing a change in Luke.

He put on a smile, albeit it was obviously forced. "I know that officer. He's a good chap. Let me find out what the issue is. It could just be something as simple as wanting to notify businesses of a planned power outage."

"At this hour?" Jade questioned.

Luke knew that his line was unlikely, but he didn't want to worry Jade. As if sensing that he wasn't telling her something, she looked back at the officer and then to Luke once more.

"Wait here," Luke requested of her. "I'll be back in a minute."

Harry brushed Willow's hair with his fingers, content to hold her. He didn't have any inclination to get dressed and leave. It was a new experience for him. There had been plenty of women in his past and after they had been together, the date came to its conclusion and he would excuse himself or fall asleep to avoid deep conversations. But with Willow it was different. She was different.

He had known her such a short time, but he had learned more about her than he had with women he had known far longer. He knew she preferred to wake up with a cup of coffee mixed with sweet cream, and he was still trying to figure out where he would find that in England. After her coffee, she said she liked to do a sun salutation and he wasn't quite sure what that entailed, but he knew he would wake up at dawn to try it. And, she mentioned that people should never randomly give a pet a name, but instead, should ask their pet what its desired name should be. Part of him thought it was sheer craziness and another part thought it made complete sense.

She nuzzled his neck and he maneuvered to kiss her mouth yet again. "Are you happy?" he asked, wanting to ensure she felt comfortable with what had transpired between them.

"I'm very happy. But..."

He propped himself up on his elbow to meet her gaze. That one word made his heart pound a bit harder with concern for her well-being. "What did I do? Or what can I do?"

"You did everything," she assured him. "You are wonderful. The 'but' is that I'm feeling the effects of jet lag; I'm hungry yet again. Le Pont had pies cooling on the counter and I didn't want a slice earlier, but now I'm craving one. Do you think it's too late?"

Harry reached for his phone on the bedside table to check the time. "They're still open and I would do anything for you."

"Wow, you sound like a boyfriend."

Harry's eyebrows shot up. That he wasn't expecting. But as Willow looked at him with the most carefree expression, he couldn't help but return her smile. "Willow, you aren't afraid to say what's on your mind. Until now, I haven't been particularly open with my feelings. I've never attempted a headstand. I've never had an in-depth conversation with animals. But I do know, that with you, I would try anything. And what's more, I think I've waited my whole life for you. So I agree, I think that makes me your boyfriend."

She beamed at his words. "This is a very good reason to celebrate with pie."

Chapter Thirty-One

FIVE YEARS AGO...

"I thought you were taking the night off," Elizabeth said upon seeing Luke turn up at the restaurant. "Emma left a note in the kitchen."

"She thinks I'm just whipping up something at home, but I'm surprising her with her favorite dish. We're out of parmesan," he explained the reason he was at the restaurant.

"Cacio e Pepe?" Elizabeth asked, knowing the answer before Luke could confirm that he was making the simple pasta flavored with cream, pepper and parmesan. When he nodded, she added, "Good choice. Help yourself to parmesan, but promise to save me some."

"Of course. I thought you were having dinner with Mary and Vera."

Elizabeth nodded. "Mary felt a cold coming on."

"I hope it's nothing more than that," Luke answered.

"Vera said she just needed a night in. So, I'm going to drop off some of today's soup before I head home."

"Sounds good. I need to hurry or Emma will wonder where

I ran off to. I'm surprised she's not home yet. She walked to Stow-on-the-Water about an hour ago."

"Maybe she got to talking instead of just selecting our winter arrangements," Elizabeth mused. "We've known James for years. He could talk the ears off a crop of corn."

Luke smiled at her colorful description, but his smile faded as a police car pulled up outside the restaurant. Its flashing lights reflected on the pavement, damp from the early evening drizzle. The colors from the patrol car's lights blended with the festive lights that Elizabeth had hung over the front door and windows to welcome the approach of Christmas.

Elizabeth tensed seeing the officer approach. His hunched shoulders indicated that his visit wasn't a cheerful one. Luke opened the door and the officer presented his badge as Elizabeth and Luke waited for an explanation about his presence. The officer was young and seemed unsure of how to best continue with the reason for his visit.

Elizabeth broke the silence. "Can I help you?"

Still the police officer hesitated as if bracing himself for the part of the job he hated most. He took a deep breath and stoically told them that an accident had occurred.

———

Luke felt as if he had been sucker punched. Tears poured from his eyes. He turned to Elizabeth and saw that she was crying as well, shaking her head back and forth. It couldn't be true. What this officer was saying just couldn't be right. Denial, the first stage of grief, hit both of them instantly.

But his words were clear. His demeanor professional. Had he been a friend, his factual recall of the accident would be considered cold. Elizabeth started to bristle about his interruption of their evening and for what... certainly he was at the wrong business. Anger. The second stage of grief came swiftly.

Luke listened to her argument in shocked silence, too numb to respond. "Certainly there must be some mistake," Elizabeth spoke while searching the officer's face. Bargaining. The third stage of grief. Luke once heard that a person could maneuver from one stage to the next in an instant and then vacillate back and forth amongst them. He had heard this, but never thought he would have to consider it. These thoughts pounded his mind as he tried so very hard to block out the conversation occurring in front of him. Elizabeth's sobs and anguished voice rose.

Again, she was struck by the officer's age. He made a mistake, she insisted. "How long have you worked on the force?" Her question was meant to imply his inexperience caused him to confuse the facts.

But in spite of their tears, their shaking shoulders, the rise in their voices paralleled with the disbelief of their whispers, still, the officer continued to speak in a quiet voice, doing his best to calm them during this storm of their lives. He offered more details in spite of how difficult it was to relay them. "Our investigation shows that she was crossing the A29 at the top of Bibury Hill when she was hit by a vehicle. The rain caused the ford to rise making it necessary for vehicles to slow down. However, witnesses on the scene identified a black BMW driving recklessly. The driver died at the scene."

"But you don't know that it was Emma," Elizabeth pleaded. She turned her attention away from the officer, away from the bad news. "Luke, call home! See if she's come back yet." And then, realizing that the officer was still there, she spoke to him once more. "We're going to check. You'll see that there's been a mistake."

"I'm sorry, Ma'am. She had her I.D. on her. Let me escort you both to John Radcliffe Hospital where she's been taken."

Luke turned to Elizabeth, who was already shrugging on her coat. "She'll be alright," he assured her, feeling the pangs of denial return.

Chapter Thirty-Two

IN THE POLICE CAR, NOBODY SPOKE. THE OFFICER drove with the car's lights and siren on to get through the early evening traffic.

Luke tried to process the information. Emma had been walking. She often cut across the motorway. It wasn't that dark when she left. There had to be a mistake. But one piece of news had him doubting his resolve that she was alright. The driver had been in a black BMW. Certainly there were hundreds in the city. Still, Luke couldn't help himself. He had to make sure.

"You said the driver died at the scene?"

"Yes, sir," the officer answered.

"What was his name?"

"I'm not sure that next of kin have been notified, sir. I can't say any more until then."

"Please, officer," Luke spoke in a tone that wasn't much above a whisper.

The officer knew how hard this must be on Elizabeth and Luke. This is when his youth and inexperience had gotten the best of him. He reasoned that they were in pain, and the name would be released soon enough anyway.

"Allen," the officer replied.

Luke exhaled. He didn't know anyone named Allen. The news about Emma was still horrendous, but it would be unfathomable if he had a personal connection to her accident.

And then, just as Luke took Elizabeth's hand and gave her a squeeze of reassurance, the officer spoke again. "His surname was Allen. Roger Allen."

Luke felt dizzy with the information. He had assumed the officer relayed the driver's first name. But it wasn't the case. Roger… his father's long time friend and drinking companion who had accosted him earlier that day. "Was anyone else in the car?" Luke asked.

The officer confirmed what Luke feared. "There was a passenger. Clive Barrows has been taken into the station for questioning."

Luke held his head in his hands and bowed his face towards his lap. "I'll never forgive him. That bastard! Oh my God, Elizabeth. What has he done?"

Luke and Elizabeth sat in the hospital waiting area. Empty paper coffee cups were stacked on a table in front of them, growing with the hours they had been there. The wall clock indicated it was now past one o'clock in the morning. But in spite of the hour, they were wide awake waiting for answers about Emma's condition.

A nurse led them down the hall where Emma had been transferred from surgery to a room in the Critical Care Unit. Her frame looked frail due to the machines that were attached to her arms and hummed in rhythm with her breathing. Helping to support that effort was an endotracheal tube that had been taped in place. In spite of the probes and contraptions, her eyes were closed serenely.

When Elizabeth and Luke were led into the room, Elizabeth gasped slightly at the sight of Emma, while Luke immediately went to her side. He took her hand in his own and waited for the doctor's news. After a moment to give them time to adjust to seeing Emma, the doctor approached quietly. "I'm sorry to tell you this hard news. Emma sustained severe internal injuries. She lost a lot of blood when her spleen was ruptured."

Luke and Elizabeth shook their heads in disbelief and covered their faces as their tears leaked down their cheeks. Lowering their heads, they listened as the doctor's horrific account continued. "We repaired the damage to her spleen, but I'm afraid she experienced cardiac arrest in the process due to blood loss. We were able to resuscitate her heart, but she is left without brain activity due to the loss of oxygen. I'm afraid that only the machines are keeping her alive."

Elizabeth pointed to the monitors, one indicating heart rate and another showing blood pressure. Both seemed to be functioning as normal. "But look," she said, insistent in her belief that Emma would be alright.

The doctor nodded sympathetically and placed a kind hand on her shoulder. "I know it seems as if she is just sleeping, but without the machines she will not regain consciousness. Without the machines, her heart will fail again and she will never be the same."

Luke gently released Emma's hand and turned toward the doctor. "Can she hear us? Would it help if we spoke to her?"

"She is brain dead. She will never regain consciousness. She has no chance of recovery."

The doctor placed a hand on each of their shoulders. After delivering his final piece of information, he attempted to offer comfort, although there was none to provide. "When you're ready…" he said quietly. The remainder of the sentence was left unsaid, but the meaning was clear. He was giving them time to say their goodbyes.

Luke and Elizabeth held tightly to each other. Wrapped in her arms, Luke began to shake. It was the first time since they received the news that he had truly fallen apart. He couldn't speak and so she held him.

Finally, he uttered the words, "I'm so sorry," over and over. "Elizabeth, I wanted to ask her to marry me. I was going to come to you and get your blessing. But I didn't because of my father. Nothing good ever comes from being near my family. You are probably cursing the day you met me."

Elizabeth looked at Luke firmly. "Listen to me. This was an accident. You are not your family. You're a good boy, Luke." Tears spilled down her own cheeks as she said the words.

She continued to speak to him with a motherly tone, remembering the years earlier when she took him in. He continued to hold on tightly to her and in turn, she ran her hand down the back of his head. They cried together and then turned toward Emma's bed, each taking one of her hands.

"She loved you, Luke. Even without marriage to Emma, you are family."

He nodded and tried to stop his tears and offer comfort to this woman who stood before him, showing him love when her own heart was breaking. He looked at Elizabeth, saw her strength and compassion, that which she had shown him when they first met and never allowed it to waiver, even now. "Elizabeth, you are my family, too."

Luke and Elizabeth stood on either side of Emma's bed, staring at the girl they both loved so dearly. If it wasn't for the breathing tube still in place, she would look peaceful.

Elizabeth knelt next to the bed to be closer to Emma's ear and placed a gentle hand on her cheek.

"My sweet girl… you will always be with me. I love you now and forever." She rose and looked to Luke for support as well as to indicate it was his turn to say goodbye.

Just as Elizabeth had done, Luke bowed down to be level with Emma's bed and didn't hesitate to speak his heart. His words came out freely, even in front of Elizabeth.

"Emma, I loved you so much." Then he shook his head. "No, I can't say loved. I *love* you." He emphasized the word. He looked up at Elizabeth helplessly. She nodded at him to continue.

"You are the best thing that ever happened to me," Luke continued. "You will always be a part of my life. May you be at peace." The last word broke from his voice with a choke. Luke struggled to get to his feet and he hung his head as he reached for Elizabeth. They stood by Emma's bedside holding each other in support.

When they composed themselves, they gave a small nod to the nurse indicating they were as ready as they could be. As the nurse disconnected the leads from the machines, the humming noise stopped. The line indicating Emma's heart beat continued in a mocking way giving Luke and Elizabeth one more moment of false hope, until it went flat indicating she was gone.

Elizabeth leaned down and kissed her daughter one last time on the cheek. Luke did the same, bidding her goodbye to her final resting.

Chapter Thirty-Three

THE NEXT DAY WAS A SOMBER ONE. ELIZABETH LEFT
the house early to place a sign on the restaurant indicating
they were unexpectedly closed. She returned home to find
Luke in the main house, sitting on the couch looking out the
large window to the backyard.

"I made a pot of coffee. Would you like me to get you a
cup?"

"No, no," she was quick to answer. "Stay where you are;
I'll join you. Emma loved sitting there just as the morning sun
rose."

Luke nodded and made room for Elizabeth, offering her a
few cushions, and then settling back again. He wondered
aloud how long the house would feel empty.

"We'll always miss her," Elizabeth answered.

Luke nodded again as he inhaled deeply, trying to be as
strong for Elizabeth as she was for him. After a moment, they
settled into silence, but it was shortly interrupted by a knock
on the door. They both looked at each other questioningly and
then Luke rose.

Elizabeth recognized the voice of the police officer who

broke the news and escorted them to the hospital. She stood when Luke brought him back to the main room.

"I'm sorry to interrupt your morning." The officer seemed just as ill at ease as he had been the previous night. "I know this is a very difficult time and I'm sure you want your time to grieve, but I thought it was important to deliver news of our findings."

Immediately, Luke and Elizabeth took their seats on the couch again and instinctively gripped hands. The officer took a deep breath and continued, "Roger Allen, the driver of the vehicle, had a blood alcohol level above 80 milligrams, the acceptable sober limit in the United Kingdom. We can confirm that his passenger's was as high, but since he was not the driver, he's been released. We can't prosecute."

Luke and Elizabeth hung their heads in heavy sorrow.

The 'temporarily closed' sign remained on the window of the restaurant, but Luke came to clean and stock shelves, anything to stay busy. When the bell over the door chimed, he imagined it to be Elizabeth, who like him, would have a hard time not coming in and feeling useful at a time when they both felt so helpless. But as he pushed open the double doors leading to the dining area from the kitchen, he saw his father.

Without a thought, he crossed the room to him and laid a powerful punch against Clive's jaw. Clive fell to the ground and the area where Luke's fist connected reddened immediately, the discoloration adding to a black eye and a deep abrasion on his cheek, both probably results of the accident.

"Get up! Get up you worthless piece so I can pound you down once more." Luke stood over him, both daring and goading his father to rise.

From his vantage point on the floor, Clive yelled to Luke.

"I didn't kill that girl." His speech was slurred, either because of the punch or evidence that he was still feeling the effects of the evening. "You got to let her go," he stammered.

"Get up!" Luke insisted.

Clive ineffectively pressed himself onto his forearm, but still remained prone on the ground. He gazed up at Luke with a lazy eye. "Justice has been served. Roger, my lifelong friend is gone too."

His words sent Luke into a frenzy. He dropped on top of his father and punched him repeatedly, one fist and then the other, each connecting with a loud pop. He didn't even hear Elizabeth enter the restaurant until her shouts increased.

"Luke! I said to stop!"

Once assured that his father was pummeled into silence, Luke rose and began to steady his breath. He looked down at his father who had passed out and then to Elizabeth.

She took Luke's hands, turning them over to inspect the damage he inflicted upon himself. "Luke, you'll end up in prison. I can't lose you, too."

He nodded, and threw his arms around her. They stood for a moment until Luke replied. "You're right. He's not worth it." He bent over and grabbed his father's legs, then dragged him by the feet and out the door. Once outside, he threw a pitcher of water over Clive's face to rouse him. When it had the desired effect, Luke hissed, "Get on your way. The police may have released you, but I know you're not innocent. You were both drinking. You could have insisted that neither of you drive."

His father spat out a wad of blood and looked Luke in the eye, but didn't dare reply.

"Justice?" Luke repeated his father's offensive word, low under his breath and took a final step toward his dad again. With satisfaction, he saw his dad shrink and scramble backwards. The first time he had ever backed down to Luke. "There is no justice until you take your dying breath."

Chapter Thirty-Four

Over the years, Officer Vallens had developed into a more than competent member of the police force. He understood the delicate nuance of when to let something slip and when to tow the line. There were nights when he encountered noisy and loitering teenagers and he sent them on their way knowing that their parents' wrath would straighten them out. But if those same teens were ever found to be drunk and behind the wheel, he would haul them to the station for an immediate overnight stay.

The devastating news he delivered to Elizabeth and Luke didn't just change their lives, it changed his. He had been on the force less than a month when he found himself on duty that terrible night. After Emma's accident, Officer Vallens stopped into the restaurant once a week out of concern for Luke and Elizabeth. Then, out of kindness, he continued to stay in touch, coming in before work for a morning coffee and pastry.

Over the years, his patronage of Le Pont grew and he became a regular customer, often stopping in for a late dinner before ending his day. He never pried into Luke and Elizabeth's life, nor did they with his. Their conversations were focused on daily pleasantries of how are you and notes about the weather. But there was always the unspoken knowledge that Officer Vallens had helped Elizabeth and Luke move on with their lives.

Luke filled a to-go cup with coffee and two sugars, just as he knew Officer Vallens preferred it. He headed across the street and handed it to him. "What brings you out?"

"Hiya Luke… it's not a social call, I'm afraid."

Luke furrowed his brow and automatically glanced across the street at the restaurant where Jade waited. It was then that Harry and Willow made their way towards him, walking hand in hand. Luke was surprised to see them, but also relieved at the timing.

"Everything okay?" Harry asked.

"Just getting to that," Luke answered back. "Hey, Jade is inside and probably could use the company. I'll be back in a minute."

Willow was already looking anxiously toward the restaurant for Jade, and Harry answered on behalf of them. "No problem. Take your time."

As they walked off, Luke kept his poker face in case Jade was watching, and tried to read Officer Vallens. In truth, he never considered his patronage 'social' but more part of his duty. Not knowing what to say and fearing the worst, like Harry, Luke inquired if everything was alright with the property.

"Do you know the owner? Does he ever come by the restaurant?"

"The owner's wife is there now."

Officer Vallens followed Luke's gaze. "You mind introducing me?"

"Sure, but what's going on?" Luke hesitated and then

explained, "We've become friends. If it's something troubling, perhaps I can be of help."

Officer Vallens replied, "In that case, you should be there for her. Let's go across the street."

Luke had heard that heavy tone years earlier and would never forget its implication. In his bones, he knew bad news was coming.

Willow was seated with Jade, trying her best to calm her. Harry was there for companionship, knowing better than to get in the middle of a tense conversation between long friends.

"I know something bad has happened," Jade fretted. "He's been gone for over a day."

"He may have just over-indulged and has been sleeping it off at a hotel," Willow offered in her soothing voice.

"Then why the police?"

"Like you said, something as silly as permits," Willow answered.

"Look," she pointed to Officer Vallens and Luke approaching the restaurant. "That's not the look of someone wanting to speak to me about permits. They'd send a letter or post a sign."

As Luke and Officer Vallens crossed the street and entered Le Pont, Jade anxiously rose from her place at the table. Luke cradled her in a hug and without question she allowed it. Neither one of them seemed concerned about the impression they would give to Willow and Harry. Given the ambiguity of the situation, Luke simply acted on instinct because his gut told him that something was very wrong.

He gave her shoulders a light squeeze. "Jade, let's sit down again at the table." His voice was gentle, but firm.

"Jade, do you want us to leave?" Willow asked.

"No, of course not. You know everything about me. There's no reason to hide anything now." Turning to Harry, she nodded, indicating that he should also stay.

As much as Officer Vallens had become a fixture in the neighborhood, Luke knew he didn't stay for casual conversation and as far as he knew, he had never poked around the old property before. He held Jade's hand in support for what was to come.

With the four of them seated at the table, Jade indicated it was alright for the officer to proceed. She looked directly into his eyes and took a deep breath, steadying herself.

"Mrs. Grainger Thomas?" Officer Vallens confirmed.

"Yes. He's my…" The last words choked in her throat as if saying the word husband wasn't something she had uttered in many years. She simply nodded and implied she wanted the officer to continue.

"There's been an accident. Your husband was involved. And, Luke…" the officer turned his attention, "your father as well."

Luke had suspected as much. He was taken back to five years earlier when this same officer spoke those same words. He knew that his father and Grainger had become thick as thieves, and he started to seethe even before Officer Vallens provided more details. Luke's voice was calm, but tight with his anger. "Was he driving?" He spoke the words slowly and distinctively, speaking each one with a pause between.

Although Luke had never given anyone on the force a lick of trouble, the officer knew how this situation could quickly change Luke's resolve and calm. Believing it best to delay the answer to that specific question, the officer continued with his account.

"Both the driver and the passenger were killed instantly. I'm sorry, Ma'am." He knew better than to offer apologies to

Luke, but unaware of Jade's long and tumultuous history with Grainger, he spoke as one in his position would — with professional courtesy.

Yet, Jade looked confused. The news didn't register. "What are you saying?"

Still holding her hand, Luke turned toward her. He pulled her in close and held her in a hug. He understood all too well that this sort of news always seemed improbable upon hearing it. It was as if there were two types of people — those preconditioned to believe the worst and the ones who maintained hope for a brighter future. And then there existed his complicated thoughts about his father where he simply hoped that the man wouldn't bring any more pain to those around him.

Jade bent her forehead to Luke's shoulder, needing the comfort, but not altogether understanding. After a brief pause, Luke explained. "What Officer Vallens is saying is that my father and Grainger were together at the time of their death."

Luke continued to hold Jade, but looked over her shoulder to Officer Vallens with the obvious question in his eyes. He insisted on knowing the truth, and Officer Vallens had known him for too long to not be honest.

The officer nodded his head. "Your dad was behind the wheel."

Jade met Luke's gaze. Neither seemed to know how to react to each other's loss. A myriad of emotions passed in her expression, and she said as much with her silence. Anger about Grainger's drinking. Fear of what the future held. And naturally, grief.

Grief was the most complicated because Grainger had not been kind to her. Still, she was married to him and now she had to tell Emilie the news. She just shook her head in silence and then bowed it to Luke's shoulder once more.

"Again, I'm sorry for your loss," Officer Vallens spoke quietly. "I apologize for what I'm about to say, but I have to ask you to come with me and positively identify your husband."

He turned his attention back to Luke. "Luke, we've made the identification of your father, but for official purposes, you need to come as well."

"Willow… can you pick up Emilie tomorrow? She's at a sleepover. I'm not ready to tell her." Jade's thoughts were flowing freely and the panic rising in her voice.

"Text me the address. Don't worry. I'll look after her," Willow assured her friend.

They stood and followed the officer outside. Luke locked the door to the restaurant and hung the sign indicating they would re-open in the morning. He didn't intend to take time off.

Chapter Thirty-Five

FIVE YEARS AGO...

The vicar bowed his head and tossed a small amount of dirt onto Emma's casket. "May you go in peace and may God be with you."

The outpouring of attendees was vast despite the rainy weather. The day was as gloomy as everyone's mood. Elizabeth and Luke held hands and accepted the sorrowful greetings from friends, neighbors, and local business owners who filed along in a line to pay their respects.

Mary and Vera each placed a flower on Emma's casket, handed to them by James who also provided a beautiful standing spray of roses. Ben Mason cautiously approached Elizabeth and took her hand. "Elizabeth, I'm so sorry for your loss. There are no words that will take away your pain, but please know that I'm thinking of you."

In an uncharacteristic manner, she hugged Ben close to her chest before getting control of her emotions and pulling away. "Thank you. It means a lot to me that you're here."

Ben stayed by her side another moment, then unsure of what else he could say, he moved aside giving way to George and Brianne who followed next in line. George was never very good with words or crowds, but he offered heartfelt condolences. "I'm so sorry," he said simply and shook his head side-to-side. Brianne spoke in a tone much more reserved than she normally displayed. "If we can do anything, please let us know."

The sheer number of people from the village who had come out touched Elizabeth's heart. For over an hour, she and Luke accepted the condolences of their community. Then, Luke wrapped his arm behind Elizabeth's back, ensuring that she wouldn't slip on the wet grass of the memorial park. They made their way to the car park with the other guests, a parade of black cloaked individuals. "I've invited people to come back to the restaurant," she said to Luke quietly.

"But… I haven't prepared anything."

"I know," she patted his arm. "I want you to be surrounded by people who care about us and not focus on anything except Emma. Nico offered to bring over some platters." She paused, then with a choke in her voice added, "To think I used to be so competitive with him. Especially when Emma told me his moussaka was one of her favorite meals.

As if knowing they were speaking of him, the owner of the neighboring restaurant came over. "My dear, Elizabeth, I'm going to leave now and pick up the food. I'm bringing a few extra dishes that Miss Emma always loved. I never told you this, but occasionally she would pick up orders of Greek lemon soup if you ever had a cold."

"She did?" Elizabeth's eyes opened a bit wider. "She told me that it was a recipe she had experimented with."

Nico smiled kindly. "I know." He leaned in and whispered conspiratorially, "We agreed that you were more likely to eat it if you thought she made it. Emma loved you very much, Elizabeth. She was the only person, other than my own daughter, who I've taught how to make that recipe."

"Thank you, Nico. We'll see you at the restaurant."

Le Pont bustled with activity. The front door was in continual motion with the arrival of friends. They brought platters of food or loaves of bread to be eaten now or frozen for later. Elizabeth and Luke never expected the outpouring of gifts considering they were in the business of feeding others.

The food, people, and holiday decorations nearly made it seem like a festive event. Although in her sadness, Elizabeth had wanted to take down the holiday decor. A tree was decked out in the corner and absently, she touched one of Emma's favorite ornaments. It was a sleigh with bells on it that Emma always hung in a position where it would be brushed against and therefore, would chime. She reached out to steady the ornament and then retreated into the kitchen where she found Luke.

"I just came to check if any platters needed refilling," she said as way of explanation for not socializing. But in truth, no explanation was needed. Luke was there because he also wanted a reprieve from talking.

"People have really turned out to support us," he noted.

Elizabeth nodded, adding, "They say it's supposed to be a celebration of life."

"She would have liked this," Luke replied. "Lots of people, eating, festive with the holiday season…" his voice grew weary and melancholy.

They stayed silent for a moment, watching Nico direct his people around the kitchen, expertly navigating the scene as he would in his own restaurant. He had platters of food cooking in their ovens and even more arriving from guests. He approached Luke and Elizabeth. "We know you won't be serving these to your customers, but you could if you wanted to take a break for a week or so. Or, bring them home and freeze them so that when you eat them, you're reminded of the many people who love you."

Choked with emotion, Luke allowed himself to be pulled into Nico's massive chest for a bear hug. The heavy set man gave Luke's frame a squeeze for good measure. When they parted, Nico smiled broadly. "Never underestimate the power of a hug."

Luke nodded, "I believe you… if I didn't, you'd squeeze the living daylights out of me."

Elizabeth smiled too, the first one since the accident. It was exactly what was meant to happen when people gather to offer support and kindness. "Shall we say more hellos?" Elizabeth motioned to the activity of the restaurant, and Luke agreed.

The chatter was loud throughout the restaurant. Luke and Elizabeth joined a table of neighbors to dig into the food. And like wearing a smile, eating a proper meal was something they hadn't done since receiving the awful news. Although their sadness was present, it felt good to be among friends, and the talk eventually blossomed into happier conversations.

As was typical for December in England, the daylight turned into darkness by 4 p.m. Elizabeth and Luke had returned home. The exhaustion of the day had taken its toll on both of them so Luke retreated to his cottage, giving Elizabeth her space in the main home.

He paced in his sitting room, turned the television on and then off again. He sat down with a new cookery book to peruse recipes, but even that didn't hold his attention. He glanced up at the roof when he heard the soft rain start to fall and was taken back to when he and Emma had dodged a storm. He considered lighting a fire, but couldn't be bothered to make the room warmer. The cold matched his heart, and after only an hour of solitude, he heard a quiet knock at his door and opened it to find Elizabeth.

"Come in, you're getting wet. You shouldn't be out in the rain. I could have come to the main house."

"I just couldn't focus on anything. The place seems so empty."

Luke nodded, knowing just how she felt. Although Emma had passed a week ago, now that the funeral arrangements were completed, there was nothing more to do but grieve.

"Shall I put the kettle on?"

"Please," Elizabeth agreed and went to sit on the couch.

After a brief spell, Luke returned with two steaming mugs of tea along with a plate of finger sandwiches that Nico had sent home with him. The bigger dishes were deposited in Elizabeth's kitchen and the freezer of the restaurant. He offered the plate to Elizabeth and she accepted an egg salad sandwich wedge.

Before she could speak, Luke took a deep breath and addressed her quietly. "Elizabeth, I've been thinking over the last week… I'm wondering if it would be easier on you if I moved out of the cottage and looked for other employment. Of course I would stay on at the restaurant until you replaced me."

Elizabeth looked gutted. "Why would I want to replace you and why in the world would you want to move out?"

"I hardly think you want me around as a reminder." Luke leaned back on the couch, putting his head in his hands. "When you see me, do you think of my father?"

Elizabeth reached for his hands and took them into her own as she had done so many times when something was amiss. "Dear one, that is the farthest thing from the truth.

222

You made her happy. I could always tell how in love you were with each other."

Luke wiped a wayward tear away. "Being here — the house, the restaurant — I see the memory of her everywhere. I don't know if the pain will ever go away. And I'm sorry to even utter that statement. I can't imagine how you feel."

Elizabeth didn't say anything, but simply nodded. "Losing a child…," she paused. "I don't know if a greater pain exists, but I do know that yours is also immense."

"There's no place I'd rather be than surrounded by her memory, but I don't want to make this harder on you."

"Being alone would be harder, Luke." She looked at him expectantly, hoping he would change his mind. "I think you need my help and I know that I need yours."

Luke nodded and they sat in silence for a few moments. Luke took a sandwich and topped up Elizabeth's teacup. "Thank you," he finally said.

"You'll stay?" she took his hand.

"If you're sure."

"Of course, I am. When I gave you a place to stay… a refuge from your father… I started to think of you as a son." She wrapped her arms around him as he did to her. "Luke, this is your home for as long as you want it."

Chapter Thirty-Six

Jade sat draped in a blanket that Luke had wrapped around her. A cup of tea was placed in front of her, and he lit the fireplace… little things that he hoped were comforting. He knew she was in shock and trying to process what happened. As such, he insisted that she not be on her own.

She leaned back against the soft leather sofa while he sat in a matching club chair opposite her. Those two pieces of furniture were the only things that Luke had changed in the tiny cottage from when he moved in. There was comfort in the familiarity. The fireplace hearth remained stocked with cut wood and it burned throughout the winter. One of his favorite paintings by Emma hung prominently above the mantle.

Jade realized that she had been silent for ages, and she wasn't sure what to say. They had each lost someone, and both were at odds with their complex emotions. Finally, she looked at the painting above them. "It's beautiful. Was it also done by Elizabeth's daughter?"

Luke nodded. "Do you want to see some others?"

Jade nodded and he led the way to a small closet where he

carefully removed a painting gently draped in a cloth. When he revealed it, Jade could see the depiction of Luke lying on his back, his arms crossed behind his head, the way he often did after rowing.

"It's you."

He nodded rather solemnly and pulled another painting from the closet, the one of the couple leaning within the crevice of the Radcliffe Camera building.

Jade admired it, and then peered closer. "Is that you as well? They look… they're obviously in love."

Luke sighed heavily. "I've wanted to tell you something, but I thought it would sound presumptuous. You were married; I had no business falling for you." Luke looked back to the painting. "Elizabeth's daughter… Emma… was my girlfriend. This was her last painting."

Jade looked at Luke, knowing there was more that he wanted to say. "Are you okay?"

"Her death came at the hands of a drunk driver; my father was involved." He watched her expression with his admission and then continued. "He wasn't the driver, but he never suggested they take a taxi… and I'm sure he didn't this time either."

They stared at each other, not knowing how to navigate their emotions. Jade crossed to the fireplace and warmed her hands, suddenly feeling a chill. Luke ran his hands through his wavy hair and exhaled his breath, as if finally exorcised from the pain his father had caused.

Jade turned and gazed once more at Emma's painting. "Is it the two of you?"

Luke shook his head. "She told me it wasn't meant to be us, but rather the representation of love. She insisted it wasn't finished, but she could never put her finger on what it needed."

Jade felt a myriad of emotions, but was determined to

maintain her composure. "She'll always be in your heart, as she should." Giving the room one last glance, she started to gather up her purse and coat. "I should go."

Luke caught her hand. "Please. Don't leave like this." He wrapped his arms around her, and she rested her head on his shoulder. They held each other close, and Luke spoke his truth. "I loved her, but she died five years ago. I never thought I would love again. Until you."

As much as Jade felt her heart soar, she pulled away from his embrace. "Luke, it's just not right for us to be together now." She brushed a tear from her cheek, no longer able to prevent it. "The accident is too fresh."

He nodded. "You had many years together."

"No, it's not that. He wasn't a good husband or father. But the accident has made so many difficult memories resurface."

Luke wished he could take back the thoughts that had escaped him. "The accident… It was bad timing then… and now."

"I think we need time apart. Being with me will always remind you of your father. I'm going back to Los Angeles."

She turned to leave, reaching for the ornate door handle, but Luke placed a hand on her shoulder.

"Jade?" There was something he desperately wanted to say, but again the timing felt off. Instead, he whispered, "I'll miss you."

"I'll miss you too."

The right person had come into her life at the wrong time. She didn't look back, her footsteps quickening as she made her way down the path, the threat of more tears too real to ignore.

Five years ago, Luke had endured a pain so profound, he never imagined he could survive anything like it again. But as he watched Jade's silhouette recede into the distance, he realized he had been wrong.

Chapter Thirty-Seven

Willow and Harry enjoyed an afternoon picnic on the banks of the River Widenbrush. Harry had picked up Willow's idea of comfort food from a local pub: burger, chips, and a bottle of merlot. Harry also asked Luke to prepare American style chocolate chip cookies for dessert. With Jade back in California, he knew it was likely that Willow might also return, especially since she came to England for her friend.

Jade had insisted that Willow continue her house exchange in Bourton Bridge as it was too soon for the other party to give up Willow's place in Los Angeles. Still, Willow expressed that she was worried about her friend. With the threat of her leaving, Harry wanted any remaining time to be memorable. He decided to add a bit of California flair to their meal — guacamole as a topping for her burger. In spite of his initial insistence that burger toppings should never be green, after trying it, he was hooked.

When Willow saw the spread, she mused at how easily they had started a routine together and learned each other's preferences. Proving her point, she took the top bun off their burgers and placed a few crisps inside the sandwiches, then spread the bun with the avocado mixture. Harry expertly mixed a helping of ketchup and blue cheese dressing for their chips.

As he held one for Willow to try, she said, "There's no better way to enjoy French fries… chips, as you say. Why doesn't Luke serve them this way?"

Harry smirked. "We didn't go to a fancy culinary school, so I don't think he trusts our simpler taste."

Willow took a bite of her burger, and seemed to digest this thought. "He landed okay in spite of his upbringing." Harry raised his eyebrows, but neither questioned nor confirmed her statement. "Jade told me about his dad. I know it's wrong to speak ill of the dead, but honestly, it seems like Luke is better off."

Harry nodded. "Clive was a mean bugger. I made a point of doing my work while trying to avoid him."

In spite of their relationship being new, they were comfortable with each other. Willow took a bite of her burger; Harry used his napkin to wipe a bit of stray guacamole from her cheek. She smiled at his thoughtfulness; and in turn, he didn't seem to mind that food always found her cheek. After a moment, she asked, "Can I share something else?"

"Of course."

"Simply put, Jade is better off too. And this isn't just an opinion. It's fact."

Harry hadn't heard such seriousness in her voice before. He met her gaze, "Did you see something between them?"

"Constantly. Grainger never had a kind word for her. He was small-minded and abusive. But he knew I had his number and barely tolerated me. But if Jade ever spoke against him, the way I did, I'd see bruises appear on her arms."

Harry let out a low whistle. "That's rough. I assume she stayed for Emilie's sake?"

"Yeah, and now she's in their old house alone. The memories can't be pleasant."

"I know someone else who isn't happy about her absence."

"How is Luke?"

"He mopes around. He loves his work, but now it's all he has and he pours himself into it."

She reached for another chip and stirred the sauce in thought. "I don't think there's anything wrong with them dating. Screw that societal idea of a distinguished waiting period after someone's passing. It's probably leftover from some Victorian era custom."

"Queen Victoria's mourning over Prince Albert," Harry confirmed.

"There you have it! And when was that?"

"Mmmm, 1861, I believe. It's been awhile since my school lessons."

Willow nodded, knowing that Harry helped make her point. "And how long did she mourn?"

"That I know, without a doubt; it was 40 years!"

"That's insane. It's half a lifetime!"

"Some would see it as romantic?" he reasoned.

Willow smiled. "I love your romantic side. But…Jade and Luke… a mourning period shouldn't apply to them. Jade endured years of a loveless relationship."

"And Luke suffered far too long in his grief," Harry agreed.

"They have to get together." Willow started to twist the wrapper of her straw. It was one of many habits that Harry found adorable, like when she did squats while brushing her teeth and read the last page of a book first to ensure it ended happily.

"I love you, Willow. You have to have faith."

She smiled at him. "I believe you… because I love you so much."

In his past, declarations of love made Harry nervous. But

with Willow, it was different. Not only had he wanted to hear it from her, he was the one to say it first. And he didn't want to stop there.

"Willow…" he took the twisted paper from her hands, "I love how much you care about people, your laugh, your smile, your sexy dimples, everything about you." He dabbed one end of the paper straw into his wine and attached it to itself to form a paper ring. "This ring was once a simple straw wrapper. But I know on good authority that it had big aspirations in life."

Amused, Willow played along with his story. "Did it now?"

"It dreamed of one day becoming a symbol of love." He wrapped the little piece of paper around her fourth finger of her right hand. Then, he got down on one knee. "Although I'd love to honor its noble dreams, I think your engagement ring should be made of platinum."

Willow's face lit up in a huge smile. "My what?"

"Will you marry me?" He reached into his back pocket to produce a beautiful diamond ring set in a platinum, filigree band. It looked to be an antique. "This was my mother's, but if you would rather have something more modern…"

"Oh my goodness, Harry. It's beautiful."

"And?"

"Ab-so-darn-lutely!" She paused and chuckled under her breath. "This is a pretty elaborate gesture to bring my friend and your friend back together."

He placed the ring on her left hand, where it belonged. "This is about my love for you. But Luke and Jade being brought together would certainly be a very happy side effect."

Chapter Thirty-Eight

LUKE ARRIVED HOME FROM THE RESTAURANT, BUT before heading to his cottage, he took a £50 bill from his wallet, placed it in an envelope, and slid it through the letterbox. Elizabeth peered out the window upon hearing the creak of its metal cover. She saw Luke's downturned mouth and sad eyes. Opening the door suddenly, she spoke with exasperation. "When are you going to stop?"

"This is my last installment, so I guess now." His voice had a considerable edge to it.

Elizabeth shrugged her shoulders. "I wasn't referring to your payments. I meant your depressing demeanor. I've gotten used to splurging on myself thanks to your stubbornness."

"Typical. I spend years standing my ground and look where it gets me."

"Are we still talking about payments for a flat that was offered for free, or why you and Jade aren't... you know."

Luke opened his eyes wide in horror. "I'm not talking about that with you." As an afterthought he asked, "What do you know about it anyway?"

"Jade came by the restaurant the following morning to say

goodbye. When I suggested she have breakfast and wait to see you, she said she was in a hurry. It wasn't like her, so I asked if everything was okay. She just said that you two had an awkward moment the night before and it was best that she leave."

Luke bowed his head and exhaled his breath. "I guess I didn't handle things quite right. I was having trouble forgetting…" his voice trailed off as if he didn't want to put words to his thoughts.

"Are you talking about your father or her husband?"

When Luke still didn't answer, Elizabeth threw out an even harder question. "Luke, what is this about? Tell me it has nothing to do with Emma."

"It's not about my father or her husband. I'm better off without my father and Jade is certainly better off without someone who verbally and physically abused her. But their death brought everything rushing back to me about that night five years ago."

"I understand that, but it's been five years. It's time to stop blaming yourself for what happened to Emma."

Luke simply shook his head, the thought of doing anything else being unfathomable.

Elizabeth continued. "It wasn't your fault that she went to the florist that day. It was her choice. Just like it was her decision to take the short cut. It wasn't your fault that your dad had been drinking with Roger Allen, another drunk."

She paused to see if her words resonated with Luke. Noting his still downcast eyes, she spoke with more conviction. "Listen to me. You couldn't control Emma's decision to go on that errand or walk back on that motorway, and you couldn't control your father's decisions. He's gone and it's time to let everything go with him."

He looked at her sadly. His voice barely above a whisper as

if the words in his mind were just too painful to utter. "Including her?"

Elizabeth smiled gently. "Emma or Jade?" She took Luke's hand. "You've kept Emma in your heart for years. She would want you to be with someone, and so do I."

"Maybe Jade and I are both too broken."

"Broken can be repaired. You're not the same young man who snuck into my storage room. I just applied a little glue to your life. Maybe that's what she needs."

Luke shrugged his shoulders. "Emilie has probably settled back with her friends, and Jade will most likely sell the property and be done with this chapter."

"And maybe she'll decide to keep it. Don't be so quick to put an ending to her story."

With his phone in his hands, Luke stared at it momentarily and then looked away, deep in thought. "Idiot," he mumbled to himself. "It's just a stupid text. Not that big a deal." He repositioned the pillow that was behind his head and gave the phone another glance. Finally, his thumbs manipulated across it.

I miss you.

"Too needy," he said to himself. He thought a moment longer, then tried again.

I'm thinking of you.

"Seriously?" he said aloud. "Too creepy."

With each text that he wrote, he would read the words with dissatisfaction and promptly hit delete.

"Jade, if you need anything, I'm here."

He read his words and finally satisfied, hit send. He repositioned the pillow across the mattress and turned over prepared to go to sleep. It was late afternoon in Los Angeles, and he turned the light back on with the sound of the incoming text.

I was going to text, but I was worried you wouldn't be happy to hear from me.

He read her words and immediately texted back. *I wish you were here.*

Her response, *I booked a flight back,* brought a smile to his face. And even though she added, *It's just a short trip,* filled him with hope.

———

The following day, Willow waited until an appropriate time in Los Angeles to reach out. Hearing the phone, Jade leaned it against a vase so that Willow and she could share a FaceTime call. She lifted her coffee mug as a toast to her friend and hunkered down in her chair to catch up. Taking a sip from her mug, she stated, "I miss your coffee. Why was it always better than mine?"

"Because I took time to grind my own beans, used filtered water, and bought that yummy sweet cream in the lavender carton." Willow winked at her and took a sip from her own coffee. "I hate to rub it in, but my coffee is even more decadent here. I now use full cream with a dash of maple syrup as there's no sweet cream or half-and-half. Ahh, but you might not know that trick because you had a personal chef prepare your morning coffee."

"Personal chef," Jade tried to scoff off the comment. In truth, she wanted to ask about Luke, but instead led the conversation away from her personal life. "That must be delicious. When I was there, I was envious of people pouring double cream over their dessert. Very decadent."

"You should enjoy your one life," Willow said pointedly. "Speaking of which…," Willow nearly broke the news about her engagement, but then took in her friend's sad eyes. It wasn't like either of them to hold back, but the distance made it harder to share. Some topics needed to be followed up with a hug, and to Willow, this felt like that time. She decided to play it safe.

"How are you doing? You look quite busy."

Jade picked up an empty cardboard box and placed wrapped dishes inside it, wishing she could also pack up her feelings. Somewhat avoiding the real answer, she replied, "This is a daunting task," and waved to her kitchen cupboards. "Nobody needs three sets of dishes," she said, obviously trying to busy herself.

"You're packing?"

"Just... organizing. Giving things to charity." Jade paused to blow her nose. "His clothes... but also these things," she waved her hand to a myriad of dishes and glassware. "Things from our wedding... presents from people who expected us to stay married."

"Jade, you can't blame yourself for an accident."

"I know. But, I also know that there were many times before the accident when I didn't want to be married." She let her admission hang in the air. She had ample time to reflect on her emotions, and she couldn't shake one of the stages of grief that plagued her. Guilt.

Jade picked up her phone to see Willow closer. "Well, there you have it." She couldn't escape Willow's concerned expression, but she misread the thoughts behind it.

"Jade, I will say this again. You are not to blame for his death, and certainly not for the demise of your marriage... which occurred beforehand."

A tear creeped down Jade's cheek, and in uncharacteristic fashion, she let it all out. "I felt like I couldn't do it any longer. The fighting. The drinking. The lack of respect. I wanted to escape. Willow, you always saw him for what he was. Somehow, he never bothered to hide it from you."

Willow wore a wry smile. "I guess that's why he never liked me."

"Well, he wasn't very likable himself. It was a difficult marriage. That's why I'm so confused. I don't feel guilt in the way that people who have lost someone do… like they wish they could have done something to prevent it. I feel guilt over my sense of relief. But, then I think of Emilie, who lost a father."

Willow couldn't hide the roll of her eyes. "Please. When did he ever act like a father?"

"She'll still grow up without him."

Willow muttered, "Probably a good thing."

Jade ignored the comment and turned back to the box she was packing, carefully placing the dishes inside. Watching her efficiency from an ocean away, Willow bridged the subject that was on her mind. "I think you should come back to Bourton Bridge. Let me help you heal and enjoy that one life of yours."

"Willow, I got so wrapped up in my worries, I didn't tell you… I booked a flight."

"You did?!" Willow said with more enthusiasm than Jade felt.

"I'm not coming for pleasure… I need to get things in order with the property. Sell it, I guess."

Willow shrugged her shoulders. "Grainger was an ass and an idiot, but that purchase might have been the one thing he did right. The building is in disarray, but it has potential. You could make it wonderful, Jade. Think about it."

"I did come to appreciate the charms of Bourton Bridge," Jade mused.

"Bourton Bridge… or a particular person in that village?"

Jade smiled. The first one in a long time. "I shouldn't feel this way."

"He's kind and handsome, so why the hell not?"

Jade shrugged and shook her head, unable to say the words that clouded her mind.

Willow raised her voice ever so slightly. "Jade, listen to me. You deserve love. I watched you throughout your marriage, and that wasn't love." She lowered her voice to a gentler tone. "It was abuse."

Willow let the words sink in and Jade nodded accepting them. "Grainger didn't break you, Jade. You found the strength to persevere. Maybe you did it for Emilie, but it's time you did something for yourself. You've been lucky enough to find love, so get back to England and claim it."

Chapter Thirty-Nine

LUKE BUSTLED AROUND THE RESTAURANT, FEELING happy for the first time since Jade left... because he knew she was returning. He carefully measured out spices — a mixture of cardamom, cinnamon, cloves, and ginger. Adding a small amount of honey, he tasted the thick paste. Elizabeth arrived and eyed the dark concoction.

"What are you making?"

"A marinade for tonight's duck," Luke answered while whisking his bowl briskly.

Elizabeth dipped a finger into it for a taste. "Good... but some plum syrup would make it great," she said definitively.

Luke narrowed his eyes at Elizabeth and then his bowl. He also took a small taste and he immediately nodded. "You're right."

"We have some preserves in the outside storage cupboard from last Summer's bounty that will be perfect."

But rather than go to the storage, Elizabeth suddenly sat down at the massive island. In a voice that wasn't her usual self, she asked, "Do you mind retrieving it?"

"Of course not." Luke swung his jacket on before heading

out to the storage area. Upon his return he noted that Elizabeth was still seated. "Are you alright?"

To make light of his concern, Elizabeth reached for a bowl and began shelling peas. "I'm just a little tired. Anyway, don't focus on me."

Luke nodded, and within a moment Elizabeth seemed back to herself, offering a few tips related to the duck. When it was in the oven to roast, Luke sat down by her side. "Elizabeth, you haven't had a check-up in a while. Maybe you should?"

"I'm fine," she insisted, but something in her tone made him question the truth of her statement. As if sensing his hesitancy, she deftly changed the subject away from herself. "I haven't seen you experiment in the kitchen for quite awhile. It's nice to see you a bit more..." she shrugged her shoulders, trying to find the right word. "Jovial," she finally landed on. "You seem lighter, happier. By any chance did you hear from Jade?"

Luke paused trying to figure out the most delicate way to confide in her without making her angry that he hadn't shared his news earlier. "She's arriving tomorrow."

"Tomorrow?! Why didn't you tell me? Where is she staying? What about Emilie?"

"Whoa... the flat she rented was still available, so she'll be there. Emilie is coming. And, I didn't know of her plans until yesterday."

And then to Luke's surprise, Elizabeth grabbed him by the arm. "Come on; we have a lot to do."

Whatever had ailed Elizabeth seemed to have passed and she was as spry as usual. Luke watched in amusement as Elizabeth rounded the kitchen to grab a pad of paper and started making a to-do list. He encouraged her to slow down by putting his hands up, but she ignored him. "Elizabeth, where's the fire? What do you think needs to be done?"

"Well, it's all fine and dandy that you're finally smiling, but it's not going to be a permanent fixture if you don't convince her to stay. I've seen surveyors eyeing up the property. Do you know if she is selling, leasing, or what?"

"She's deciding when she gets here."

Luke reached for a basket of fresh carrots and shook his head in dismay. "Our new prep chef was supposed to have these peeled and julienned first thing this morning." He located the peeler and started to work on the first carrot.

"Will you put that down?" Elizabeth seemed more agitated than Luke would expect.

"It's okay; I'll speak to him."

"Luke! I'm not concerned about vegetables. We're talking about your life." She took the peeler from his hands.

Luke's gaze softened, a small smile crossed his features. "I want her to stay. I want to tell her what I should have said before. That is, if I have your blessing."

Elizabeth smiled and placed a hand on his cheek. "Emma loved you, Luke. I love you. Now it's time that you give yourself permission to love again. You have my blessing and then some."

Jade had poured her second cup of coffee and Willow was now snacking on a packet of crisps when Jade realized they had been on the phone for over an hour. "Willow, you must be getting tired of listening to me rattle on. And, you look hungry. I've talked right through your lunchtime."

"First of all, I've dealt with time differences my entire life. I would spend the summers away and have to stay up late to talk with my American friends… just like now. And second, we're not done yet."

Jade grabbed her phone from the kitchen counter and with

her coffee in hand, she took both items into the living room and plopped onto the couch. "Okay, but I'm warning you… you'll get tired before I do, so I'll save you the trouble now. Luke and I…," she paused. "Willow, we both have too much in our pasts."

"Hogwash! The two of you are meant for each other. I see it; Harry sees it. Why can't you see that he's smitten with you?"

At the mention of his name, Harry passed into the frame of Willow's phone. "Oh hey, Jade," he waved, walking past shirtless.

Jade responded with a casual, "Hi Harry," and then opened her eyes wider to Willow and mouthed O-M-G.

Willow smiled. "I know, right? He's such a hottie. Hurry back to your handsome bloke so you don't have to ogle mine."

"I wasn't ogling." Jade paused in thought and sipped from her mug. Finally, she voiced what was on her mind. "I'm worried that when Luke sees me he thinks of the accident — this one and Emma's."

"That's a stretch."

Jade shook her head vehemently. "Grainger and Clive were drunk."

"And Luke's father was a drunk long before he met Grainger." Willow sent Jade a sympathetic look and after a pause, she changed her tone. "Jade listen to me. That sadness you talk about in Luke… it's what makes him a good man. Yes, I'm sure he still has somber moments when he thinks of Emma because they were in love and she was taken from this world too soon. But I see the way he looks at you too. You've made him realize that love is possible again."

"How can you be so sure?"

Willow smiled at her friend. "I see the way he gets tongue-tied around you. The way his face lights up when you're near.

And now that you're not in England, he's different. It's as if a part of him is missing. That part is you. And you know what else?"

"What?"

Willow smiled big, her tone moving from somber to playful. "You, my sweet friend, are a catch!"

Chapter Forty

JADE ARRIVED AT HEATHROW AIRPORT FEELING THE exhaustion of the long journey. In spite of the steep fare into Bourton Bridge, she hailed a black cab. Her budget was stretched thin, but practicality had to win out. The thought of Emilie navigating trains into Oxford and then making their way to the tiny village seemed far too exhausting. Instead, she took in the smell of the leather seats and closed her eyes with Emilie sprawled out across her lap. She let sleep take over without worry of packing, people, or her purpose. She just allowed herself to be and trusted that the cab driver would be honest and drive directly to their flat.

"Wakey wakey, Madam; We're here."

The cab driver's voice woke Jade from her slumber. She fetched around in her purse for the English notes that she had saved from her previous trip. "Thank you," she said, handing them over. "Can you just give me a minute to carry her inside?" She indicated Emilie, who had yet to fully wake.

"You take the young'n inside and I'll grab your bags," the driver kindly offered.

Once inside, Emilie stirred as Jade placed her on the couch. "Are we home?" she asked.

Jade was surprised by Emilie's willingness to call it home. She wondered if the long journey had confused her.

Answering back, she clarified, "We're at the *English* home." Jade realized that she hadn't even used the pronoun 'our' because she hadn't yet considered it more than a temporary stop in their lives. She added, "Let's get to bed."

With familiarity, Emilie padded down the hallway, holding a worn stuffed animal that had accompanied her on the long flight for comfort. "Can we go to the restaurant tomorrow for breakfast? The one where Luke works? I want a super choco-latey hot chocolate like only he makes."

"Sure, that sounds nice." Jade smiled to herself, thinking that indeed it did.

———

The combination of jet lag and thick curtains created an environment meant for sleep. When Jade finally woke, she looked at her phone and saw that it was already half past ten o'clock in the morning. If they didn't get a move on, Le Pont would be finished with breakfast service, even if Emilie had gotten used to Luke's willingness to make her favorites at any time. But that was before. Jade couldn't ask for special treatment after everything that had happened.

She went across the hall to Emilie's room and was surprised to see her bed empty. She glanced in the bathroom, but it was empty as well. Finally, Jade went into the kitchen and saw Emilie with a ceramic mug on the table in front of her.

"What are you doing?" Jade asked.

"Having my morning cup of tea," her daughter answered as if it were the most obvious thing in the world.

"You drink tea?"

"Everyone in England starts their day with a cup of tea." With an afterthought, she added, "Or coffee. But I prefer tea with lots of cream and sugar. I found the sugar still in the cupboard, but you need to buy cream."

Jade smiled. "We can go to the grocery store after breakfast. How long have you been up?"

Emilie stared at the big iron clock that hung on the wall. "About an hour, I think. The little hand was on the nine."

Jade retrieved a tea bag from a glass jar on the counter and dropped it into her own mug. The electric kettle purred in no time, and after Jade poured the hot water, she joined Emilie at the table. She closed her eyes while taking a sip of her tea, trying to get control of her burgeoning nerves that arose with the thought of seeing Luke.

"So, you like tea?" Jade mused, sipping her own slowly.

Emilie admitted, "I prefer hot chocolate the way Luke makes it."

Jade nodded, knowing perfectly well that it wouldn't be long before Emilie insisted they leave. As if on cue, Emilie asked, "Wouldn't you prefer a latté?"

Jade knew she was beat. "Give me half an hour to shower and get ready."

Emilie rolled her eyes. "I've been up for an hour," she reminded her mother.

"I guess I needed the extra sleep. You're such a good girl to let me lie in. I'll make it twenty minutes. Pinky promise." They squeezed fingers and Jade turned to get ready, her heart pounding with anticipation.

Chapter Forty-One

WHEN JADE AND EMILIE CAME THROUGH THE DOOR of the restaurant both Elizabeth and Luke hurried to greet them. Elizabeth surprised Luke by embracing Jade in a big hug, an uncharacteristic gesture for the refined, French woman. But, as Elizabeth grew older she had become more open with her emotions.

"It's so good to see you, my dear," she said to Jade. "And Emilie, how did you find your flight?"

"It was long," Emilie admitted.

"Well, in that case, let's get you fed. Your favorite table is open." Elizabeth pointed to a sunny, corner spot facing the street.

Both Luke and Jade stood awkwardly until Emilie settled onto the bench seat and Elizabeth returned to the kitchen for glasses of water. Then, Luke met Jade's eyes. "It's good to see you."

Jade smiled. "It feels surreal to be here on my own."

"Come 'ere," Luke opened his arms and Jade walked into them. He held her close and laid his cheek on top of her head. "I missed you so much," he whispered.

She looked up and nodded. It was a small gesture that she felt the same, even though she was hesitant to define their relationship as more than friendship. He gave her hand a gentle squeeze and turned in the direction of the kitchen. Speaking over his shoulder, he promised, "I'm going to make you a perfect welcome breakfast. Guaranteed to rectify jet lag fast."

She watched him walk away, and was surprised that he looked even more handsome than she remembered. His shoulders were broad in his white shirt. The black trousers that completed his work uniform made his waist look trim. Even his forearms were ripped with muscles. She had noted his white teeth when he smiled at her, his defined cheekbones and jawline, and those green eyes… Every time he looked at her, she felt beautiful under his gaze. She sighed involuntarily.

"You like him," Emilie taunted.

"What?" Jade brought her focus back to her daughter, and in protest to her comment insisted, "No, I don't. Well, I mean I do like him. He's a very kind person, but that's all."

Emilie wrinkled her nose at her mom, daring her to disagree. "You like him."

"This is childish," Jade whispered. "And he's coming back, so zip it."

Emilie laughed as Luke returned.

"What did I miss?" he asked, placing a hot chocolate in front of Emilie, served in the French manner that was a cup of steamed milk and a small silver pitcher of sweet, thick melted chocolate. Emilie poured the entire contents into her cup and then picked up the delicate silver spoon with a long, engraved handle to gently stir until combined.

"Nothing at all," Jade answered and stared at Emilie as if to say, 'Don't you dare,' but her eyes smiled as she spoke.

"Almond latté," Luke spoke, placing the drink in front of Jade.

The delicate almond scent immediately wafted upwards as Jade brought the mug to her lips. A small almond biscotti, just the size of a pinky finger, rested next to the cup. Jade smiled and took a bite.

"How is it?" Luke asked.

"Just perfect."

"Hopefully the rest doesn't disappoint," he said, moving aside when one of the servers arrived with their meals. "Jade, you have avocado toast with a light pesto drizzle and poached eggs on top. And, it is resting on a granary bread that came out of the oven just this morning."

"You go to a lot of trouble," Jade commented. "I would have been happy with just the coffee."

Luke rolled his eyes and smiled. "My boss is a bit harder to impress than you. The homemade bread goes with the territory of running this place. I hope you enjoy."

Wondering if she had been forgotten, Emilie tugged at Luke's apron and looked up at him with saucer eyes.

"Don't worry," he assured her. At that moment, another plate arrived. "French pancakes… crepes. Lightly sprinkled with lemon juice, dusted with powdered sugar, and served with strawberries and chantilly cream on the side."

Emilie immediately dipped her finger into the cream and then picked up her knife and fork. "I'm so hungry! Thank you, Luke."

"I'll leave you to it." He made his way to the kitchen, but from time to time, peeked through the port window to make sure they were happily eating. Elizabeth noticed his long-distance attentiveness. "Aren't you going to check in with our customers?" she asked goading him on.

"Thomas has the floor," he replied with a nonchalance that didn't fool Elizabeth.

"Hmm, you made your point. So what's the plan?"

"The plan?" he asked.

"Are you spending the day together? You're off work in an hour." She jutted her chin toward the large clock that hung on the wall.

"I'm not sure. I didn't want to push myself on her. She's going through a lot, coming back here to deal with the property… I think she's seeing a solicitor about it. But I don't know when."

"Do you know where?"

"We haven't really… talked."

Elizabeth rolled her eyes at him. "Let me fix this." Elizabeth whipped off her apron, wiped down her hands as if she meant business, and headed out the kitchen doors.

"Wait!" he reached for her arm. "You can't 'fix this' because I don't know what 'this' even is."

"That's a bit obvious and also why it needs fixing. You stay here." She handed him a carrot and peeler, and headed into the dining room.

After launching into some casual conversation, Elizabeth discovered that Jade's appointment for legal advice was indeed that same afternoon in London. Reminding Jade that the jet lag might get the best of her, she offered to look after Emilie and suggested that Luke escort her. Initially, Jade refused, but Elizabeth cleverly reminded her that navigating the train lines in a city that was still rather foreign might cause her to be late.

An hour later, Jade was seated next to Luke. The light pressure of his thigh against hers once again brought his muscles to mind. She inadvertently closed her eyes, remembering the strength at which he navigated his punting boat through the river. The memory of it, mixed with the motion and sound of the train, lulled her into a state of relaxation. Elizabeth had been right as usual. She was thankful that Luke had willingly accompanied her as she was finding it difficult to keep her eyes open.

"We get off at the next stop," Luke said, gently rousing her. "By the way, you've made Elizabeth very happy."

Jade opened her eyes, not even realizing she had drifted off. "How so?"

"She loved getting to know you and Emilie. When she heard about your return, she was excited to babysit. He paused for a moment, then added, "She always wanted grandchildren."

Jade looked over at him, noticing those muscled forearms again. Perhaps it was her tiredness, or maybe her recent talks with Willow, but she felt a lack of inhibition suddenly. "I always thought I would have more than one child, but my marriage wasn't equipped for it." She added mischievously, "At this time, I'm just interested in how babies are made."

Having just taken a gulp of his coffee, Luke coughed, and turned to Jade in surprise. "Sorry, went down the wrong pipe."

Jade smiled, knowing her words had made an impact. She switched to a more demure tone. "I do appreciate you coming with me. I hope it isn't too much trouble."

"I can promise you that there's no place I'd rather be…. unless it's…"

Jade blushed, recognizing an innuendo when she heard one. But as they exited the train station and started toward the London offices of her solicitor, her mind went back to the issue at hand. "Luke, the laws are different here than in the States. I'm hoping there aren't any surprises."

But he liked this new playful side of Jade and wasn't ready

to let it vanish quite yet. "No, I think you'll find our laws of attraction are similar to yours."

"Luke…"

"There won't be any surprises from me, and your solicitor has an excellent reputation. It'll be fine, and I'm right by your side."

Chapter Forty-Two

JADE AND LUKE SAT ACROSS FROM WILLIAM Barrett, senior partner of Barrett, Godfrey, and Townsend Solicitors. He wore a stern expression and in turn, Jade looked as if she might break down in tears.

"This is not what I expected," she said, her shoulders sagging and her eyes cast downward.

Mr. Barrett nodded his head and removed his glasses. Placing them on the desk, he picked up his phone and dialed his secretary, requesting some coffee for himself as well as Jade and Luke. "I wish I had something better to report. But it's about perspective; it's not all bad."

"What do you mean?" Jade implored. "I'm trying to process what you've told me and I don't see another perspective. Mr. Barrett, please correct me if I've misunderstood. You're telling me that I can't sell the property because there are conveyance documents, but no recorded deed."

Mr. Barrett sighed heavily. "Yes, this is more complicated than you were led to believe. There's also the issue of your residency, lack of a UK work visa, and perhaps the most pressing matter... You owe more on the property than its current market value. Even if you got your documentation in order, I don't see a sale being feasible."

"Feasible?" she repeated his careful choice of words. "What does that mean?" The alarm was clear in her voice. "Can't I do a short sale? Where I sell for less than what's owed on the mortgage based on buyer interest? You know, just to cut my losses?"

Barrett sighed and shook his head. "When you retained me while still in the U.S., I started my research." He spoke bluntly. "There is no serious buyer interest. Yes, there have been surveyors eyeing the property, but they're hoping it will go on the auction block."

Jade looked to Luke with panic in her eyes. "And, that's bad?"

"Let me explain," Mr. Barrett continued. "In England, you can't just sell a property for less than the mortgage and as of right now, there aren't any buyers. You don't want it to be on the auction block. You won't get anything out of it. In order to sell for less than the mortgage value, the lender who holds the mortgage must approve the sale." Mr. Barrett nodded as if the situation was totally clear and understandable.

But for Jade that was far from reality. "And? Did they? Did they approve?"

"No, I'm sorry, Jade. After speaking to them on your behalf, they have informed me that they won't agree. Apparently, they were led to believe by your former husband that he was quite established financially. They do not believe that you are in dire straits."

Jade sat quietly, processing the information presented to her. Finally, in a voice both resolved to a bad situation and unwilling to succumb to it, she spoke. "Mr. Barrett, my husband was an alcoholic and a liar. Had he not passed, we would probably be getting a divorce. My situation is far from what he led the bank to believe.

Luke had been seated next to her, quietly taking in the information. She looked at him for support.

"Mr. Barrett…," Luke spoke clearly, "Is there a scenario in which the lender would reconsider?"

Barrett looked to both Jade and Luke. "It will take months of non-payment before they think you are serious," the solicitor answered.

Jade knew the repercussions of the statement. "You mean seriously in trouble. If I don't pay, I will devastate my credit. I can't do that when I'm a single mother. My life is too… precarious."

Barrett leaned his elbows onto his massive desk and interlaced his fingers, placing his hands under his chin. He exhaled a deep breath, trying to decide how best to deliver more news that was certainly not going to be well received. "It's not just the problem of selling the property. You can't readily work in the UK either. If it were just a matter of getting a work visa, you would still need to find someone established in business to sponsor you."

Luke shrugged his shoulders as if it was a no-brainer. "Elizabeth. She emigrated from France and knows the challenges first-hand."

"I can't ask Elizabeth to sponsor me. She hardly knows me."

Luke did his best to convince Jade otherwise. "You know that's not true. She couldn't wait for you to return. All I do is talk about you. After me, she's your biggest fan."

Jade suddenly seemed to forget she was at the solicitor's office. She smiled and a light blush spread across her cheeks. "You talk about me?"

"I do," he squeezed her hand. "And, you wouldn't leave Emilie with someone 'who hardly knows you.' You're too good of a mother for that."

Jade looked at Mr. Barrett expectantly, but again, he simply

254

shook his head. "It's not as simple as just working in the UK. You're trying to generate income from a real estate transaction without setting up roots. That could be considered a business."

Jade placed a finger next to her temple and took a moment to consider the situation. "Surely Grainger must have come across this same stumbling block. Didn't he file the right licenses or whatever was needed?"

"Apparently not. He paid the down payment on the building, but construction was performed under the table." The solicitor paused, "Like I said, perspective... you could start again and do it right."

Jade looked at him, considering her response. "It sounds as if I don't have much choice." She turned to Luke. "What do you think?"

"I'm not impartial, Jade." His eyes told her that he felt about her the way she did about him.

Barrett added gently, "It would be a shame to sell, in my opinion. It's a lovely, historic building, and with a little imagination and time, it could be great once again." He paused to let his words sink in.

Jade's thoughts were brimming with legalities, but questions surrounding her personal life pressed to the forefront of her mind. "Were you hoping that I was coming back for good?"

Luke released the breath he had been involuntarily holding and smiled. "Yes Jade. I'm in love with you and haven't been myself without you."

She grabbed his hand and gave it a squeeze. Turning her attention back to business, she smiled at Mr. Barrett, "Sorry about our moment."

"No apologies necessary. I don't often get declarations of love in my office. It's a nice turn of events."

Jade's hands no longer subconsciously drifted to her

temples to ward off a headache. She reached for her phone and leaned forward to show Mr. Barrett a photo. "This is a rendering that I did for fun. I think the property's style is well-suited for conversion into a boutique hotel. I would naturally keep the farmhouse appearance and historical elements, but add modern conveniences." She looked at her solicitor expectantly. "What would need to be done first?"

"The business license needs to be re-filed, and you need a start-up visa. I can do both for you."

"What's a start-up visa?" she asked the lawyer.

"It's quite simple. It's for individuals with no business experience who want to establish and develop a new business in the UK. After two years, you convert it to what's called an innovator visa… when you have £50,000 to invest."

For the first time, Jade saw some humor in her situation. "Well, a lack of experience… I should qualify for that."

Luke said directly to her, "Don't sell yourself short, Jade. Remember those talks we had, when we walked along the river? Your ideas are brilliant, and there isn't another hotel in the immediate area."

Mr. Barrett interjected, "I can introduce you to my banker at Lloyds. The loan you have on this property isn't very forgiving. But, Simon, my banker, is a good guy and top notch in his field. He could probably convert the existing one to something fixed with lower interest."

Jade nodded, as much to herself as the gentlemen in the room. She was turning a corner and as such, her voice was confident and direct. "I contacted a realtor in the States. The market is good so the sale of my property should be swift and more lucrative than renting it. The life insurance policy will give me breathing room with other living expenses. The loan will be used for the renovation. I just need to work efficiently."

Barrett cautioned her, "But Jade, to do it right takes time.

You had mentioned that your ex-husband attempted a four-month renovation. That was never realistic."

Jade nodded, then turned to Luke. "Do you think this is more than I should bite off?"

He shook his head emphatically. "You're creative. You have amazing people skills. You were meant for this."

Over the years, Grainger had done his best to destroy Jade's confidence. Now was the time when she needed to regain it and flourish. She raised her eyes upwards, offering a silent prayer. "From thinking I was going to sell the property to now, converting it into a hotel…" She let the thought linger, digesting the idea while hearing how it sounded to say it aloud.

When she first came to England, her ideas had fallen on deaf ears, but now the planning was in her hands. Early on, she had recognized that a renovation and subsequent sale would provide a one-time payout, but a hotel would give her financial stability with recurring income well into the future.

There was a change in Jade's demeanor and mindset. The woman who came to England on the heels of her husband was now a hotelier. She lifted her chin and sat up a bit straighter. Her eyes shone with excitement, and a smile graced her delicate features. She had accepted her predicament, and refused to be daunted by the task ahead.

She looked Mr. Barrett in the eye. "If you wouldn't mind, I'd like to end this meeting the way I should have started." She held out her right hand, determined and strong. "I'm Jade Thomas, owner of the new hotel in Bourton Bridge."

Chapter Forty-Three

LUKE INDICATED THEIR TRAIN STOP. WALKING down the platform hand-in-hand felt much differently than when they had left for London. They exited the station and turned onto a street that took them along the River Widenbrush. "Want to relax a bit?" he asked.

She nodded and followed him to the banks of the river, and to her surprise, to the boathouse where his shell was stored. He threw it over his shoulder easily. Handing Jade one oar, he carried the other. When they got to the head of the river, he held the small boat steady for Jade, and once she was settled, he climbed in and used the oar to push off.

She watched Luke's strong arms propel the boat forward. The sound of the oars cutting the water provided a peaceful rhythm. Occasionally, they passed another rower and Luke would nod his head in greeting. When there were no other boats nearby, he took a break from rowing and allowed the narrow boat to float along peacefully. "This is how I sort out my thoughts. When things were tough…," he paused, and she knew he was referring to when he lost Emma, "this would give me clarity."

Luke settled onto his back, placing the oars in their oarlock, and closed his eyes. The silence was comfortable. For a few minutes they enjoyed the sound of birds and the gentle lapping of the water against the boat. Luke peeked open one eye and smiled upon seeing Jade gaze in his direction.

"Want to try it?" He indicated the oars.

"Not sure I have your upper body strength."

"You were checking out my biceps," he replied cheekily.

"Maybe a little."

He smiled and indicated a spot in front of him. "Sit here."

Jade maneuvered between his legs and rested her back on his torso. She accepted the oars from Luke, positioning her hands just below his. "We just lean forward and then pull back," he said, guiding her.

Their first attempt caused the small boat to go sideways, but Luke took control and steadied it. After a few more attempts, they developed a rhythm. When Jade seemed to tire, he took over, maneuvering the boat in long, swift movements. After returning to the boat house, they took a moment to sit on the shore. Jade laid her head on Luke's shoulder. When he tilted his head, he could feel her cheek against his. In that moment, he wanted to kiss her so badly. He wanted to ignore every bloody British expectation about decorum and public displays. He didn't care that people were meandering about. He knew firsthand that life was short, and he didn't want this moment to pass. He was falling in love with her.

It felt right to tell her except for one nagging thought that weighed on his mind. Until the solicitor explained the situation fully, Jade was prepared to sell the property. There had been talk of Grainger. She expressed doubt about staying in Bourton Bridge. And then, of course, there was the memory of the night before she left for California.

Jade was equally quiet. Part of her hoped he would turn his head toward her. But another mindset told her to be wary. She was newly widowed and had to think of Emilie. He hadn't dated since Emma. And now, she needed to focus on a new business. So many reasons not to get involved, and yet her heart told her differently. And damn if she didn't want to listen to her heart.

She pressed up against him a little more. He felt her soft curves melt into him and it gave him hope that they could make a relationship work. Her breathing was audible. His thoughts were decidedly less innocent than when they were rowing.

"Luke?" her voice was a quiet whisper, sexy as hell and reminding him that her mouth was so terribly close.

"What are you thinking about?" he pressed, wanting to be sure he was reading the signs correctly this time.

Jade shrugged her shoulders. "The usual… If it's too late for a cuppa? If I'm crazy to take on the renovation. And, whether you like this shade of lipstick?"

He placed his hand under her chin, slowly bringing her face closer to his. He let his mouth just barely grace hers until he couldn't wait for the kiss any longer. When they pulled apart, he indicated her mouth, lifting his chin toward her. "That is the most beautiful shade of lipstick I've ever tried on."

Forgetting the rowers and joggers, the walkers and picnickers, he held her tenderly, and it most certainly felt like love. Their lips brushed against each other once more and Luke whispered against her mouth. "I should have never let you leave."

She looked up at him, and simply said, "I'm here."

They stood up and carried on down the river bank hand-in-hand, and in that moment, he knew that he would do anything for her.

Chapter Forty-Four

HAVING SPENT MORE TIME TOGETHER THAN APART in recent months, Harry had asked Willow to move in with him. Some might say they were moving quickly. They argued that they had seen enough bad relationships to recognize that theirs was a good one.

Testing out their new domesticity, they had decided to cook their specialties for each other. The fact that neither was much of a cook didn't dissuade them from friendly competition. "You are going to love this taste sensation," Willow promised with confidence. "In fact, I'm willing to bet that you'll start asking for it, showing off the recipe to your friends, and maybe… just maybe, you'll convince Luke to put it on the menu at Le Pont."

Harry peered at Willow's preparations with a look of serious doubt. He eyed the baking sheet and the streaky bacon that Willow had placed in soldier formation. On the counter, she gathered other ingredients: brown sugar, a shaker of black pepper, and a jug of honey. But none of those items gave him as much cause for concern as the big jar of peanut butter that Willow had introduced into his kitchen.

"You know that peanut butter isn't really a thing in England. It smells funny."

Willow ignored his critique. "This dish will change your mind. By the way, it's technically pronounced like one word."

"You're sure?"

"Very. It's an American staple. Kids who are just knee high to a grasshopper ask for it. And therefore, the two words are pronounced in kid speak as if they are melded together. Kinda like us," she smiled and stood on tippy toes to kiss his cheek.

"How so?"

"Like this… pee-nuh-budda. Not peanut with a distinct T. And certainly not *butter* with two distinct Ts."

"So you're making my point. This is not a dish that the royal party would ever ask for and certainly not eat."

"Well, they're missing out."

She sprinkled each slice of bacon with brown sugar and popped them under the broiler. After they came out of the oven, she sprinkled on black pepper, ensuring it blended with the melted, brown sugar. "Now watch this…" She reached for the peanut butter, spread an ample amount on top of each strip and then smiled. "And the final touch…" she grabbed the honey jar and drizzled a substantial amount over the peanut butter bacon strips. "Try it!"

Harry knew he was in love. He had absolutely no desire to eat peanut butter ever. He had even less inclination to eat it with bacon, but Willow's enthusiasm and zest for life was contagious. He reached for a strip and held it up as if in a toast before taking a bite. "Wow!"

"Don't sound so surprised. I told you that my dish was going to beat out your dish. Peanut butter and bacon is not only delicious, it's also versatile enough to be consumed at any meal."

Harry finished his slice and reached for another. "Willow,

this is the best. And you're the best. I'm just going to eat this entire platter of sweet fatty goodness and admit that my avocado toast recipe can't hold a candle to this."

"Jade loves these," Willow said, holding up a slice. "Probably Luke would too!"

Harry kissed her cheek, loving her exuberance. "How could anyone not?"

As they weaved their way through the quiet streets, Jade chatted about design ideas, while Luke pointed out various structures. "That warm colored stone is limestone…" he motioned towards a building, "Bourton Bridge, and Oxford for that matter, is known for it."

Jade nodded, happy for the education. "If I source local materials, perhaps I'll save some money?"

"Most definitely. And you'll preserve the history of the area."

Jade nodded to herself, deep in thought. "Grainger and I didn't agree on a lot of things, actually most things. He wanted the property done up with a modern motif… mirrors, chrome, dark accents… he said that equalled luxury."

"What do you want?" Luke asked. "It's yours now."

"It's not that I don't like luxury, but this was once a working farmhouse. It has history that should be highlighted. It can be comfortable without being ostentatious. I want to use interesting textiles and pottery from local artisans… reclaimed wood from historic barns and tapestries rich in history and color."

She described her ideas freely. A comfy couch to beckon people to sit. Soft music to place guests at ease. The scent of flowers to relax weary travelers. And a welcome drink to chase away the blues… lemonade in the summer or warm cider in the winter.

When she was finished, she asked, "What do you think?"

A strand of her hair had fallen across her face, and he gently tucked it behind her ear, a quiet smile spreading across his lips as he remembered the first time he'd seen her—the way the wind had played with her hair. "I know you can do it," he said in a tone that filled her with confidence. "Create your vision. This is your chance."

As they continued their way back to Le Pont, they paused atop Bourton Bridge where Luke kissed her again. Even when they pulled apart, Luke maintained a subtle connection, gently running his thumb over the back of her hand.

After a moment, she met his eyes and whispered, "Luke, it's been a long time for me… for this. I want to be ready, but this is a big deal for me. I feel like I'm not going to just fall for you, I'll plummet."

"I feel the same."

Her words grew more urgent. "But I have a child. It's one thing for you to spend time with me and help with the hotel, but Emilie… if she sees us… socializing…" she opted for an appropriate word. "She may get the wrong idea."

"What idea would that be?"

He knew he had put her on the spot, but this was new territory for him as well. He had spent the last five years keeping his heart securely inside his chest and this was the first time he was offering it up to a woman. He didn't see this as a fling, far from it.

"Kids get attached…" was all she offered.

"And what about you?" he pressed. They were playing a romantic chess match with neither one wanting to make the wrong move.

Jade shook her head, indicating she wouldn't budge,

although a smile crossed her lips making her true feelings known.

He decided to man up. "After Emma died, I avoided attachments for fear of losing someone. I was more comfortable treading water, than diving into life." He gathered his thoughts. "But I realize now that I wasn't biding my time. I was reflecting on life and love, and healing myself so that when true love presented itself, I knew what was real. This isn't a fling, Jade. And yes, I want to *socialize* with you."

She loved that he could be serious one minute and tease her the next. She laughed, but admitted, "I'm just kind of scared to jump."

"You know what? We're going to fix that." He pointed to the water below. The bridge wasn't very high, but still she looked at him as if he were crazy.

"Oh no way," she said. "That's not what I meant by falling."

"I know what you meant, and Jade, I'm crazy about you. Maybe if we fall… take the leap together, it won't be so scary. There's actually a tradition here. In May, specifically on May Day, couple's jump together. Now, that tradition has been tempered and most people gather to sing traditional hymns, but a few of the wilder ones still carry out the jump."

She looked around and saw a number of young couples walking away from the bridge, hand-in-hand, laughing. Luke indicated one couple who was soaking wet and Jade's eyes opened wide. "You're serious? And you're insane. I'm not going to…"

"Jump," he said simply. "Let this be cathartic. "If we can do this, we can tackle anything life throws at us."

"But it's not May Day. It's November and that water looks damn cold."

She watched the faces of the couple who had dared to

jump into the water in spite of the season. She turned back to Luke, a question in her eyes, but no words on her lips.

"You'll know that you can handle anything. Also, there's an assortment of chef's clothes at the restaurant. Do you trust me?" he asked, indicating the bridge.

She took a brief pause, but without hesitation she answered. "I trust you," and took his hand preparing to jump.

Chapter Forty-Five

Luke and Jade walked toward the restaurant, a blanket wrapped around their drenched figures.

"How are we going to explain this?" Jade whispered urgently.

"The wet clothes or this?" He held up her hand and leaned in to kiss her cheek.

Jade started to speak, but froze when she noticed Elizabeth rounding the corner with Emilie in tow, rather than where she expected them to be, safely tucked within the restaurant. Instinct took over and she dropped Luke's hand. But she wasn't quick enough for Elizabeth's eagle eyes.

The strong-minded woman walked directly up to Jade and Luke, and starring Jade straight in the eye, she reached for Emilie's hand and then changed her gaze down to the little girl and smiled broadly.

When she looked back at Jade, she spoke with a point to be made. "Showing someone you care about them is not something to be hidden."

"Were you two holding hands?" Emilie asked.

"Did I see a kiss land on her cheek?" Elizabeth followed suit.

Jade looked to Luke and then shrugged her shoulders. "Yes, just like you two."

"It's not the same," Emilie said wisely. "Miss Elizabeth didn't want me to get hurt crossing the road. You two like each other."

"Don't forget that I like you too, Emilie." Elizabeth winked at her.

Elizabeth led Emilie inside the restaurant and Jade could hear Emilie ask, "Why were they all wet?"

"I have no idea, dear. Sometimes grown-ups are silly."

Elizabeth sent Luke and Jade a know-it-all smile as she gathered up two sets of chef's whites. After they had changed into dry clothes and Jade took Emilie aside, Luke checked in with his beloved mentor. "Speaking of silly... Elizabeth, did you get yourself to the doctor for a check-up?"

"His office called to inquire if I could postpone until next week. Apparently an emergency came up and since I'm right as rain, I agreed." Luke sent Elizabeth a concerned expression, but he knew her stubborn side.

"I guess there is no point in arguing with you," he finally acquiesced.

"True. And your outing has placed you behind schedule so scoot," she said indicating that the kitchen was waiting.

Jade sat at her favorite table reflecting on the visit to the solicitor's office while Emily reviewed her math lessons. Emilie was anxious to reacquaint with friends she had met during their first visit and the local school had an opening just after the winter holidays. In the meantime, Jade was home-schooling Emilie and Elizabeth, who had embraced her role as a surrogate grandmother, helped as well. Everything was falling into place with the restaurant at the center of their lives. Elizabeth called out math problems to Emilie. Luke taste tested dishes that bubbled on the stove. Jade made copious notes and lists, and although the task was daunting, it filled her with excitement. She could hardly believe how much her life had transformed.

Occasionally, she could hear Luke give instructions to Thomas, and in turn, the sous chef would respond, "Yes chef." The restaurant ran smoothly and Jade took it all in, wondering if she would be able to replicate a similar standard at her boutique hotel. Her ideas were percolating when she suddenly noticed Elizabeth standing very still, gripping the edge of a nearby table.

Jade had been around Le Pont long enough to become accustomed to the constant movement of the staff. Sous and prep chefs moved throughout the kitchen, seen through the port holes of the kitchen double doors. Waitresses scurried throughout the dining room, ensuring that every need was met. And Elizabeth was always on high alert to catch any mistake before it happened. Activity and movement were the staples of the restaurant business. But it was the lack of movement that drew Jade's eye to Elizabeth and fear struck when she saw the woman's ashen complexion. "Luke!"

A second later, Elizabeth inadvertently released the plate she held. Jade's voice and the clamor of the plate's crash alerted Luke. When he realized that it wasn't a waitress misstep, he rushed from the kitchen. "What's wrong?" When she didn't answer, he placed a protective hand under her arm, and then as if in slow motion everything changed. He caught Elizabeth as her knees buckled and she slumped over.

Luke eased her to the ground and pulled his phone from his pocket. Jade had rushed to help, taking Luke's phone. "9-9-9 … emergency code for the UK," he said with urgency. Jade called for help, and Luke placed his ear near Elizabeth's mouth to listen for her breath.

Chapter Forty-Six

JADE CRADLED AN ARM AROUND EMILIE, PULLING her body close while Luke sat on her other side. The hospital waiting room was empty, yet they had chosen chairs right upon each other to take comfort from each other's presence. They waited in stoic silence for news of Elizabeth's condition.

She had only lost consciousness for a matter of seconds, but they insisted on taking her to the hospital. When the ambulance arrived, Elizabeth was aghast at "all the fuss." Finally, she agreed to cooperate with the paramedics after negotiating a quick tour of the emergency vehicle for Emilie.

After a long two hours, Elizabeth, seated in a wheelchair, was brought to the waiting area by her attending physician. "This chair is hardly necessary. I can walk."

"It's just our policy," her doctor said with a slight Indian lilt to her voice and a pleasant smile on her face.

Elizabeth did a slight eye roll and then addressed the group. "You see? Fit as a fiddle," she announced, smoothing down non-existent wrinkles in her skirt. "Just a little dizzy spell. I was probably dehydrated, that's all."

To Luke and Jade's relief, the doctor seemed to agree, and

turned to speak directly to Elizabeth out of respect. "Unfortunately, dizziness and imbalance is normal as we begin to get older. Our vestibular system begins to decline. It's nothing to worry about at this point. If it continues, however, we may want to check for Meniere's disease, an inner ear disorder," she explained.

Elizabeth nodded her head, appearing satisfied that her attempt at making light of the situation was valid. "There you have it. Nothing to worry about." Turning to Luke, she said, "You didn't need to fuss and I didn't need to close the restaurant."

Before Luke could argue, the doctor helpfully stepped in. "But Elizabeth, as your physician..." she said delicately, "you might want to consider handing off a little more work." Then turning to Luke she added, "Symptoms tend to worsen with fatigue."

With that declaration, Elizabeth indicated that she had enough attention lauded on her and stood up from the wheel-chair. Her gaze at the three adults surrounding her dared them to argue. With her polite restraint, she turned to her doctor. "Thank you for your time. I'll consider taking a few days off." Then turning to Luke, she said, "Let's go home so the doctor can attend to patients with real issues."

Although Elizabeth wanted to check on the restaurant's inventory, Luke convinced her to go home with the caveat that he would get to the restaurant early the following day. She fumed for a moment, but when Emilie declared she was tired, Elizabeth acquiesced, admitting that the day had worn her out.

"You're sure you feel alright?" Luke asked.

"Yes, you can stop worrying..." and in her teasing tone,

"and stop pestering me." Turning to Jade she added, "Can you do anything to make him relax?"

Jade smiled as Luke shook his head. He had long known that arguing was futile and now, Jade was learning Elizabeth's idiosyncrasies as well. When the car pulled into the drive, it was Emilie who brought Elizabeth out of her gloom. "We have scones for a cream tea," she chirped happily, heading to the kitchen.

"That would be lovely. Thank you, little bird."

Their interaction gave Jade reason to pause. She knew that people handled stress differently. For years, she had seen Grainger erupt into anger when he was over extended. Once, Emilie asked him to a tea party, but he was busy and barked an excuse. *"Use your stuffed animals. Like your mother, they have straw for a brain and just sit around the house."* Jade still remembered the exchange. Elizabeth certainly didn't react to stress at the restaurant. She took everything in her stride. Yet, Jade couldn't help but worry that she was placing too much pressure on her.

"You okay?" Luke touched Jade gently on the shoulder, noticing she seemed far away.

She lowered her voice to a whisper. "Asking Elizabeth to make Le Pont the official restaurant of the hotel may be selfish on my part. It serves me, but is it good for her? You heard the doctor. She should be doing less, not more."

Elizabeth may have had an off day, but her hearing was sharp as ever. "Jade, just because I took this afternoon off work, don't think I'm ready to retire." She patted the seat next to her. "Come here, dear one."

Jade obeyed and took a seat next to Elizabeth, who surprised her by wrapping her arm around Jade's back. It had indeed been a long day, and although she tried to keep a stiff upper lip, Jade felt a wayward tear weave down her cheek.

"What is this about?" Elizabeth asked.

Jade just shook her head, afraid to speak for fear that more tears would fall. Finally, she took a deep breath to compose herself. "I haven't had a mother in years. I'm not trying to replace Emma, but it feels so good to have you in mine and Emilie's life."

Elizabeth nodded, and to Luke's surprise she reached for a tissue and dabbed at her own eyes. Before she responded to Jade, she met Luke's gaze and knew that he innately understood what was going through her mind.

"You're the first girl since my Emma that Luke has taken a shine to and having you around is a tremendous comfort. I'm not about to overstep my boundaries, but I would love to help you… as I would help my own daughter."

Elizabeth leaned toward Jade and lightly touched the pendant that hung from her neck. "This is beautiful. A Halcyon?"

"It was my mother's. She gave it to me when I was just a child and she was sick. She told me that the bird symbolizes tranquility, and that even in the toughest times, peace is attainable if you have faith."

Elizabeth nodded. "You must have found it quite serendipitous to find Halcyon Cottage. There's something I want you both to see. I'll be right back," she promised as she hurried toward the kitchen.

"Elizabeth, you're meant to rest. I can retrieve whatever you want," Luke called to her.

"You'd never find it. I'll just be a moment."

"What is 'it'?" Jade sent Luke a questioning glance as they waited for Elizabeth to return. When she did, she held a large envelope, slightly creased and a bit worn with time.

"I brought this home from the restaurant recently. It was tucked safely away in the filing cabinet." She gave Luke a meaningful glance. "Other than canned goods and bags of flour, the cabinet was the only thing housed in the storage room... until you."

Luke smirked, knowing that she referred to the nights when he snuck into the storage room to sleep and hide from his father. That seemed like another lifetime ago. He was too young to stand up to his father, but not too young to fall in love with Emma. His heart warmed at the memory of how she and Elizabeth changed his life, and how he grew into being his own man.

Elizabeth opened the envelope with care. As she looked at its contents, she steadied her emotions with a deep breath. Inside were a child's drawings and school report cards, hand-made mother's day and birthday cards. There was also an envelope with cursive writing of a more mature age that read, 'For Luke.'

"It's from Emma," Elizabeth explained. "She didn't want to give it directly to you."

"When did she write it?"

"She wrote it when she knew she was in love with you."

Emilie had since left the room to watch television, and with the turn in conversation, Jade felt she should also leave. "I'll just go and check on Emilie," she offered.

"Jade, please stay. You should be here," Elizabeth said gently. "You see, Luke, Emma and I had a long talk about love and life. She never knew her father, and always asked me why I never remarried. I told her that after he passed, nobody compared to him and I decided I would be married to the restaurant."

She turned back towards Jade, "So you see, it gives me great pleasure to provide good food to people."

She pressed the creases from the letter and continued her story. "Emma grew up understanding it was rare to find true love. She told me that if anything should ever happen to her, that I was to wait until the right moment… when someone special entered your life, and pass on her letter."

Elizabeth nodded to herself and said, "I feel this is that time."

Jade had wondered if she could ever measure up to such a deep love. As if reading those thoughts, Elizabeth said, "I made a choice to spend my life alone with memories of my first love. But Emma said she would never want that for you, Luke. It was a testament to her character… to live and love until one's dying day." Elizabeth paused and released a light chuckle, "She often tried to set me up."

"You know Ben is into you," Luke interjected.

"That's ridiculous."

"You like the same books, the same television shows… he's well traveled…" Luke could have gone on, but Elizabeth shut him down.

"This talk isn't about my love life," she pointed out.

"So you admit that a love life for you isn't out of the question," Luke mocked.

He and Jade shared a conspiring glance, but seeing their minds brew with ideas, Elizabeth responded, "He's just a friend. Enough about me." Handing over the letter to Luke, she added, "Take your time as you read this. Jade, shall we check on Emilie?" The two women left Luke alone to revisit his past.

Chapter Forty-Seven

FIVE YEARS EARLIER...

Emma gazed at Luke as he lay on his back in the small punting boat. She happily took photos of the scenery, and secretly of Luke, as he rested. With eyes closed and his muscular arms crossed behind his head, he appeared completely at peace as the sun shone on his face. Inspired by the day and not wanting to disturb Luke, she reached into her bag for paper and pen.

Luke, when I'm with you, the summer sun shines a bit brighter and the dark days of winter aren't as lonely.

You once told me that you never thought to bake treats because sweetness was missing from your life. But now that you do, I taste the love behind each bite. That kind of love is here, even when you can't see it.

It is the sun that warms your face and the gentle rain that refreshes

your spirit. Always bake your sweet scones and share them with someone who loves you as deeply as I do.
This is my ethos for you.

Hearing Luke stir, Emma quickly placed the paper in its envelope and wrote his name on the outside before safely tucking it into her bag. "Hello, sleepy head. You dozed off."

"What time is it?"

"That all depends. Is dinner prepped and ready to go?"

Luke looked at his watch. "Yes and no. Prepped but not ready. I need to get back."

He pulled himself up, grabbed the oars and easily glided the punting boat through the water. At the dock, Luke got out first and helped Emma so that she didn't get wet. He pulled the boat slightly onto the shore and picked it up and over his shoulder as if it weighed next to nothing. Emma smiled and shook her head in amazement.

"You think this is impressive? One day I'm going to pick up up and throw you over my shoulder."

"Promises, promises," she teased.

"You don't believe me?" Luke set the boat down and lunged at Emma. She squealed and tried to run away, but Luke's arms were too long and he was too fast. He caught her hand and pulled her to his body. "Promises are meant to be kept. Give me a second. Don't move."

He reached for his phone and found a slow, romantic song and clicked the play button. He crooked his finger at Emma and when she was near once again, he lifted her off the ground and swung her around. When he stopped, he held her a foot off the ground and gazed up at her. "God, I love you." When her feet were planted once again, their kiss was immediate. And when they broke apart, she replied, "I love you, too."

Luke and Emma arrived at the restaurant to find Elizabeth in full preparation mode. A prep cook stood nearby, frantically taking notes as she dished out instructions. She placed her hands on her hips and sent Emma a sideways look as she approached.

"Don't blame him; blame me," Emma said before her mother could complain about their tardiness.

"This is becoming a habit with you two. Good thing Luke had the sense to prep the meal early." Turning to Luke she added, "And, I had a taste of your bolognese sauce. It's perfection as are the short ribs. But… I don't see any accompaniments." She wagged her finger to make her point.

"I'm on it." Luke removed a clean set of chef's whites from the staff cupboard. As he headed into the kitchen, he called back to Emma, "See you after work?"

Emma gave a thumb's up and began to lay the tables, setting vases with fresh flowers from James' local flower shop and white linens. She went about her work with more reserve than Elizabeth usually saw in her daughter.

"Are you alright?" Elizabeth asked over her shoulder.

"I'm great," Emma reassured her. "But, can I ask you to do something for me that might seem odd? And, can I ask you not to question it?"

"That does sound odd. But yes, I suppose." Elizabeth looked at her daughter with concern, but Emma offered a reassuring smile.

"Don't be worried. I just want you to give this to Luke… one day. It's unsealed. You can read it." She handed over the letter she had written earlier and waited in silence while Elizabeth scanned the words.

"One day?" Elizabeth questioned. "This sounds… Is there something you're not telling me? Are you okay?"

Emma nodded her head to reassure her mother. "Everything is fine. And I hope this will never materialize. I just wrote it because I love Luke so deeply. And I know what kind of person he is... loyal and decent. So much so that I want to make plans for his future."

Elizabeth opened her arms for Emma to walk into them. "I love you so much, sweet girl. May I never have to hand over this letter."

Emma squeezed her mother's waist. "I love you, too."

Chapter Forty-Eight

Elizabeth dried her eyes after seeing Luke's reaction. He bent his head and closed his own eyes to regain composure. Then, he nodded to Elizabeth, indicating he was alright. He folded the letter with care and placed it back in its envelope. Elizabeth reached for his hand, once again taking on the role of mother and mentor. "She loved you so much, Luke. So much so that she wanted to make sure you always had love in your life."

Luke took in a deep breath, but couldn't get the words out. Finally, he found his resolve. "I used to tease her when she spoke about signs and fate. I never believed in that sort of thing the way she did. Maybe it's better that way. If I knew that fate was going to take her from me, I wouldn't have been able to live in the moment the way she did."

They could hear Emilie laughing from the next room and Jade's voice telling her a story. On Elizabeth's insistence, they had started to make themselves at home in the kitchen. Each day, Jade would make Emilie lunch and Emile would share the cooking lessons that Luke had imparted. "If you want to

believe in fate, then find comfort that they were sent here…
for both of us," Elizabeth said wisely, angling her chin toward
the kitchen.

"I never thought I'd find someone to fill the hole in my
heart, until I met Jade." Luke said the words almost
sheepishly.

"Luke, I'm happy for you. She fills my heart with joy as
well. And Emilie… it's like having the granddaughter I always
longed for." Elizabeth smiled and paused. "You know, Willow
asked me if she and Harry could have their engagement party
at Le Pont."

"They're engaged?"

"I thought you knew. Well, they only told me so I could
reserve the restaurant. Let Willow tell Jade. And maybe, you'll
find some inspiration from this news."

"It's a little soon, don't you think?"

"Pretty fast for Willow and Harry too," Elizabeth shrewdly
pointed out.

"True. Maybe this will satisfy your romantic notions? It's
not a ring, but more like a promise…," Luke revealed a jewelry
box he had hidden in his pocket. He opened it to reveal a delicate bracelet with a heart charm and the letters L + J engraved
on it. Elizabeth gave his arm a squeeze. "Let me spend some
time with Emilie. You do your thing."

Luke went to sit by Jade and whispered, "I have something
for you." Then, turning to Emilie, he added, "I think Miss
Elizabeth said something about hot chocolate in the kitchen."

Emilie smiled and scurried away with rocket speed, leaving
Luke and Jade alone. He held out the small, wrapped package.
"Open it."

Jade looked at him with an uncertain expression. "Luke?
There's been so many changes in my life. I…"

"Don't worry." Knowing what she might think and not
wanting to either disappoint, nor scare her off, he added,

"When I propose… and I will… you'll be ready for it. Just open it."

She nodded happily and pressed her finger against the tiny silver button on the front of the box. It opened to reveal the Tiffany style bracelet. "It's beautiful. I love it. Will you…," she held out her wrist for him to fasten it in place.

Luke's fingers worked deftly and when the bracelet hung off her wrist, he said, "I'm not going to lie. If you had decided to go back to California, I would have booked the next flight as well. I love you, Jade."

Jade looked at him in awe. "I can't imagine being there while you're here. I love you, too."

Jade realized that she had found so much more in England than a business. She found a family — one that she and Emilie had desperately craved. Tea hour turned into the dinner hour and Luke called in an order for takeout. It was unusual for them, but having closed the restaurant early, a good Indian takeaway was in order. Luke ordered their favorites: Chicken Tikka Masala, Lamb Rogan Josh, and Peshwari Naan — flatbread sweetened with sultanas, almonds, and coconut.

As they settled down to wait for the delivery, Elizabeth called Jade over. "You know we have something in common," she started, "besides our love for that guy," she joked and indicated Luke. "We're both stronger than we look. You've proven it and this little hitch that occurred to me, is just a temporary pause. So, hear me out. If you're going to turn that dilapidated barn into a chic boutique hotel, you need help."

Jade nodded, knowing Elizabeth was right. "Trust me… I'm well aware. It's a big undertaking."

"Let me take some financial pressure off you. After all, your hotel is going to give me a lot of business so it's in my best interest to make sure this happens. Use the remainder of your flat's lease to pack. Then, you and Emilie should move in here. Emma used the cottage as her artist's retreat, and I'd like to honor her by using it as a creative venue and remote office. I've been avoiding spending time there, but I'm ready."

"Moving in is a big step," Jade replied.

"Jade, you can keep your place if you like, but in two short months you will have to renew the lease and start paying rent."

"How did you know?" Jade stared at her in amazement.

"I heard you talking with Willow. Bourton Bridge and all of the Cotswold villages come with pricey rentals. You can stay at my place free of charge and I'd love to have you. I have three extra rooms, which means Luke can be in the main house too." She knowingly raised her eyebrows and whispered so Emilie couldn't hear, "Of course, you don't have to make use of all three."

Jade felt a blush rise in her cheeks, but threw her arms around Elizabeth and ignored her embarrassment. "Thank you."

Chapter Forty-Nine

ELIZABETH AND LUKE HAD DECIDED TO WELCOME Jade and Emilie into their home by throwing a small dinner party the following evening. Willow and Harry arrived and joined the others in the kitchen where they all took part in preparing mini pizzas. Luke had prepped the dough earlier. Jade had cut up vegetables for a salad. And Elizabeth had made a tiramisu that would rival any traditional English trifle.

They gathered around the old butcher block island to decorate their pizzas and eat them as they came out of the oven. "I hear we're celebrating?" Willow spoke between bites.

"I'm moving in," Jade said with a coquettish smile. There was a time not so long ago when Jade thought happiness was just a fictional idea reserved for romance novels. But now, as she stood in the midst of this room, she looked at the people around her and knew that she had found her happy place.

Luke opened his arms to her and she walked into his embrace. Jade had always been careful to hide her affection for Luke when they were at the restaurant where Elizabeth and Emilie might observe them, but this time she lifted her mouth to his without hesitation.

"Hey now," Willow mock protested. "You think we came over here to watch you make out? We've got news of our own."

Luke immediately broke eye contact with Harry. Elizabeth started rearranging the flowers in a vase. Then, Jade bit her lower lip, a habit Willow had seen for years whenever Jade tried not to reveal something.

"Elizabeth? Why do Luke and Jade look like cats who have eaten the canary?"

Elizabeth placed her hands together in confession style. "I had a very good reason, dear. Luke is my chef. I had to tell him that a party was scheduled."

Willow nodded, and then turned to Luke. "And Luke? Do you have something to confess?"

"And I had a very good reason, too," Luke added.

Jade laughed. "Don't let him fool you, Willow. His reason for spilling the beans is that he can't keep a secret. They were both acting so weirdly. I dragged it out of them."

Willow shrugged her shoulders. "I guess surprises are overrated."

Harry held up Willow's left hand. "You may know the news, but you haven't seen the proof." Willow's engagement ring caught the light and shined as brightly as the happy couple's smiles.

"Oh Willow!" Jade exclaimed and went to hug her.

Luke gave Harry a hearty pat on the back. Elizabeth retrieved the bottle of champagne she was chilling. After glasses were poured and the group toasted to everyone's good fortune, Willow asked for everyone's attention. "Harry and I think the perfect venue for a wedding would be a charming hotel in Bourton Bridge… your hotel."

Harry continued, "So, we want to contribute to your renovation by putting down a deposit."

Jade was speechless. Willow and Harry's news solidified

her plans. She now had a goal beyond simply making the property financially viable. She wanted to give her best friend the wedding of her dreams.

"Let's do this!" Jade smiled big at her friends who were gathered, the man she loved, and the woman who had become a maternal figure to her. "Since you're all gathered here, I want to run an idea past you… especially you, Elizabeth."

All eyes were on Jade as she continued. "I was brainstorming names. After all, we can't keep calling it 'the property'," she mused. "As a partner to Le Pont… *the bridge* in English, why not simply *The Bridge Hotel*?"

"Let's raise our glasses." Luke refilled everyone's flutes. "To Jade and The Bridge Hotel."

Jade continued, "To Elizabeth and Le Pont… our official restaurant."

It was Elizabeth's turn next. "And to Willow and Harry… who have given us a kick in the pants to get this renovation started."

The group moved into the sitting room and gathered around the fireplace. The Fall weather brought a chill in the evening air. Luke put another log on and the room started to warm with the crackle of the flames.

"This is my favorite season," Jade noted. "Pumpkin lattes, pumpkin bread, Thanksgiving dinner around the corner… well, if I were in California."

"I'll make you a Thanksgiving dinner," Luke promised.

"Since we're talking about holidays…" Willow hedged. "Do you think we could plan for a Christmas wedding?" Willow noted the sudden worried look on Jade and Luke's face, and quickly added, "Next Christmas…"

"Fourteen months…" Jade murmured. "Harry, I've been wanting to ask you something… will you be my contractor and foreman?"

286

"Jade, I would be honored. And you're a sly one… now I have to make sure you're happy as well as Willow."

Jade asked, "Is the timeline possible?"

"Not just possible, but probable. And Jade…it'll be done right."

She sent Harry a relieved smile and then turned to give Willow a big hug. "We're going to throw a Christmas wedding in the Cotswolds."

Epilogue

Each morning, Luke prepared a pot of coffee for the household before leaving to open the restaurant. Although today was decidedly busier than usual, he still planned to check on George at the corner co-op shop. In the last year, George had started to show signs of slowing down, but it served him well as people in the village made more of an effort to support the shop, along with chalking up his grumpy demeanor to old age. As Luke scooped out the coffee beans, he smiled to find a note from Jade hidden within the canister.

"Can't wait to see you on this special day," it read. The swirl of her signature followed by x's and o's set a smile onto his face. Jade had been bubbling with both excitement and nerves as this day approached. It was the hotel's soft opening, marked by Willow and Harry's wedding. But Luke had a surprise of his own planned for her. He grabbed his coat and pulled his hat down over his hair that had recently acquired a couple of grey strands amongst his dark waves. Jade said it was sexy, but he rolled his eyes whenever she flattered him, and humbly replied that sisters Mary and Vera seemed to like it too.

It had been over a year since Jade arrived in England and first set eyes on the building she would come to own. Back then, the lane was black tarmac, uneven and riddled with potholes. Unkept ivy covered the walls and once removed, a dingy stain remained in its place. The grounds, which consisted mainly of weeds, were punctuated by a few garden beds that hadn't been home to vegetables for years. Their wood enclosures had rotted and the translucent cloches that once protected them were frayed and torn. Years of neglect had taken its toll on the 17th century farmhouse and its grounds. Jade came to see the building as a mirror to her own soul. Hardship had occurred, but the structure was solid. She came to believe in her abilities to turn it around and Luke played a large part in building up her confidence.

Luke had forged his own way in life. Out of necessity and survival, he carved out a more promising path for himself. And although he had much experience with painful times, he now viewed those days as a barometer for recognizing better ones. For years, he buried his emotions and maintained a sunny albeit stoic exterior, but it was only when he fell for Jade that he recognized it was safe to let his feelings surface.

Together, they journeyed on a course to healing. Over the last year, they watched the construction crew's progress. As pot holes were filled so were the holes in their hearts. The dirt on the walls was washed clean and the darkness of their pasts vanished. Sweet peas were planted along twisting walkways as a reminder that life was sweet and they had turned a corner.

As he made his way, Luke hummed a tune and stopped upon seeing Ben. "You're chipper," Ben noted.

"I've got a lot to be happy about. My best friend is getting married and I'm helping my girlfriend," Luke said emphasizing the word.

"You're a lucky guy."

Luke gave Ben a knowing glance. "I'd say you are too."

For the better portion of a year, Ben arrived at Le Pont every morning pretending to be there for a coffee and a croissant, when in truth, he was only there for Elizabeth. And although she maintained an air of French resoluteness when it came to love, she warmed to Ben's method of romancing her. Coffee and croissants turned to afternoon lunch and soon, Ben suggested that she might join him for dinner. With a shrug of feigned indifference, she replied that nobody could eat French food everyday, even though it was superior.

Ben answered Luke, remembering his first real date with Elizabeth. "It was that Indian dinner that won her heart," he said with a smile.

Luke shook his head. "Come on, Ben. She doesn't even like Indian food. You won her heart and you know it."

"Like you, I'm a lucky guy. I'll see you at the wedding."

"You didn't have to do this today," Jade chided. "Don't you have a wedding to get ready for?"

"You've done so much for me, Jade, this is the least I can do," Harry said, carefully carrying a painting up a ladder. "This is important... for you and Luke," he said.

He carefully hung the painting over the grand fireplace. It was one of the last paintings that Emma had worked on, and one of Luke's favorites. He explained that Emma didn't feel it was complete, but with Jade in his life, Luke said their story had finally been told. Jade had worked to carefully put the final touches on the painting, adding subtleties that showed the couple's faces, and now that Harry hung it in place, she stood back to admire it.

"Do you think Luke will like it?"

"Without a doubt," Harry confirmed. "Jade, I can't thank you enough for trusting me with the hotel. And to think that I'll be getting married here."

"You better get on your way. You can't be late for your own wedding."

———

Harry left and no sooner, Jade's phone rang with a call from Willow.

"Happy Christmas Eve!" her friend said in her whispery sing-song voice.

"Christmas wishes right back at you. Are you ready?"

Willow laughed. "I am. How is The Bridge Hotel doing? I can't believe you've banished me from seeing it."

"I want your wedding to be magical." Jade gazed out the hotel's bay window, her heart fluttering with equal anticipation as she watched Luke arrive in Le Pont's catering van. Each glimpse of him still sent a thrill through her, but today felt especially significant. After more than a year of planning, The Bridge Hotel in the heart of the Cotswolds was ready to welcome guests.

"Wait until you see it, Willow. I hope you'll be so happy."

"Jade, I'm already happy. Not just for me, but for you as well. I'll see you soon."

Jade had truly found a home in Bourton Bridge. The village had not just witnessed her renovation of the farmhouse, they helped shape it into a boutique hotel. Mary and Vera sourced antiques for the lobby. James suggested plants that would bloom throughout the year. And Elizabeth and Luke were with her every step of the way.

"Those look lovely," Elizabeth noted as Luke entered with

the platters of food. "I don't think there's anything left for me to teach you."

"That's quite a compliment," Luke replied. "You'll have to turn your attention to Thomas and put him through the ringer," he said, stifling a laugh.

"Oh stop. I'm not that tough."

"True, but I think Ben has something to do with your gentler demeanor."

"Ridiculous. I've just mellowed a bit."

The tables were decked out in white linens with centerpieces made of white roses, pine branches and silver candles. Chairs were tied with silver and white bows and a long white runner covered the pathway where Willow would walk to meet Harry. The wedding ceremony would take place under an ornate iron gazebo decorated in twinkling lights and branches with bright red berries from the Yew trees that bordered the property. It was the perfect effect for a Christmas Eve wedding.

Their friends and neighbors gathered and waited for Willow's entrance with anticipation. With the exception of sisters Mary and Vera, none of the guests had immediate family. The group was unusual in that respect, but their bond was unmistakable because they had chosen their connections to each other.

Elizabeth had come to be a mother figure to Luke and now sat in the front row with Ben, who looked adoringly at her, as he had every day in the restaurant for the last year. Next to them was James, who provided the flowers. He had become acquainted with Nico, owner of the Greek restaurant, after Emma's death when they worked together to make all of the arrangements. Their relationship that started as business had progressed to something more meaningful and they were looking to move in together.

George and his wife were seated behind them, along with their new lodger, Wilfred. George had finally warmed to the cat and brought him everywhere with him. Brianne from his shop seemed subdued, partly because she had resigned herself that Luke was now taken. Yet, when Thomas arrived and took the seat next to her, she brightened considerably.

Over the years, Officer Vallens had become a familiar and trusted figure in the community, and Willow had asked him to officiate the ceremony. As she prepared to walk down the aisle, she caught sight of him standing beside Harry, offering her a small, reassuring nod of support. On the other side of Harry stood Luke, the best man.

Jade had arranged for a string trio made up of violin, viola and cello to play during the ceremony. Their beautiful music began, Emilie's signal to lead the procession as flower girl. She dropped red petals along the walkway, leading to the gazebo matching the branches with red berries. Jade proceeded after Emilie, locking eyes with Luke, and quietly wondering if she would have a walk down the aisle one day. Jade also wore a red gown, striking against her pale skin. Although the color was unusual for an English wedding, Willow wanted something to remind her of her parents' background from Hong Kong. The color was known for celebrations and a symbol of good fortune. It also added to the festivity of the holiday season.

Then, it was Willow's turn. It was Jade's idea to have the music stop rather than change when Willow walked down the aisle. She knew her friend's beauty was so striking that people would hold their breath watching her. Her gown was designed by Moniquel Huillier — simple satin without lace or adornments, just an hourglass bodice leading to a glorious expanse of fabric. Matching white satin gloves rose to her upper arm revealing only exposed shoulders and décolletage. Her bouquet was striking in contrast, red roses in a tight nosegay. When she reached the gazebo, Jade took her bouquet and Willow clasped hands with Harry.

It was a short ceremony, but Officer Vallens perfectly captured the sentiment of the day, speaking of friends and future.

———

After the guests departed, and Willow and Harry left for their honeymoon, Elizabeth, Luke, Jade and Emilie settled in the hotel's club room, a cozy space where Jade hoped future guests would enjoy a brandy by the fireplace or afternoon tea. The decor featured rich jewel tones, dark woods, and a restored double-sided fireplace with the opposite side opening to a conservatory.

Emilie started to slump against the cushions of the plush velvet sofa. "Before you get too comfortable and fall asleep right here, I have a surprise for you."

Emilie perked up and looked at her mother. "What kind of surprise?"

"A really good one," Jade teased. "How would you like to sleep here?"

"Here? As in right here?"

"Almost…here, in the hotel." Jade held up an ornate room key. "It's all ready for you. You can be the first to try it out."

Emilie beamed as she took the key and bounded off the sofa. "Thank you," she said and leaned towards Jade to kiss her goodnight. It filled Jade with tremendous pride that Emilie had adjusted to her life in England so well. She had too. She smiled as Luke placed a protective arm around her shoulders.

Spying the doe-eyed looks transpiring between Luke and

Jade, Elizabeth excused herself. "I think I'm going to turn in for the night." She held up another key that Jade had given her earlier.

After Elizabeth left, Luke added another log to the fireplace. When he returned to Jade's side, she sighed with happiness. "I couldn't have done this without you. After New Year's we officially open. This is truly our last night alone here."

"How do you want to spend it?"

Jade looked at him with a mischievous gleam in her eye. Her mouth formed a seductive smile and it was all the hint that Luke needed. He wrapped his arm around her waist and pulled her in close. When their mouths met, a soft moan escaped from Jade. A moment later, he led her to one of the rooms upstairs, where their clothes landed in a heap on the floor.

"You are so beautiful," Luke said, barely above a whisper. He didn't speak another word, he just laid her on the bed and layered kisses down her neck to her stomach, and then lower still. Being with Luke was so different than any of her previous experiences. His loving was passionate and slow. As he moved on top of her, he entered with such gentle tenderness. They moved in unison, her breath matching his, her hips rising to meet his. Their passion rose until a flood of release overtook them both and after, they laid in each other's arms declaring how much they each loved the other.

***

In the morning, the sun shone a stream of light down one side of the bed, acting like Jade's alarm. She smiled at the memory of the previous night and stretched her arm to Luke's side of the bed. He rolled over and kissed her gently on the cheek. "Thank you."

She looked up at him. "For what?"

"For just being you. Merry Christmas. Will you open this, please?" He reached under his pillow to display a small, black jewelry box adorned with a gold button.

"Where did that come from?" She took a deep inhale as she took the box from Luke. Looking to him for a sign of what was to come, but having an inkling already, she pressed the button and the lid opened. A diamond ring shone brightly in contrast to the black velvet interior. It was a simple ring, but somehow, that only intensified its beauty.

"Luke…" she uttered, "it's beautiful."

"Jade, I love you. I love everything about you. Your determination and strength. Your compassion and kindness. Will you marry me?"

To Luke, Jade always looked the most beautiful when she smiled, and from the moment he met her, he was determined to bring a smile to her face. Staring back at him, her smile touched his heart. "You know I will. Yes!"

When Jade and Luke came downstairs to the lobby's club room where they had gathered the night before, Elizabeth and Emilie were waiting. Elizabeth pointed to a basket that was bursting with focaccia, cheeses, chutney, and fruit. "Thomas dropped this off to thank us for inviting him to the wedding and introducing him to Brianne. Apparently, they hit it off."

Luke surveyed the basket. "Thomas made focaccia? Where did he learn to do that?"

Elizabeth coyly remarked, "We all have secrets."

On cue, Emilie regarded her mom. "You never sleep this late."

Elizabeth raised her eyebrow and added, "Nor do you, Luke. Strange that you both overslept on the same day."

Luke took the opportunity when Emilie wasn't looking to shoot Elizabeth a look. A light blush rose to Jade's cheeks as she avoided Elizabeth's glance. "Well, this looks delicious," Luke said, stepping behind Jade to reach for a plate from the sideboard. As he did, he gave her hand a squeeze behind her back. When she didn't readily release his grip, he took the hint.

"We have some news," Luke started.

"Oh?" Elizabeth commented.

"Another surprise?" Emilie added.

"Why are you two acting so coy?" Jade asked.

They both shrugged their shoulders as if they were the ones with a secret rather than Jade and Luke. Finally, Luke took Jade's left hand and held it up for all to see.

Without a word, Emilie presented her palm toward Elizabeth, who reached into her purse to retrieve a five pound note.

"You're kidding," Luke said. "Making bets with a child?"

"It was her idea," Elizabeth stated meekly.

Jade knelt down to Emilie and wrapped her in a hug. "How did you know?"

"We've had this bet going for months," Emilie confessed. "I said it would be Christmas; Miss Elizabeth thought it would be New Year's. It's about time," she beamed.

Elizabeth embraced Luke and as she did, whispered in his ear. "I couldn't be happier for you… my sweet boy."

After tidying the room and closing the fireplace flue to keep away the chill, they were ready to lock up the hotel until its official opening in January. Elizabeth had all the trimmings for a traditional Christmas dinner at home. A year ago, none of them could have conceived that home would be such a happy place. They had all experienced a journey of healing… their own Christmas miracle.

As they drove down the lane with the hotel standing proud behind them, Elizabeth voiced what was on everyone's mind: "Is it too soon to plan next Christmas Eve's wedding?"

The End

Continue the Love Story

READY FOR ANOTHER HELPING OF LOVE?

Life in Bourton Bridge is getting sweeter with your favorite chefs cooking up surprises in book 2.

— secrets emerge
— trust is tested
— and one choice could change everything

Follow Luke and Jade's continued love story.

Download *Winter in Bourton Bridge* (Book 2) and see what happens next.

A Request

Firstly, thank you for picking up this book.
Thank you for reading it.
Thank you for giving this book series a chance.

And most importantly, thank you in advance for leaving a review. Word of mouth is imperative for authors. I truly appreciate your willingness to help others discover the community of Bourton Bridge.

— *Mia*

Acknowledgments

Writers spend a lot of time on their own — lost in their thoughts, creating stories and characters. I truly appreciate the support of readers and friends who remind me that writers might spend time in solitude, but they are never alone.

To Linda — You were with me from the beginning of my career as a novelist before I even knew this life would exist for me. Bouncing story ideas past you and hearing yours in return is my favorite way to spend an afternoon.

To Marina — I have long admired your work. To have you as one of my first readers of this book means the world to me. I always say that time is the one thing that nobody can give you. The fact that you took your time to read my book is a huge gift.

To Ginelle — You have the greatest eagle eyes I have ever known and the patience to always sift through my early drafts. I appreciate you, our friendship, and your astute observations.

To Gabbs — It's a sign of a real friend when I can disappear from the writing world, come back, and pick up with you right where we left off.

To Victoria — When I think of the book world and my

community, you are the first to come to mind. Thank you for your years of support.

To Casey — You have been so generous of your time. Thank you for being an early reader and offering your heartfelt advice. There will always be a hug waiting for you in California.

Also by Mia Fox

Bourton Bridge Series

Bourton Bridge, Book 1

Winter in Bourton Bridge, Book 2

Spring in Bourton Bridge, Book 3 (Coming Soon!)

Hollywood Hotties Series

Alert the Media

Keeping Up

.

www.ingramcontent.com/pod-product-compliance
Lightning Source LLC
Chambersburg PA
CBHW061939170626
46813CB00006B/2465